TEARS
ON HER
GRAVE

BOOKS BY D.K. HOOD

D.K. HOOD

TEARS ON HER GRAVE

bookouture

Published by Bookouture in 2024

An imprint of Storyfire Ltd.
Carmelite House
50 Victoria Embankment
London EC4Y 0DZ

www.bookouture.com

The authorised representative in the EEA is Hachette Ireland
8 Castlecourt Centre
Dublin 15 D15 XTP3
Ireland
(email: info@hbgi.ie)

ISBN: 978-1-83525-709-8
eBook ISBN: 978-1-83525-708-1

To the members of the D.K. Hood Readers' Group.

PROLOGUE

HALLOWEEN, TWELVE YEARS AGO

Stanton Forest, Black Rock Falls, Montana

"A river of red ran down the mountainside and poured into the water, turning Black Rock Falls red. Each Halloween he returns. At midnight you can still hear his laughter and see his ghost holding up a severed head dripping with blood." Wyatt Twotrees looked from one to the other. "Stay close to the fire or you'll be next." He dropped the ax he was holding into the sandy soil and everyone fell silent.

The river glistened black and resembled a tar pit with a heat shimmer. From the surface, mist rose up in white spirals like skeletons crawling from their graves. The army of ghouls marched through the forest, coming closer with each step. Only the ring of light from the bonfire held the creatures at bay. Suddenly afraid, twenty-one-year-old Abby Jaye leaned closer to her boyfriend, Cole Peters, the quarterback from the college football team. As a five-star recruit, his place in the NFL draft was guaranteed and they'd already planned for her to follow him wherever he went. She drew his attention away from another horrific tale of the Whispering Caves Axman and kept her voice to a whisper. "I need to pee and I'm not going out there alone. I can't just go behind a tree, everyone will see me. Can we walk along the trail and find some bushes?"

"We're only staying until one, just in case we see a ghost, but if you gotta go, you gotta go." Cole chuckled. "Although those guys would frighten a ghost away." He indicated to his friends, all wearing hideous Halloween masks. "I'm not sure why they wore them here. They're all crazy." He stood and held out his hand. "Come on then. There's a clump of bushes along the trail near the caves."

Abby pulled out her phone, and using the flashlight, they wandered hand in hand some ways from the fire, followed by hoots and hollers from their friends. She squeezed Cole's hand. "They figure we're heading to the caves to make out."

"Maybe we should." He gave her a lopsided grin. "Or are you too scared to be alone with me on Halloween?" He held up both hands. "See, no ax."

Giggling more with nerves than fun, Abby twirled her fingers. "Turn around and walk some ways away. I'm not peeing in front of you. It's embarrassing."

"I can never understand that about girls." He turned his back and started walking away in the darkness. "Us guys don't care. We just line up side by side."

Abby found a suitable place and turned off her phone's flashlight. As she pulled up her jeans, a thump and a low groan came from the direction Cole had walked. She fumbled for her phone and the light lit up the area. Ahead, the path where he had gone was empty. How far had he walked? Had he tripped over a tree root or something? He'd mentioned his phone battery was low and they'd been using hers all the way here. She looked behind her. The glow of the fire seemed a mile away. "Cole, where are you? Stop messing around. It's creepy out here."

As her flashlight moved over the dark opening of the cave, it reflected in the sharpened blade of an ax. Had Wyatt Twotrees slipped up ahead of them to play out his Whispering Caves Axman story? The hairs on the back of Abby's neck rose as a shape emerged from the forest. All the boys were wearing their team jackets and, apart from Cole, a Halloween mask. It was difficult to tell them apart in the dark. "Is that you, Wyatt? I can't find Cole. I figure he went inside the cave. Did he walk past you?"

"Let's take a look." He pulled a flashlight from his pocket and shone it inside the cave. "After you." He bent and picked up an ax leaning against a tree. "Better safe than sorry, right?"

Trembling, Abby nodded. She'd known Wyatt since grade school and had no reason not to trust him. Taking hesitant steps, she moved into the cave. The darkness surrounded her and critters scattered in all directions as they rounded the first bend. Terror gripped her at the sight of a figure crumpled on the sand. Blood soaked the back of the familiar jacket. She took a deep breath to scream and run away, then the cold metal of the ax smashed into her shoulder. Crying out in pain, she turned and dropped her phone, but the flashlight lit up the hideous mask.

As the ax rose high into the air, she grappled with her attacker. "Why are you doing this? Did you kill Cole?"

The masked attacker chuckled and shoved her away. "I wish I could kill him a thousand times but now it's your turn."

The caves went deep into the mountain, she could run and hide. Abby shook her head. "No!" She ran at him, clawing at his neck, and as he pushed her away, her fingers closed around his fraternity pin. When he shoved her hard, it came away in her hand. She fell hard on the dry sandy soil and, winded, rolled over, trying to get her feet under her, but he used his boot to knock her back to the ground. She didn't have time to scream as a swish followed by the cold sharp steel of the ax struck the back of her neck and darkness surrounded her.

ONE

PRESENT TIME, MONDAY

Spring in Black Rock Falls was a special time for Sheriff Jenna Alton. As the landscape changed from a blanket of white and the land came back to life after a dormant winter, she snuggled behind her husband, Deputy Dave Kane, and sighed with delight as their baby kicked Kane's back. The baby was strong, and once the first tiny flutters arrived, they'd quickly moved into noticeable kicks. They'd tentatively started to discuss names, being too scared beforehand in case anything happened to their precious bundle. As a couple, they carried the burdens of totally different past lives and the threats that went with them. Her time as DEA Agent Avril Parker had vanished after cosmetic surgery, a new name, and being placed in witness protection after bringing down a cartel. Kane on the other hand was still considered an active government asset, although his appearance had been dramatically changed, as had his name, but his time as a black ops sniper and later as a Secret Service agent protecting POTUS meant he carried a bounty on his head. He'd been forced to leave Washington, DC, after a car bomb killed his wife and unborn son and left him with a metal plate in his head. An empty coffin had been buried and the headstone held the name of the person he'd once been. A name he wouldn't reveal to anyone, not even Jenna.

After trying for over a year to start a family, they'd adopted Tauri, a beautiful boy with Native American bloodlines that linked him to their good friend Atohi Blackhawk and Kane's wife Annie's ancestry. They'd loved the boy the moment they'd laid eyes on him and he'd become a light of their lives.

The weather was still freezing and frost coated the windows. The thought of getting up for work made Jenna snuggle under the blankets.

"I can feel our baby insisting I get up and do my chores." Kane chuckled. "I know you're awake, Jenna. I can feel you wiggling around behind me." He slipped out of bed. "Why don't you go to the bathroom? I'll put on the coffee and make you a decaf before I muck out the horses." He bent down and kissed her. "Okay?"

Jenna looked into his deep blue eyes and smiled. She still couldn't believe they were married. "You trying to win the best husband award this week?" She giggled. "Trust me, no one comes close to you."

"Well, thank you, ma'am." Kane grinned. "It's nice to be appreciated." He headed for the kitchen.

It was five after six, and Tauri would sleep until seven. She could set her clock by him. At five years old, he was big for his age, taller than most by a head and as bright as a button. He could speak two languages and Kane was teaching him Spanish. Being multilingual was another one of Kane's attributes and he spoke maybe nine or more languages. She'd lost count. Apart from being skilled in too many ways to mention, Kane's six-five frame and two hundred seventy pounds of muscle made him stand out in a crowd. As a father he was incredibly patient and caring. In her heart, Jenna understood he wanted a mess of kids, but for now they'd be content with two, and if more came along, the more the merrier.

She used the bathroom and decided to have a shower. When Kane came back it would be the first thing he would do. By the time she came out, her coffee, in an Aunt Betty's Café travel mug to keep it hot, was sitting beside the bed. She sipped as she dressed when her phone buzzed. It was the 911 service patched through to her phone. "Sheriff Alton."

"I'm sorry to trouble you so early, Sheriff. This is Jud Lime. I'm with the flood watch. The river broke its banks overnight and Main is flooding. Not deep enough to hold up most folks but we believe the melt has unearthed some graves, somewhere high in the mountains. We have bodies floating in the river. There are two and they look old and wrinkled. They're fully clothed and one is wearing a college jacket." He took a deep breath. "Two of my team hauled them out and carried them to dry ground. We're not sure who to call to deal with them."

Frowning, Jenna picked up a pen on the bedside table and took down the details. "I'll call the medical examiner. He'll be along as soon as possible. Can you cover the remains and have someone stay on scene with them? I don't want people to start panicking."

"Not a problem. We've just taken over this shift. We'll keep watch to see if any more come along. We'll be relieved here at ten, so you have plenty of time."

Thankful for the mayor's flood plan for this year, Jenna sighed. "Thank you. I appreciate it. One of my deputies will be along soon and I'll call Dr. Wolfe right away. He'll get his team out to collect the bodies." She stared at the clock. "Let me know if any other bodies show." She disconnected and called Shane Wolfe, the medical examiner and Kane's handler, to explain the situation.

"Okay, we're just about through eating breakfast. Give me a second." In the background, Jenna heard him speaking to his daughter Emily. "I know you've been working all night, so it's up to you." He paused for a beat. "Ah, Jenna. I'm on my way *with Emily. She figures even after the midnight shift she can manage another hour or so now she's eaten. Catch y'all later."*

As usual, Wolfe moved into action without delay. He and his daughter Emily, currently in her first year of residency at Black Rock Falls General and an ME in training, lived only minutes away from the river and would get there well before she could. She disconnected and called Chief Deputy Rio to take over in her absence. She finished the call as Kane walked back into the room. Their dog, Duke, a bloodhound, came into the bedroom, turned around three times in his basket and collapsed with a long sigh. Jenna looked at Kane and explained the situation. "I'll get Tauri ready and start breakfast while you're in the shower."

"Drink your coffee, and then get Tauri ready." Kane stripped off, dropped his clothes into the hamper, and headed for the shower. "I'll cook when I'm done. Rio can handle things until we arrive. Wolfe will be there. We have time to feed our son before we leave."

Reluctantly, Jenna nodded. She liked to be in the action, but Tauri came first and she had a fine team she could trust. Although delegating jobs she could do herself had always been a problem, her mothering instinct usually kicked in. She smiled. "I'll call Nanny Raya and tell her we'll be dropping Tauri by early this morning. You're right, of course, but if it's a murder, I'm in boots and all."

"You'll always be the sheriff, Jenna." Kane smiled at her over one shoulder. "I wouldn't have it any other way."

TWO

The town had changed dramatically in the last week or so, from a winter wonderland to a wet, muddy, flooded landscape. Gray slush lined each side of the blacktop, and water rushed along the gutters at an incredible speed. The drains couldn't cope and muddy water gathered in slippery slicks across Main, getting deeper by the minute, as Wolfe arrived in town. He'd left his van at home and taken the truck. The cargo space was large enough to carry two bodies and it would negotiate the flooding with ease. It didn't take long to find the flood-watch crew but it seemed the mayor had workers from various departments out early to deal with the local flooding. At one end of Main, at least two backroads had barriers across them warning of the floods. They climbed from the truck and Wolfe approached the men standing beside a tarp spread out over something on the grass.

Flowing from high in the mountains, the river was one of many that originated from Black Rock Falls. Wolfe headed to one of the men and flipped open his cred pack. "Dr. Shane Wolfe. I'm the medical examiner and I'm looking for Mr. Lime."

"That would be me." Lime nodded and his mouth formed a

thin line. A man in his forties, strong in build, wearing a slicker and rubber boots up to his knees squelched across the soaked ground toward him. "The sheriff said you'd be along."

Moments later a sheriff's department SUV pulled up behind Wolfe's vehicle and Chief Deputy Zac Rio, an ex-gold shield detective from LA, stepped out and nodded to him. Rio had recently been promoted to cover for Jenna and Kane when the baby arrived. A very experienced detective, he had a retentive memory, which made him excellent to have along at crime scenes. Wolfe turned to Lime. "Okay, as Chief Rio is here, we can go ahead without the sheriff. Where are the bodies?"

"Under the tarp." Lime pointed.

Following his pointed finger, Wolfe turned to Lime. "That's all I need for now. We'll be in touch if we need any other info. Thanks for calling it in. Let me know if any more bodies show." He handed him his card.

Glad he'd doubled up his thermal socks beneath the rubber boots, Wolfe squelched through the sodden grass toward the two lumps under a tarp. He glanced at Emily. His daughter and Rio had drifted apart after dating for a couple of years. "You okay working with Rio?"

"Yeah, it wasn't like we were engaged or anything." Emily shook her head. "We hardly dated. I care for him, but I don't love him. He's fine with it. We're still friends. In fact, nothing's changed apart from we can date other people if we feel like it."

Relieved as Rio walked to their side and nodded to Emily, Wolfe bent to remove the tarp and reveal the bodies. The smell of death hit them in a wave, mixed with the smell of damp soil and mold. He took in the damage to the necks and heads, the local college football jacket with the year in a circle on the chest, and looked at Rio. "If that date is correct, these bodies are twelve years old. They've been preserved, dried out likely after being buried in sand." He looked up at the clouds swirling around the mountain and the water still gushing through the forest. "Likely buried in a cave close to the river. The melt somehow washed them out."

"We have a melt every year." Emily frowned at the bodies. "Why did it happen this year?"

"Many reasons could cause a cave to fill with water, a cave-in for instance." Rio rolled his shoulders. "The seismic activity in the mountains over winter was intense. We know about the avalanches, but we don't know if the tremors caused cracks in the mountain. The cracks fill with snow and the ice expands and increases the fissure. When they melt, if it was over a cave, it makes sense the force of the water flowing down the mountain could wash out a cave. It's not unusual for that to happen. We'd just need to find the cave. It might be dangerous."

Wolfe looked from one to the other. "That all makes sense but it's likely there'd be no evidence left behind there now. If the water gushed down hard enough to move two bodies from a grave deep enough to hide them from wildlife, the cave could be washed out down to the rock."

"We don't know that for sure." Emily frowned. "There could be evidence all over. I figure we need to find the cave." She looked at Rio. "Do you have an opinion?"

"Jenna will insist on finding the cave. She leaves nothing to chance, especially in a double homicide." Rio crouched down and peered at the bodies. He tipped up his Stetson and squinted in the sun at Wolfe. "Those are nasty wounds."

Pulling body bags from his kit, Wolfe straightened and then tossed one to Rio. "We'll get them back to the lab and I'll see what I can find. From my observation, the sand dried the bodies and the water has hydrated them some. This's why they appear so distorted." He pulled on gloves and handed a pair to Rio. "Seems to me, y'all have to hunt down the names of two college kids who went missing twelve years ago. That might prove difficult. Before Jenna took office, the sheriffs didn't do much in the way of investigating anything, let alone keep records. I figure the old newspapers would be the best place to start."

"I'm sure Jenna will organize everything when she arrives." Rio took the feet of the first victim and lifted it into a black body bag and Wolfe zipped it. "One male and one female. Someone's kids." He frowned. "Maybe finding them will give their families closure."

Wolfe nodded. "And finding their killer will give *me* closure." He bent to lift the body of a small young woman into the bag. Her wet long dark hair brushed his arm as if trying to get his attention. He examined her face. It was undamaged but squashed a little from pressure, but her eyes were open, opaque, and staring. A gold chain hung from her neck and he discovered a heart-shaped locket tucked inside her jacket. He went to fold her hands inside the bag and shook his head in surprise. Her hand was locked tight around something. It glittered gold in the thin sunlight. After laying her down inside the bag, he went to his kit and took out a small evidence bag, and with gentle care, pulled out the item from her clenched hand. He looked at Emily. "Maybe she's been holding on to a clue to her murderer for all these years. Poor souls. I mean to find the person who did this. Call Norrell and tell her I'll need her assistance right away."

"Okay." Emily made the call.

His fiancée, Dr. Norrell Larson, a forensic anthropologist who worked in the medical examiner's building, would assist with the dating of the remains and be able to interpret the conditions where the bodies were buried.

They carried the bodies to Wolfe's truck and slid them inside. The stink of death would be difficult to remove from the interior. He looked at Rio. "We're done here."

"I'll call Jenna." Rio pulled out his phone. "There's no need for her to rush here. There's nothing to see." He yawned explosively. "If you don't need me, I'm heading to Aunt Betty's for breakfast."

Wolfe pulled down the hatch of his truck and removed his gloves. "I'm good, thanks. Tell her to head to my office around ten. I might have something to tell her by then."

"Sure." Rio walked away, splashing through the mud with his phone pressed to his ear.

Wolfe turned to look at Emily. "Darn, I actually like him."

"He's a nice guy and will make someone a really great husband." Emily rolled her eyes. "I'm waiting for fireworks. Jenna said when she first kissed Kane it was like the fourth of July. When I meet a guy who does that, I'll know." She put both hands on her hips and stared at him. "Now can we get these bodies back to the morgue? If I don't get some sleep soon, I'm going to fall flat on my face." She pulled open the door to the truck. "You did mention how hard it was getting through a residency at a hospital. I'm aching in places I didn't know existed."

Wolfe smiled at her. "It will be worth it in the end."

"I sure hope so." Emily leaned back in the seat and closed her eyes.

THREE

After receiving Rio's call, Jenna disconnected and looked at Kane. "We don't need to rush. Rio has handled everything and Wolfe has taken the bodies to the morgue. He's calling in Norrell to assist. He said to drop by around ten and he might have some information for us." She brought him up to date with the finer details.

"Do you recall anyone mentioning two college kids going missing when you arrived here?" Kane added crispy bacon to plates of pancakes and set them on the table before adding maple syrup to Tauri's stack and sitting down.

Jenna shook her head. "Nope. The records, as you know, are practically nonexistent. We'll need to check news reports once Wolfe has given us an approximate year they died."

Adding butter to her pancakes and then the maple syrup, she sucked the sweet nectar from her finger and hummed in contentment. Having a ferocious appetite was, as Wolfe had insisted, quite normal after many weeks of morning sickness. She exercised every morning. Kane had found a suitable program for pregnant women and she followed it religiously most days, unless an emergency arose, which hadn't occurred until this morning with the murders in the snow. They'd already booked birthing classes for her third trimester. Although she understood the mechanics, Kane had, as usual, wanted full immersion in the birth. She smiled at Tauri. "I'm sorry we woke you so early. We had a call from the office, but Uncle Zac is handling it." Her deputies were family, and Tauri had given all of them the title *uncle*.

"Mommy." Tauri swallowed a bite of pancake and then swirled a strip of bacon in a few drops of syrup on his plate. He appeared totally engrossed and wasn't looking at her.

Jenna sipped her milk and looked at him. "Is something wrong, sweetheart?"

"Will you still love me when the baby comes along?" He lifted golden eagle eyes to search her face. "One of my friends said his mommy and daddy got angry all the time when his sister arrived."

"Maybe it's because babies take a lot of time." Kane smiled at him. "At first, Mommy might not be able to do so many things with you because she's feeding the baby or changing its diaper. They cry and need to be held. It's what mommies and daddies do, but it doesn't mean we stop loving you. That can never happen."

Swallowing the lump in her throat, Jenna met Tauri's gaze. "You're my sunshine. I could never stop loving you, not if we have another ten babies. Just think how fun it will be to have a baby brother or sister to play with. Babies always need a ton of attention when they first arrive, but in no time, they are crawling around the floor getting into mischief. It will be strange and new for all of us, but Mommy and Daddy have lots of love to share."

"We'll have fun watching them grow." Kane grinned. "You can help them learn how to crawl and walk. Maybe even teach them some words. You'll be their big brother and they'll look up to you to show them how to do things."

"Okay, that will be fun." Tauri stuffed the bacon into his mouth and then sucked his fingers.

Jenna looked at Kane and smiled. "We don't argue now, do we? Nothing will change. We could never ever stop loving you."

"It's funny." Kane rubbed the back of his neck and looked at her. "My mom told me my sister asked the very same question when they told her about me."

Jenna chuckled. She did know Kane was from a military family, just not which one. She'd discovered he'd had a sister, who'd been murdered. "Oh, I can just imagine the answer in your family. It would be 'That's need to know.'"

They finished up and headed into town. Brown water swirled through the ditches alongside the highway, spilling across the blacktop in dirty slicks of dirt and gravel. The gray snow piled from the last pass of the snowplow was filthy and crumbling as the water rushed by. Her fleece-lined rubber boots were proving to be good protection against the freezing water spilling everywhere across the ground. It was just as well, as her leather boots always ended up wet or stinking in this weather. She'd filled a bag with a few changes of clothes and boots to leave at the office, and was glad she'd taken the trouble when she took in the threatening sky. "Is that snow or rain coming? If it gets any wetter, the town will be isolated. In all the years we've been here, the last two have had the worst weather I've ever seen. Now the mountain shudders every few days. How long before we get a mudslide like last time?"

"The forestry has been planting new trees all through that area." Kane glanced her way before returning his attention to the road. "The wildfire we had a few years ago destroyed much of the vegetation, vines, and roots that created a net around the soil. It will take time to regrow enough to prevent the mudslides." He sighed. "I'm thankful they don't harvest the trees here. Logging and mudslides go hand in hand."

They drove to Nanny Raya's house and Jenna made sure

Tauri was settled. She took her to one side and told her about Tauri's question. It was something they could talk about. Her son had a great connection with his nanny but sometimes kids liked assurance from someone outside the family. Confident that Tauri was happy, she kissed him goodbye and they headed to the office. "Park around back, just in case it starts raining."

"Sure." Kane drove into the parking lot. "I'll take Duke for a walk. I'll be along soon." He opened the back door and lifted the bloodhound from the seat.

Jenna watched them go and then went inside. She waved her deputies upstairs to her office and then dumped their extra clothes and boots into the locker room. She hurried back into her office. "I know this is a cold case, but we owe it to these kids to identify them and find out who murdered them. We'll treat this like any other case."

"We're assuming they died twelve years ago." Deputy Jake Rowley had been with Jenna since her first day in office. He started out as a rookie straight from college. She'd trained him, and Kane had shared his skills with him as well. It had been time well spent. Rowley was a fine deputy.

Jenna nodded. "It's what we're assuming as the college jacket worn by the male has a year embroidered on the front. It could be an old jacket, but Wolfe will make a determination."

"Rio said the inside at the front was like new." Rowley raised both eyebrows. "There weren't any decay marks from the body either as the victim was bundled up in sweaters. So we know this happened late fall to winter."

"Yeah, it was kind of creepy, like old, wrinkled people in college clothing." Rio shrugged. "I figure we start with news-paper reports from twelve years ago and see if we can find anything."

Collecting her thoughts, Jenna nodded. "That's a good idea, but first up, we use the townsfolk's memories. People who have lived here all their lives would recall kids going missing." She looked at Rowley. "Do you remember any kids going missing?"

"I do vaguely recall the incident but not enough to give you the answers you need. These are college kids and I'd have maybe been in high school." Rowley ran a hand through his curly brown hair, making it stick up in all directions. "My early teenage years and younger were taken up by chores rather than watching the news. I was raised on a ranch. It was school, chores, assignments. That's about all."

The door opened and Kane walked in with Duke on his heels. The bloodhound went straight to Jenna and placed his head in her lap. She absently rubbed his cold ears and turned to Rio. "We'll use the media to assist us. It's a mystery the news channels will love, so Rio, use your experience with the media and get them to run a story for us. With luck, you might not need to be in the library archives searching through years of old newspaper articles."

"The families should still be around." Kane slid into a chair and crossed one boot onto his other knee and leaned back, making the wood groan. "I figure what we need is college year-books from ten to twelve years ago. From what you mentioned to Jenna, the faces wouldn't be recognizable."

"No, they are kinda squashed and thin." Rio swiped a hand under his nose. "They kinda look like leather. Wolfe believes they were desiccated, which is why they're intact. If they were buried in dry sand, that could account for it."

Jenna swallowed bile. "You mean mummified?"

"I do believe so, yeah." Rio met her gaze. "I figure one was on top of the other because, as Jake mentioned, the jacket of the male and the front of the female's coat are in good condition."

"So their killer dug a grave and rolled them in on top of each other?" Rowley paled. "There are thousands of caves all around here. We'd never find it, not with rivers bursting their banks and landslides all over."

Two people died and then the killing stopped, or did it? Jenna ran possibilities and scenarios through her mind. She moved her attention to Kane. "Motive?"

"With college kids, likely a lovers' quarrel." Kane shrugged. "Jealousy runs high in that type of scenario, or maybe it was a prank or dare that went wrong. We're only assuming one person is involved in the murders. It's not easy to dig a grave deep enough to prevent wildlife from eating the remains. It's possible but multiple involvement is an angle we can pursue."

As usual the think tank with her team turned up multiple ideas. "Okay, so we have a starting point. Rio, you get onto the media, and Rowley, you hunt down yearbooks from the local college going back about twelve years." Jenna checked her watch. "When you're done, Rio, contact the local newspaper and find out if they have any online archives available going back twelve years. I do recall their mentioning something about making the online archives available to the public for a small fee."

"Do you want me to mention that we've discovered bodies in the media release, or do you just want to ask for anyone to come forward who recalls anything about college students going missing approximately twelve years ago?" Rio glanced up from his notes.

Jenna tapped her pen on the desk, thinking for a beat. "Maybe just ask for information at this stage as we don't want the parents of these kids to find out through the media that their missing children have been discovered floating in the local river."

"Gotcha." Rio closed his notebook and pushed to his feet. "If there's nothing else, I'll get right on it."

Jenna held up her hand. "Fine, but wait up. I'm going with Kane to the medical examiner's office to view the bodies and get his determination on the age of the victims, and Norrell is going to give us some idea of when they were buried." She stood. "I'll leave you to handle things until we get back. If Cade and Piper want to help out on the hotlines again, I'd be very happy to have them back in the office."

Rio's twin siblings both had ideas of going into law enforcement but in different areas. Cade was pursuing a law degree and Piper's career choice was to work in an area that protected abused men, women, and children. They usually welcomed any exposure to the day-to-day running of the sheriff's office. Jenna paid them an hourly rate for their assistance, and as it was spring break, they were usually happy to drop by.

"I'm sure they'd love to help Maggie out again. Each time they work here, it's more experience they can add to their résumés." He turned to go. "I'll call them."

Jenna looked at Rowley, who was getting slowly to his feet. "Is there anything else you need, Jake?"

"No, I just wanted to share some good news." Rowley blushed scarlet. "Sandy is pregnant. We're very happy. We both always wanted a bunch of kids."

"Maybe it will be another set of twins." Kane grinned at him, jumped to his feet, and slapped him on the back. "I'd love to have twins but I'm very happy to be blessed with one."

"Ah, well it's too early to know yet." Rowley collected his things. "She sends you both her love and she wanted me to tell you, Jenna, that she hasn't gotten sick this time."

Overflowing with happiness, Jenna went around the desk and hugged him. "Congratulations! That's wonderful news. I'm so happy for you both."

"Thanks." Rowley took a step back and collected his things. "I'd better get back to work." He hurried out of the door.

FOUR

Rain hit the Beast like gunshot as they drove to the ME's office. The few people on the sidewalk hustled along, hunched over as they sidestepped puddles. Kane glanced toward the river. The muddy overflow had reached the edge of the park and engulfed the swings. "This doesn't look good after all the drainage work the roads department completed after the last flood. It should have been able to cope with the melt."

"Yeah, maybe if it had been just the melt, but the storms we've had over the last few days and the torrential downfall is unusual for this time of the year. It's not just us. There is flooding all over the state. It's what the media is calling 'a weather event.' It seems that no one will admit to global warming. Although Montana is doing its bit to reduce emissions, it's pointless if other parts of the world ignore it completely."

Kane slowed the Beast to drive through a river of water running across the road. He wouldn't be foolish enough to drive into deep fast-flowing water, but this was less than a foot high and was overflow from a drain. He headed toward the back entrance to Wolfe's office and pulled up in front of the awning covering the back entrance. "There you go, Jenna. Watch out for the overflow from the roof. I hope Wolfe has his chopper secured up there. I could feel the wind buffeting the truck and that's unusual in the Beast."

"I'm hoping Blackhawk is okay." Jenna flicked him a worried glance. "I heard someone in Aunt Betty's Café mentioning they'd had mudslides in the res."

Their Native American friend and Tauri's onetime guardian had become part of their family since the adoption of their son. He was a person who Kane respected and admired for his skills. He valued his friendship greatly. "I'm sure if they had been in trouble, they would have called for assistance. He knows he can rely on us to help out when necessary."

"I sure hope so. When we're through here I might give him a call." Jenna slipped from the vehicle and dashed to the door. She scanned her retina and stepped inside, turning to hold the door open for Kane.

To the right of the back door there was a place to hang their slickers and leave their boots. The morgue always smelled the same: vanilla room freshener, chemicals, and a bouquet of death. No matter how hard Wolfe tried to disguise it, the smell of decomposition lingered like garlic after a visit to an Italian restaurant. They padded along the white tile passageway to Wolfe's office. Their friend was inside at his desk working on his computer. "Morning, Shane."

"There y'all are and right on time too." Wolfe smiled at them. He was dressed in scrubs with a face mask hanging from one ear. "Nice weather for ducks. I'm seriously starting to worry if my house is in any danger of flooding and it's halfway up a hill. When I look out of my window, I can see brown water all around. It's a problem with the drainage." He let out a long sigh. "The constant flow of water is picking up the forest floor, and all the pine needles, pine cones, and other debris are blocking the drains. I've never seen anything like it since I moved here. That last flood we had was just the river overflowing."

"I noticed crews out all over when we came through town." Jenna removed her jacket and hung it on a peg inside the office. "I'm sure they're doing everything possible to relieve the problem." She gave him a long look as she turned back to the desk. "Do you have an update on the bodies found in the river?"

"Yeah, I do, and Norrell is working on them as we speak." He stood and waved them toward the door. "Suit up and I'll meet you in examination room two."

Kane noticed Jenna's face had drained of color since they'd arrived. As they walked into the alcove that contained the PPEs he turned to look at her. "Are you feeling okay? I can do this alone if you'd prefer."

"It's the different smells in here. I still get an echo of morning sickness occasionally." Jenna pulled on scrubs over her clothes. "I'll add some salve under my nose and I'll be okay. I'm very interested in this case and why it isn't on our unsolved list. I searched through everything yesterday and couldn't find any mention of two kids missing over such a long period of time. You would have thought that the previous sheriffs would have made a note in one of the daybooks, but they hadn't. I'm hoping that the townsfolk will give us some information."

Confounded why the local sheriffs had neglected to keep decent records, Kane shrugged. "There's nothing we can do about it now. We'll just have to rely on people's memories, I guess." He followed Jenna to the examination room and waited while she flashed her card over the scanner. Inside, Wolfe was talking to Norrell. She had two of her assistants with her. Emily and Wolfe's assistant and badge-holding deputy Colt Webber were missing. "Morning."

Not having seen the bodies previously, the sight of the two emaciated golden-skinned corpses surprised him. They did indeed resemble mummified remains, but it was obvious they were Caucasian, and their skin had been stained by the rich golden sand from the caves. The bodies were complete with hair, but the facial features were distorted. The eyes were sunken holes with intact eyelashes. It was as if the skin had been stretched tight across a skeletal-looking face, the lips pulled back to reveal a death smile. The injuries were graphically evident. Although the skin was contorted, the deep cuts reminded him of the layers between the skin and the meat on a cured ham. Fascination drew him closer. The female lay on her back, hands held as if clutching at her head. The skull fracture on the right side was evident even to him. The male was face down, head turned to the left, and his murder had been brutal—three deep wounds in his back and one at the base of his skull. He had one arm tucked beneath his body, and the other was down beside him. Clothes were displayed along one of the countertops. It would seem by the amount of clothing that the murders occurred during the colder months.

"What have you got for me?" Jenna peered at the bodies and then moved her attention to Wolfe and then Norrell. "They look to me as if they've been attacked with an ax." She walked along the autopsy tables peering at the bodies. "Do they tell a story?" She turned and looked at Wolfe and Norrell.

"Without being able to examine the soil around the bodies for clues, or having any decomposition rates or bugs to use for comparison, we have to make a determination from the evidence we have at hand." Norrell indicated toward the clothes. "Everything here indicates a time span of approximately ten to twelve years ago. The brand names and style of the shoes, for example, are consistent in both victims. The date on the male's jacket corresponds to his fraternity pin and another we found clutched in the girl's hand." She retrieved an evidence bag. "Alpha Pi is a very respected local fraternity."

Inquisitive, Kane took the bag from her and turned it over in his hand, examining the contents. "Do you think it's possible she tore this from her killer's jacket?"

"Yeah, because there's an identical one on the male victim's jacket, which means this wasn't a random thrill kill. These guys knew each other. They were in the same fraternity and that's like a brotherhood. On the other pin, you can clearly see that there are threads of a similar blue jacket still attached." Wolfe raised both eyebrows. "This is a clear indication that when she died she was in close proximity to someone wearing the exact same jacket as the other victim. There's also a wallet and a set of keys from the male. The female has a college ID in the back pocket of her jeans. The IDs are faded but there are partial names evident. These are all great to find, but I'll need DNA or dental records to do a positive ID."

"It's a starting point at least." Jenna pushed hair from her eyes. "One thing is for sure: this was no accident."

Kane allowed the evidence to percolate through his mind and could almost envisage what had happened on the night of the murder. "The male victim was attacked from behind, which makes me believe the killer, pardon my pun, had an ax to grind. Maybe this guy had stolen his girlfriend and this was a love triangle. If this was the case, he attacked the guy from behind first—put him down and then went for the girl."

"Possible, because there are no defensive wounds on either of them." Wolfe indicated to the center wound in the middle of the male's back. "This blow would have damaged the spinal cord, and from the angle of entry of the other lacerations, the victim was on his knees when the killer finished him off. I agree with Jenna, an ax was used as the murder weapon. Not a large wood-splitting ax, but a smaller one most campers use." He turned to the screen array and tapped on his computer, bringing up images of axes he considered could have been used. "All these have the dimensions of the wounds, and the weighted head would have made them a formidable weapon."

"How do you think she managed to grab the pin from the killer's jacket?" Jenna peered at the female's remains. "Do you figure the blow to the head would have knocked her out immediately?"

"Maybe not. Her nails are broken on her right hand, and it was closed into a fist so tight even her stint in the river didn't unclasp it." Wolfe frowned. "Maybe he roughed her up some and she ran because the wound was inflicted from behind. Or she was alive when he carried her into the cave to bury her. From the X-rays, I found two blows to the skull—the laceration from the blade and, I believe, the other is from the blunt side of the ax or maybe the handle. The one that ultimately killed her was to the back of the neck."

Over the years, they'd had many callouts for disturbances concerning college students, and Kane had dealt with every type of mischief a group of college kids could get into when out together. He rubbed his chin. "I figure we're looking for a group of kids that came up into the mountains for the day or even stayed a couple of nights, camping by the river. It would be unusual for a couple to go so deep into the forest for a romantic liaison in the cold weather."

"We also found candy in the jacket pocket of the male victim." Norrell produced another evidence bag and held it up for Jenna. "The candy was long gone but the wrappers were still intact and they have pictures of pumpkins on them."

"If they were in the mountains over Halloween, it would make it easier to discover when they went missing." Jenna examined the bag and nodded. "This is looking more like a group of college kids who went into the mountains to scare themselves silly over Halloween."

"The murder weapon is unusual." Wolfe leaned back on the counter and folded his arms across his chest. "It's not easily concealed, whereas a knife would be a more suitable choice if the killer had intended to murder these people. Say we assume that he was part of the group that went into the mountains. He waits for the couple to walk off, maybe to visit the caves or whatever, and then follows them?"

"Yeah, that sounds reasonable, but what about the others in the group? They should have heard the girl screaming for sure." Jenna looked from one to the other. "Unless you believe that this murder was due to hazing?"

Kane shook his head. "I don't know about twelve years ago, but I do know the fraternities within the Black Rock Falls College are held in high regard. There's no hazing there now. It's illegal and bullies are expelled." He examined the fraternity pins. "This would be a good place to start because fraternities keep records of their members. Someone at the college would recall if one of their members went missing never to return."

"That's a good idea." Jenna pinched the nose of her face mask tighter. "If a group of college students went out on Halloween and two didn't return, you would imagine search and rescue would have been called out. The sheriff would have definitely been involved, so why can't I find even a small notation in a daybook of the event?" She turned her attention to Wolfe. "Honestly, it's as if there was a time shift or a fire because there's no logical explanation for the missing records. Either crime rate in Black Rock Falls was zero or we had a progression of lazy sheriffs. I've read through the files many times searching for information and there just isn't anything there to read. It's as if the actual files for what happened in town over that time are missing."

"I often come up against brick walls like this, Jenna." Norrell gave her a sympathetic look over the top of her face mask. "The only thing you can do is to go to the remaining sources for the information that you require. As Kane said, the college is a good place to start looking as we at least know the male victim's fraternity and his last name ends in *ers*. The college would be able to give you an exact year of when he left or vanished, whatever the case may be."

"What about the female?" Jenna peered at the line of evidence bags.

"Not much info at all, but I've tried to enhance the image of the card and I believe her name was Abby." Norrell smiled. "It's not a full name but better than nothing."

"How long do you intend to keep the details from the media?" Wolfe's attention moved to Jenna. "It's a good guess these kids went to the local dentist. If you discover their names, I'll get a positive ID."

"A media release has been issued but without any details. Get me a positive ID and I'll notify the next of kin." Jenna shrugged. "Then I'll call a media conference. Although, I can't explain about mummified remains. It would be beneficial to have you or Shane there to field the questions I can't answer."

"I don't have a problem fronting the media." Norrell smiled. "Shane will be there as well to back me up."

Concerned about the media releasing the identities of the victims prior to them notifying the next of kin, Kane straightened. "As Jenna said, our first priority is identifying the victims. The media has likely discovered the information on the missing college students. It's all over town about the bodies found in the river. It won't take them long to put two and two together and plaster the victims' photographs all over the news. That would be a terrible shock to the families."

"Leave the media to me." Wolfe shrugged. "Rio will have a list of where he sent the media releases, and I'll request that any information on the missing students should be sent either to me or to the sheriff and not broadcast until we've notified the next of kin. I'll inform y'all. Be in touch to organize a tell-all press conference in the next day or so."

"That sounds like a plan." Jenna nodded. "If we're through here, we'll head to the college and see what we can discover."

Kane removed his gloves and tossed them into the trash.

"Lead the way." He turned to Wolfe and Norrell. "Thanks." He followed Jenna from the room.

FIVE

Panic rose up the back of Josie Campbell's throat, cramping her belly and taking her breath away as the news came over the radio. It had been twelve long years since that Halloween night in the forest with her friends. Twelve long years of keeping a secret, unable to utter a word or even mention the names of the friends they'd buried inside the cave. The terrible nightmare had faded from her memory but now it was front and center. Every excruciating, vivid, and horrifying detail of that night flashed across her mind. As the newsreader requested information about anyone going missing approximately twelve years ago in Black Rock Falls, it was obvious that they'd found the bodies. With trembling fingers, she lifted her phone and called Marissa Kendrick. Many things had happened since that night in the forest. A few of the group of friends had married. All had careers and a life. Everything would be ruined if the truth came out. The phone rang and when the voice of her friend came through the speaker it was evident that Marissa had heard the news as well. "I'm guessing you've heard the news, Marissa?"

"Yeah. It was quite a shock, but think about it. It's been twelve years and there wouldn't be any evidence left to point to

us. Only our small group of friends knows the truth and I'm not guessing that any one of them plans on speaking to the cops. We all have lives now and what happened was a stupid mistake. I figure we should just go about as normal and deny everything if anyone asks us any questions. If we all stick together like we did before, no one is ever going to find out what happened."

Sick to the stomach, Josie hugged her belly. "We need to have a meeting so we can discuss what to do. We can't use the phone because I don't call the others very often, maybe once or twice every few years. It will look suspicious if the cops check out our phones and suddenly we're calling each other the moment the media releases the information. I can walk into town and use a payphone to speak to Jess. Maybe he'll be able to contact one of the others."

"Lily Jones is my hairstylist, so I'll drop by the beauty parlor and speak to her." Marissa sounded calm and in control, but she'd always been the strong one. *"We'll have to meet somewhere where no one will see us. What about the Old Mitcham Ranch, where we used to hang out at Halloween when we were in high school? I doubt it will be flooded on that side of town. We'll see if we can arrange to be there at seven tomorrow night. No one will see us there. It's very isolated."* She heaved in a deep breath. *"I'll drop by different stores and purchase a few burner phones. You do the same. Don't purchase two in the same place and use cash. We'll be able to keep in touch then and no one will know."*

Nodding, Josie sucked in a deep breath. "Yeah, that would work. I'll tell Bob I'm going to the store. He'll be watching TV and will never miss me." She let out her breath in relief. "We can exchange phone numbers of the burners when we meet up at the Old Mitcham Ranch."

"Okay." Marissa sighed. *"Don't stress. We've been doing this for twelve years and we can hold our tongues for as long as it*

takes. I'll see you tomorrow at seven. Bring a flashlight." She disconnected.

As Josie's heart rate slowly returned to normal, she stared at her reflection in the glass-fronted cabinet. The young college girl who had kept a deadly secret no longer existed. She'd worked from home as a teleworker. Her husband, Bob Campbell, was in construction and they had no kids by choice. She gathered her things together, pulled on her coat, and headed for the door. She needed to speak to Jess Hallon. She'd dated him in college, but after what happened, they'd drifted apart and he'd married and now had a son. As he was the manager of his parents' ranch, his phone number was all over town on advertisements for prime beef. Contacting him would be easy.

SIX

The rain-soaked college campus, with its wide sweeping glistening blacktop and impressive buildings, was relatively quiet. It was spring break, but the offices were always open. A few students dashed from place to place, hoodies pulled up over their heads. The dining halls would remain open for the residents as many students lived in. When Kane parked the Beast outside the office, Jenna gathered her things and, pulling her slicker over her head, climbed down from the vehicle. She turned to admire the new truck. The old Beast had been like a reliable friend all the time she had known Kane, and when this new tricked-out glossy black Beast had arrived, seeing the old vehicle being loaded onto the semitrailer had brought tears to her eyes. The new truck was literally bombproof, with bullet-proof glass and every gadget known to man. It was supplied by the government to protect Kane and now his family. It was strange, the old Beast had its own smell and, funnily enough, she missed it. It was like they'd taken a piece of her husband. Knowing she missed it, Kane had purchased her a Mustang for her birthday. All thoughts of the old Beast slipped away when the powerful vehicle, all black and shiny with stripes, slipped down from the trailer. It was a dream come true for her. She would enjoy driving it for as long as she could fit behind the wheel and reach the pedals—if the darn rain would ever stop.

"You have that look in your eye again." Kane came to her side, shoulders hunched against the rain. "Missing the old Beast?"

Self-conscious, Jenna blinked, surprised that he could practically read her mind. "It's as if we sent away a part of you. I mean, when I saw that truck, it meant you were close by. This one is magnificent, with everything we could possibly need to keep us safe, and I'm sure I will get used to it. It's just that I miss the other one."

"I miss it too, but it was getting too old and I was working on it every other weekend to keep it running." Kane pulled down his Stetson to shield his face from the rain. "We could have tried another new engine and replaced the brakes again, but when push came to shove, it may not have performed adequately to save our lives. This is the reason it was replaced and we should be very grateful that POTUS has supplied this new updated version for us." He smiled at her and cupped her chin in his warm fingers. "I'll always be close by, Jenna, and if you need me, you only need to call. You know that, right? I'm sticking right by your side, come rain or shine. You and Tauri are my priority and always will be."

Reluctantly, Jenna moved away and headed for the campus office. It was strange how small things seemed to get under her skin since she'd been pregnant. She had always imagined that the change in hormones causing mood swings was a myth, but little things seemed to play on her mind. She worried more about her family and was currently going through the fear that most women in her condition suffered: Would she and the baby survive the pregnancy? Although she had been assured she was fit and healthy and could have more children if they were lucky enough to conceive them, it didn't help her concerns. It wasn't about herself. She worried what would happen to Kane if anything happened to her. He had suffered enough heartache in his life and didn't deserve any more. Losing his wife and child in a car bombing had taken him years to come to terms with and she couldn't do that to him. The moment she'd discovered the pregnancy, she'd taken every precaution to ensure she would carry to full term. As she approached the office door she pulled her mind back into the game. As sheriff of Black Rock Falls, the townsfolk depended on her to keep them safe. She straightened her back and walked into the registrar's office. The nameplate on the front counter read: ELIZABETH HAUBOLD, REGISTRAR.

"Someone should be around." Kane rang the bell and leaned across the counter, peering into the passageway.

A woman came out from a back room wearing a tailored suit and smiled at them. "Good morning, Sheriff and Deputy Kane. What can I help you with today?"

Returning the smile, Jenna moved closer to the counter. "Two bodies were found yesterday in the river. We believe they are from twelve years ago. One of them was wearing a college football jacket with the year on it and an Alpha Pi fraternity pin. We'd like to identify them. Do you recall any of the students going missing around that time?"

"I do recall two students missing in Stanton Forest." Elizabeth tapped her bottom lip in thought. "Give me a minute. I'll pull the previous yearbook from our files and the names will come to me."

"Do the yearbooks list members of fraternities?" Kane leaned on the desk looking at her.

"Yes, they do." Elizabeth smiled at him. "I guess it's just as well because for me to give you that information, you'd need a warrant. I'll get both books."

She returned shortly after and they waited patiently for her to thumb through the pages. When she turned the book around and pointed at a fresh-faced young man by the name of Cole Peters, Jenna took out her phone and took a photograph. Moments later, she indicated to a girl with a bright smile and long dark hair eerily familiar to the desiccated body she'd seen previously. The girl's name was Abby Jaye. After taking another image, Jenna lifted her gaze. "Do you recall anything about the circumstances surrounding their disappearance?"

"In fact, I do." Elizabeth found the list of Alpha Pi fraternity members for that year and pointed it out to Kane. "There was a lot of scuttlebutt around it because it happened at Halloween. A group of students went camping alongside the river some ways from the Whispering Caves. They went up there to scare themselves silly because of legend of the Whispering Caves Axman. Apparently a hundred years or so ago, he walked the forest murdering anyone who crossed his path, and the legend goes that he wanders through the forest over Halloween murdering people." She rolled her eyes. "The thing is, a search was conducted all through that area and no one found a trace of the missing students. You see, everyone knew Cole. Being a star quarterback and a real nice boy, he was popular. One of the girls mentioned that Abby and Cole left the group before midnight. When they didn't return, she assumed that they'd left early and traveled back down the mountain. No one ever saw them again. Of course, the general consensus on campus was that she'd run away with Cole, but his vehicle was found parked near the ranger's station at the bottom of the mountain alongside Stanton Forest a few days later. The other members of the large group had no idea anyone was missing. Some noticed Cole and Abby leaving but assumed that they had gone somewhere to make out. It was a day or so later we discovered they'd never returned home." She sighed. "That's all I remember." She frowned. "I'm not sure where the idea came about that they'd run away together. Cole's future was bright. It wasn't something anyone would just throw away. I recall him being excited about his five-star rating. He'd be living the dream."

"Five stars?" Kane whistled. "He was an elite athlete."

Jenna glanced at him. "There'd be no reason for him to take off with his girlfriend. I wonder who started that rumor?" She gave him a meaningful stare. *Maybe it was the killer to throw everyone off the scent?*

"Do you recall the names of the people in the group that went into the forest that night?" Kane had been making notes and looked up at Elizabeth. "Any names would help."

"No, I gather it was a large group and it's been a long time to recall specific names, but I do know the story about the missing students didn't come out in the press until later that week—so probably November second. I watched it on TV. I recall thinking that the sheriff had moved too slow to save them if something had happened. It was different back then, not like now with so many murders. I guess he was waiting for them to show before he alerted the press." She shrugged. "I don't know."

"Well, I guess if he didn't investigate the missing persons cases, we'll never know just how long serial killers have been in town." Kane raised one dark eyebrow. "He didn't mention the students going missing at all. Did he even investigate or set up a search for them?"

"The parents and friends hunted through the forest." Elizabeth frowned. "They had flyers on trees all over but never found a trace of them."

Overwhelmed by the mountain of information that the woman had given them, Jenna glanced at Kane and then back to Elizabeth. "You've been extremely helpful. If you do think of anything else or if you discuss it with anyone and they have any other information, please contact me." She handed her a card.

As she walked back to the Beast beside Kane, she turned to look at him. "We'd better hunt down the next of kin of the victims right away to forewarn them that we may have found the bodies of their children."

"With luck, they might still be living in town." Kane slid behind the wheel. "We could access the birth records for the names we have and see what comes up."

The small breakthrough lifted Jenna's spirits. "I'll get Kalo onto it, but first I'll call Wolfe and give him the names. He can get the dental records."

SEVEN

Jenna eased onto the towel-covered front seat of the Beast and reached for a box of tissues to dry her face. The constant rain and being wet all the time annoyed her. The wet slicker seemed to cling to her all over and it concerned her that the constant wet might damage the Beast's pristine leather seats. After drying her hands, she waited for Kane to start the engine and then entered Kalo's number into the onboard computer. Using the FBI whiz kid out at Rattlesnake Creek would be the best way to get information fast. She needed the current addresses of the families of both the victims and passed on their information the moment he picked up.

"Give me a few moments. This shouldn't take long." Kalo tapped away on his keyboard. *"Yeah, I have it. They're still living at the same place, have lived there for twenty years or so."* He gave Jenna the details. *"While you're heading that way, I'll do a background check on both sets of parents and see if I can discover where they're working now or if they're working. If they're not at home, you'll be able to hunt them down there."*

Jenna heaved a sigh of relief. "Thanks." She added the coordinates to the GPS and waited for it to find a signal. She turned her attention to Kane. "They're close by. One is on School and the other on Pine."

"Okay." Kane backed out of the parking space and headed in the direction of Pine.

Pine Road had been named well. Tall pines lined the blacktop along both sides. The houses, all red bricks, built almost one hundred years ago and set back from the road, had long driveways meandering through what was once part of Stanton Forest. The picturesque houses appeared welcoming during the day, but at night the long closed-in dark driveways became threatening. She recalled a few murders that had happened on Pine over the time that she'd lived in Black Rock Falls. "The Peters' residence is first. I do hope someone is at home. There is nothing worse than going to a person's place of work and giving them bad news." She glanced at Kane. "I believe that most families would still be holding out hope that their children would walk in the front door one day."

"I figure I would be the same." Kane turned the Beast into a driveway that was little more than a tunnel of green vegetation. "At least the driveway is hard-packed gravel, some of them along Pine have deep ruts that fill with water and become quagmires."

The trees closed in around Jenna as they moved deeper into the tunneled driveway. The driving rain had been diminished to large spots of water splashing on the windshield. Here, the steaming forest was dark and foreboding even in the daylight. The hairs on the back of Jenna's neck rose as if in warning and yet she could see nothing to fear. As she turned to face forward, the Beast's lights lit up the way ahead and everything appeared normal again. At the end of the driveway stood an impressive house, which she imagined would have at least six bedrooms, reception rooms, a library, and an office. No lights shone from the upstairs windows and they stood out like the black sockets in the skulls of the two victims they'd discovered. Two of the ground-floor windows glowed with light that spread out over a small covered entrance with steps leading up on both sides. The pillars on each side of the steps made the house look very regal and an unusual design for a small town in Montana. She wondered if it had been owned by one of the town's forefathers or perhaps a banker. They stopped outside and Jenna pulled her slicker hood over her head and dashed to the front door. When Kane walked up beside her, she pressed the bell. Footsteps echoed from inside and the door opened to reveal an older woman. Her hair was dark brown, short, and stylish, but a few silver hairs were evident. "Mrs. Peters?"

"Sheriff Alton and Deputy Kane." Mrs. Peters looked from her to Kane and then back. She pressed one hand against her chest. "Oh my goodness, is this something about Cole?"

"May we come inside?" Kane gave her a sympathetic stare.

"Yes, yes, of course you can." Mrs. Peters stood to one side and waved them toward a mudroom. "Please leave your wet things in there and come into the family room. I have a nice warm fire in there and you both look frozen to the bone." She sighed. "Can I offer you a cup of coffee?"

Although Jenna would have loved a hot drink, she shook her head. "That's very kind of you, but no thank you. We have other people to visit this morning." She removed her slicker and wiped her boots on the thick mat and then followed the woman into the family room.

The room smelled of polish and wood smoke. Everything about the room spelled opulence, from the large stuffed sofas to the bronzes sitting on the mantelpiece. Artwork of scenery around Black Rock Falls covered the walls. As she walked to the sofa, her feet sunk into the deep pile carpet covering the floor. She sat down and waited for Kane to join her before turning her attention to Mrs. Peters, seated in a chair beside the fireplace. "I'm sorry to inform you that this morning we found two bodies in the river. We have reason to believe one of them might be your son."

"That's impossible. My son went missing twelve years ago." Mrs. Peters raised both eyebrows and stared at them with an incredulous expression.

"We have reason to believe that the bodies were mummified by being buried in sand approximately twelve years ago." Kane frowned. "Do you recall what Cole was wearing the night he went missing?"

"Vividly." Mrs. Peters met Jenna's gaze as her fingers busied with the folds of her pleated skirt. "As he was planning to go into Stanton Forest and camp for the night in the mountains, I insisted that he wore extra clothing. So he would have been wearing thermal underwear. Maybe one or two sweaters and his college jacket over the top."

"Did he wear a watch or a ring or anything else that could identify him?" Kane's pen paused over his notebook.

"He didn't wear a ring—he was hoping to get one after the football finals—but he did wear a watch and a fraternity pin on his jacket. He was a member of Alpha Pi." Mrs. Peters shook as she pushed a strand of hair behind one ear. "Do you believe it's my son? What happened to him? How did he die?"

Overwhelming empathy flooded Jenna. As a mother now, she completely understood what it would be like to lose a son. Having to deliver this type of news was soul destroying. She took a deep breath and let it out slowly to calm her nerves. "We don't have a positive identification yet or cause of death. He's with the medical examiner now and he'll be checking dental records. We're following up on anyone who went missing around Halloween the same year as your son. There was no watch found with the body, but he was wearing a college jacket and an Alpha Pi fraternity pin. Would you consent to a DNA test to confirm?"

"Yes, of course. Where would you like me to go?" Mrs. Peters stood wringing her hands. "I'll go at once."

"That's not necessary." Kane pulled a DNA collection kit from inside his pocket. "All I need to do is swab the inside of your mouth. The medical examiner has a DNA sequencing machine in his laboratory and will be able to give you an answer by tomorrow." He handed the kit to Jenna and then pulled on examination gloves. "I'll do the test and the sheriff will give you some paperwork to sign."

"If this is Cole, can I see him?" Mrs. Peters stood and opened her mouth for Kane to swab the inside of her cheek.

Swallowing the lump in her throat at the woman's over-whelming sadness, Jenna shook her head. "I don't think that's a good thing to do. It would be better that you remember him as he was when he left that night."

"Oh, sweet Jesus." Mrs. Peters covered her face and sat down abruptly. "He was murdered, wasn't he?"

"Like we said before, we don't have a cause of death at this time." Kane raised both eyebrows at Jenna. "Do you want us to contact your husband or a family relative who can stay with you for a time?"

"No, I'll tell him when he gets home." Mrs. Peters lifted a tear-stained face to Jenna. "I can't give him this terrible news and expect him to drive home in this weather. It's too dangerous."

Nodding, Jenna pushed aside her despair and moved on. She needed information and this woman was all she had right now. "Do you recall the names of any of his friends? Who he was with that night?"

"Not really. The boys all had nicknames, but I do recall one of the girls went by the name of Josie Grady. It's my sister's name, so it stuck, I guess." Mrs. Peters sighed. "They'd been friends since high school and Cole took her to the prom. She'd be in his group of friends, but his serious girlfriend was Abby

Jaye. I didn't see anyone the night he went missing. He left here alone and didn't mention plans to give anyone a ride, but I assume he dropped by for Abby. They were all meeting in the forest rangers' parking lot that night and that's where we found his truck." She pulled tissues from a box on a side table and patted her eyes. "I knew then that he'd never left the forest. We searched for an entire week, both families and some of the neighbors. I'm sorry to speak ill of the dead, but the sheriff back then did nothing to help find my son. He spent the entire four years in his office drinking whiskey. He was a disgrace to the badge."

Jenna stood and handed her a card. "Thank you for speaking with us. The medical examiner, Dr. Shane Wolfe, will contact you with the results."

"One thing." Mrs. Peters lifted her gaze. "Whoever this boy is, did he suffer?"

"No." Kane shook his head. "It would have been instant. If this is your son, we're very sorry for your loss and you can rest assured we will find answers."

Jenna nodded. "We can let ourselves out." She headed for the door.

The rain had eased as they ran for the Beast. Jenna climbed into the passenger seat and leaned back, allowing the information to seep through her mind. "Well, we have another name. At least that's progress. Perhaps the family of Abby Jaye will be able to fill in some of the blanks as well." She added the address to the GPS and waited for the voice to come through the speakers to give them directions.

"It's past one and you've been on your feet all day without a break." Kane headed back through the tunnel of vegetation. "I know you believe I'm being overprotective, but I'm not. I'm just following the instructions that Wolfe and Norrell gave you. Missing meals and being on your feet for long periods of time was on the list of things you mustn't do. I know you think you're indestructible, but every month that goes by from now will be more difficult for you. You're carrying a large baby, and at five months, it's evident to me that the weight is going to be a problem the further you go into the pregnancy. Pregnant women don't usually carry weapons, utility belts, and extra ammunition."

Annoyed, Jenna flashed a look at him. "So what exactly do you want from me, Dave? Do you want me to quit my job?"

"No, I want you to take regular breaks like every normal person." He followed the GPS instructions and soon they were turning into School. "That's not too much to ask, even during an investigation. It's not as if we have a psychopathic killer running loose at the moment. This crime happened twelve years ago and you need to slow down, if not for your own well-being but for that of our child."

Seeing the concerned look in her husband's eyes, she placed one hand on her rounded belly. She'd waited so long for this baby and didn't want anything to happen to it, but she felt just fine. Nodding, she relented. "Okay, I'll take regular breaks and eat. The time has gotten away from me, and I had a big breakfast. We'll speak to the Jaye family and then head to Aunt Betty's."

"Thank you." Kane pulled up outside a rambling ranch house and squeezed her hand. "I only want what's best for you, Jenna. You know that, right?"

Smiling, she met his gaze. "Yeah, but if you start calling me ma'am again, you're sleeping in the spare room."

"Okay." Kane's mouth twitched up at the corners. "That's a deal."

EIGHT

The interview with Mr. Jaye offered little valuable information. Mr. Jaye was a delivery driver and waiting for the floods to clear before returning to work. His marriage had ended in divorce a year after Abby disappeared. The stress of not knowing what had happened to their daughter, an only child, had caused the split. He didn't know the names of her friends at college and only recalled Cole because he was the other person who had gone missing. He knew his daughter was dating a member of the football team. She lived on campus after winning a scholarship and they'd been informed by the college that she hadn't returned to the dormitory after Halloween. He had no idea what she was wearing or if she had any jewelry, but she did own a gold locket her grandmother had given her for her sixteenth birthday. He recalled his wife mentioning it was missing from her belongings. The locket was heart-shaped and she'd put pictures of her mom and dad on one side and her grandparents on the other. He'd given a DNA sample and taken Jenna's card.

As they turned into Main and headed toward Aunt Betty's Café, Jenna contacted Kalo again. "Hi, Bobby, I have another name for you: Josie Grady. She went to high school with Cole

Peters and they went to the prom together. I believe she was with the group of them the night the others went missing."

"I'm on it." Kalo's chair squeaked as he slid it across the floor. *"I hope you discover the killer, but he could be dead or long gone by now. I've never known someone to go to these lengths and then stop killing, and we've covered a ton of murders since I joined the FBI."*

Shrugging, Jenna didn't care. She'd find out who was responsible and track him down. "You could be right, but these kids and their families deserve to know the truth. Call me if you find anything. I'll be in Aunt Betty's."

"Have a slice of pie for me." Kalo chuckled and disconnected.

Inside Aunt Betty's a tsunami of hunger hit Jenna and she stared at the specials on the board like a starving wolf. She smiled at Wendy, the assistant manager. "I'll have a steakburger, with fries and coleslaw on the side. The peach pie and ice cream. Hot chocolate with marshmallows and a glass of water."

"I'll have the same, but coffee for me, please." Kane placed a hand under Jenna's elbow and guided her to the table. He leaned in close. "I thought you said you weren't hungry."

Jenna removed her slicker and coat and sat down. "No, I said... Oh never mind." She looked at him. "I hope Kalo comes up with the details on Josie Grady. She might be the key to discovering everything about the night the others went missing."

Just at that moment her phone buzzed and she stared at the caller ID. It was Kalo calling back. "Okay, Bobby, what have you got for me?"

"Josie Grady, married to Bob Campbell, of Campbell Construction. She is living in her parents' house. They passed some years back and she works from home as a teleworker." Kalo cleared his throat. *"I followed her through college. There are images of her with a friend by the name of Marissa Kendrick. I'm*

hunting her down now, maybe they were both with Cole and Abby that night over Halloween."

Jenna grinned at Kane. "That's fantastic news. Do you have an address? Can you send me the details? We'll go and see her this afternoon."

"I sure do." Bobby sounded excited. *"I'll keep on the trail. It's like peeling off the layers of an onion. The more layers I remove, the more I find. I'll be in touch. Enjoy your pie."* He disconnected.

"Well, this case has just gotten interesting." Kane smiled as Wendy delivered the food. "Thank you kindly, and if you have any leftovers I could take back to Duke, I'd appreciate it. Just add it to my bill."

"Oh, we always have something for Duke." Wendy smiled and headed back to the kitchen.

Jenna shook her head. "You spoil that dog."

"Yeah." Kane met her gaze. "I figure he deserves a little spoiling."

NINE

Stomach flip-flopping and heart racing, Josie gaped out of her window as the sheriff climbed from a black truck. She'd voted for Sheriff Alton and Deputy Kane. They had a reputation of keeping the town safe and getting their man. The only possible reason they could be heading for her door would be about finding the bodies in the river. She'd never mentioned that Halloween night to her husband, Bob. It was better that nobody ever knew the truth and she couldn't trust anyone but the group of people that were there at the time. After graduation they had all decided to keep their distance, communicating only with the friends they'd had since grade school. They all figured that cutting off ties completely would only bring suspicion down on them. Pushing her shaking hands into the pockets of her jacket, Josie headed for the front door in anticipation of the knock. When she opened the door, her gaze moved up to the face of Deputy Kane. His expression was unreadable but his appearance was incredibly menacing. She swallowed hard at the man whose broad shoulders filled her doorway. He stood directly in front of her, blocking a direct view of the sheriff. After his gaze moved over her face and then over her shoulder to the passageway, he stepped to one side.

"Mrs. Campbell?" Sheriff Alton offered her a small smile. "May we have a moment of your time?"

Unsure of what to do, Josie nodded, stood to one side, and waved them through the door. The group had all decided twelve years ago to cooperate fully with any police investigation. They figured by sticking to the same story, sooner or later the cops would forget all about Cole and Abby. For the last eight years or so, they had believed this to be the case until the bodies showed up in the river. How could bodies show up in a river twelve years after they'd been buried in a cave? There should only be a few bones left by now. Nothing seemed to make any sense and the fact that the sheriff had homed in on her meant she knew something. Trying to keep a pleasant expression on her face, she led the sheriff and deputy into the kitchen. "Is it time to donate to the Broken Wings Foundation again? Time certainly does fly." She went to her purse on the counter.

"No, unfortunately we're here on other business." Sheriff Alton took out a notebook and pen from her pocket.

Acting surprised, Josie stared at them. "Has something happened to Bob?"

"Not as far as we're aware." Kane narrowed his gaze. "This is about the bodies that washed up in the river this morning. Have you been watching the news? We issued a media report earlier in the day."

Shaking her head, Josie waved them to a seat. "I'm sorry, I've been working in my office all morning and I don't have a radio on anytime during the day. What about these bodies has sent you to my front door?"

"We believe the bodies belong to two friends of yours from college who went missing twelve years ago: Cole Peters and Abby Jaye." The sheriff gave her a long look, as if studying her reaction. "I believe you were with them the night they went missing at Halloween. What do you recall about that night?"

Shaking her head, Josie looked from one to the other. "Heavens above, I can't remember what I had for breakfast this morning let alone what happened twelve years ago."

"That's very unusual because most times when a significant incident occurs, the details remain in our memories." Kane gave her a long look. "I would have imagined that two of your close friends going missing on a trip over Halloween would have been a significant memory. Just cast your mind back and try to remember what happened that night."

"First, do you remember how many people went on the trip?" The sheriff's pen hovered over a notebook and she gave her an expectant look.

Staring into space for a beat to make it look as if it were difficult to remember the past, she sighed. In truth she recalled every single minute of that night. "Well, I can't possibly give you a number because people were coming and going over the entire evening. It was dark and we only had the light from the fire. I spent most of the time with my friend Marissa. We've been close friends since grade school."

"You do recall Cole and Abby, don't you? They were in the same year as you at college." The sheriff raised both eyebrows, and her blue eyes searched her face. It was as if she were looking right through her and knew that she'd concealed the truth.

Letting out a long sigh as if all this was very boring, Josie shrugged. "I honestly don't remember very much about what happened that night. I do recall speaking to the sheriff a couple of days later. I can only tell you what I told him, although some of the details might be a little different because I can't remember everything."

"That's fine, just tell us what you remember." Kane ran a

fingertip over the rose pattern on the tablecloth. "Do you recall who organized the trip?"

Josie shook her head. "Nope. A flyer was attached to the bulletin board informing everyone that if people were brave enough to go up to the Whispering Caves over Halloween, a group would be heading up there at ten that night."

"Can you give an estimate of how many people were in the group that walked up the mountain with you?" Kane rolled his wide shoulders and narrowed his gaze.

The large deputy intimidated her and she stood and went to the counter, playing for time. She couldn't recall how many people they'd agreed to say. She turned to look at them. "Coffee?"

"No, thanks, but I'd like an answer to my question." Kane eyeballed her. "More than ten, less than twenty?"

Taking down a cup and pouring the coffee, she added the fixings before returning to the table. The cup gave her something to do with her hands, trying to avoid them seeing her trembling was becoming a problem. "I figure there was more than ten, but I don't believe it was as many as twenty, but then a few groups came along after us and made camp there, so it could have been more."

"Did you make camp near the Whispering Caves?" The sheriff looked at her across the table and then back at her notes. "They cover most of that part of the mountain. Do you recall if you camped on the highway side or on the river side of the caves?"

Why had the sheriff specifically mentioned the Whispering Caves? Concerned she'd made a fatal slip of the tongue by saying they'd made camp, Josie couldn't recall if they'd decided to mention the caves or not as a reason for being on the mountain at Halloween. She covered her mistake with a laugh. "Even as a college student I wasn't stupid enough to go to the Whispering Caves on Halloween. A group of us made camp alongside the river, not far from the old rope bridge. I recall seeing it swinging in the moonlight."

"That's a very unusual thing to remember when you can't recall who you were with that night." Kane shook his head, the disbelief on this face evident. "What was it about the bridge that made it significant to you?"

Josie gripped her cup like a life preserver, lifted her chin, and glared at him. "We were sitting around the campfire and some of the guys were telling stories. One of them told a story about the Whispering Caves Axman and how he hung a body from the old bridge, and it swung backward and forward dripping blood all over the rocks. It was windy and the bridge was rocking back and forth. People were talking about ghosts and being able to see him carrying the body toward the bridge. One thing I do remember about that night is that I was scared to death. The stories were getting very gruesome and that's around the time people started leaving. I recall it was very cold and I couldn't wait to go home."

"Look around the campfire in your mind." Kane stared at her. "Who was telling the stories? You dated Jess Hallon at one time. Was he there?"

Trembling, Josie nodded. What else could she do? "Yes, he was there. We weren't dating, that was in high school."

"Anyone else?" Kane leaned forward. "Who was Jess' best buddy?"

Looking away from Kane's penetrating gaze. Josie shook her head. "I can see their faces, but their names are gone. I'm sorry."

"When did you notice that Cole and Abby were missing?" The sheriff made copious notes in her book.

Sipping her coffee, Josie met her gaze over the rim of her cup. "I didn't know they were missing at all until days after. Like I said, couples and groups were coming and going all the time. I was spooked and Marissa was getting scared. We'd set up a small tent close to the fire. We climbed into our sleeping bags, zipped up the front of the tent, and talked until daylight. We were way too frightened to go to sleep. At first light, we didn't hang around and made our way back down the mountains to the parking lot near the forest rangers' station. I had a very old Jeep at the time and drove Marissa home. I went home and slept all day as far as I recall."

"What did you do when you discovered that your friends were missing?" Kane drummed his fingers on the table. "Did you start calling everyone? And did you or anyone you know go out searching for them?"

Shrugging, Josie shook her head. "I didn't, no. After hiking there and back, I had stiff legs."

"Hmm, you remember all about that night but you can't give us a name of anyone else who was there?" Kane leaned on the table. "Did the sheriff come by the college to take statements from everyone?"

She'd already said way too much and shook her head. "I didn't see the sheriff or hear anything that was going on until I watched the news. I figured that Abby and Cole were just two of the people who wandered off during the course of the night. I didn't hear anything unusual, no screams or people running in fear. Most people sat huddled around the fire until it got light and then we all wandered back down the mountain. It was an anticlimax after all the horrific stories that people had told about the axman. No one saw a ghost or anyone walking around carrying an ax with intent to murder anyone." She raised one shoulder in what she hoped looked like a nonchalant shrug. "That's all I can remember, I'm afraid."

"I'm sure that at that time in college many of your friends were couples." The sheriff folded her notebook and leaned back in the chair. "I've seen the yearbooks and have a list of names. I know Abby was prom queen. There's a picture of her the year before she went missing, alongside a guy by the name of Clint

Wasser. Do you recall if they were an item at the time she went missing?"

Josie shook her head. "I believe they'd broken up before Halloween. Clint was a wide receiver on the football team, so a big name on campus. He had more than a few cheerleaders chasing after him at the time. I don't know if he took anyone with him to the campout that night. I didn't move around in his elite circle of friends. I was studying and wasn't very interested in sports."

"So you do remember another person on the mountain, Clint Wasser?" The sheriff made more notes.

Horrified at her big mouth, Josie blinked. "I guess so."

"Do you believe there were two different groups in the forest that night?" Kane smiled. "The jocks and the nerds? That would have been a potentially lethal combination. I gather the beer would have been flowing in the jocks' camp and the rest of you all sat around the campfire telling ghost stories." He cleared his throat. "The football crowd can be a little wild at times. Weren't you concerned being in the forest alone with them when they'd been drinking?"

Nodding, Josie considered her reply. That was not how it went down but it sounded feasible. "I guess so, but who doesn't like a little adventure?"

"I would have expected that sort of setup to happen in high school and not in the last year of college." The sheriff exchanged a glance with Kane and then looked at her. "Okay, thank you for your time." She placed a card on the table and pushed it toward her. "If you remember anything else at all about that night, please give me a call. I'm sure the parents of the victims would appreciate knowing exactly what happened."

Standing, Josie ushered them to the front door. "I will. I'm sorry I couldn't help you any further." She closed the door behind them and leaned on it for a few seconds before dashing back into the family room to grab her burner phone from her purse. "Marissa, it's Josie. The sheriff was just here to question me about what happened to Cole and Abby. They have our names. Make sure you contact everyone about our meeting this evening. They need to know what I discussed so we can make sure we all have our stories straight."

"The guys are going to go ballistic." Marissa's chair scraped and a door slammed. *"This problem was buried and forgotten. How the heck did they end up in the darn river?"*

Josie chewed on her nails. "I don't know. Maybe they've come back to haunt us."

TEN

Cold damp air seeped into every crevice of Jenna's clothes as she walked back to the Beast. Raindrops splattered her cheeks and she pulled down the hood of her slicker, slightly annoyed by Mrs. Campbell's almost total refusal to answer questions when it was obvious that she had full recollection of the night in question. It seemed incredulous to her that someone could remember bits and pieces of a night so horrific in their lives but absolutely nothing about the two people who went missing or who else was there at the time. She tore off her slicker and tossed it into the footwell, climbed into her seat, and clicked in her seatbelt. As they drove away, she turned and looked at Kane. "I have the distinct impression that that woman is with-holding information. I know we can be a formidable couple but her hands were shaking from the moment we stepped inside her house. She was doing everything possible to avoid eye contact with us and was doing things to give herself time to reply to my questions. One thing's for darn sure, she knows exactly what happened that night and is keeping it a secret."

"My thoughts exactly." Kane turn the truck toward Main. "We need to get back to the office and discuss this with the others. Either she's covering up for the person who murdered these kids or she's involved."

Dabbing at her wet cheeks with tissues, Jenna looked at him. "There is another reason. If she does know who the killer is, she might be keeping quiet because she's in fear of her life. We don't know what happened that night, and if others were involved, there's a good chance that the killer threatened everyone. College kids do crazy things sometimes. For all we know they could all be involved with the murders and burials. It was Halloween after all, and you know as well as I do that things sometimes get out of hand. They could all be involved and therefore equally responsible. Getting one of them to break the code of silence is going to be very difficult. I guess we just keep interviewing everyone in that yearbook until we discover the truth about what happened to Abby and Cole."

Jenna's phone chimed and she looked at the caller ID. It was Wolfe. "Hi, Shane. This case is going to be a little more difficult than we imagined."

"Yeah, and it has yielded a little more evidence." Wolfe's footfalls echoed on the tiled floor in the mortuary. *"I've been working with Norrell on the bodies, and considering they've both been in the river, I can only attribute the findings to the fact that they were mummified. We discovered sand in the lungs of both victims."* He sighed. *"This makes this crime more sadistic than we'd first imagined. These kids were buried alive."*

Horrified, Jenna stared ahead at the rain-soaked blacktop. People moved around hunched against the rain or under umbrellas. Everything appeared to be normal, but nothing was normal in Black Rock Falls. Twelve years previously, two young people had been brutally murdered and their slaughter covered up. The killer or killers could still live in the same community as her. She could be raising her children in this town, never knowing if the parents of the kids Tauri played with at school had been involved. The thought that psychopaths moved among them on a daily basis chilled her to the bone. "What do you want us to do, Shane?"

"I figure if we let some of this information out to the public, we might draw out the perpetrators. There would have been others around that evening who weren't involved and don't want to be marked with the same brush. Norrell could hold a press conference and explain how she deals with the forensics of a case like this and how nothing can be hidden from science."

Jenna nodded. "Okay, make the arrangements and we'll be there. Thanks, Shane." She disconnected and looked at Kane. "I hope this works."

"So do I, Jenna, so do I." He pulled into his parking space out back of the office. "I just hope Norrell isn't painting a bullseye on her back because we have no idea how many people we are dealing with right now."

Gathering her things, Jenna climbed out glad of the under-cover area in front of the back door of the office. Being wet and cold all day wasn't her idea of fun. She headed straight for the counter to speak to Maggie. "Have we had any response to the media release this morning?"

"Yeah, the phones have been ringing off the hook." Maggie smiled and waved a pile of notes. "I'm not sure how I would have coped without Cade and Piper here to help out." She handed the notes to Jenna and leaned on the counter. "Things have settled down now, so can I send these guys home? It's been a long day for them and I don't want them to be reluctant to come by again."

Nodding, Jenna gathered up the paperwork. "Hey, Piper, Cade. Thank you so much for dropping by today and helping out. We really appreciate you being here. Maggie believes the rush is over now, so why don't you head on home and enjoy the rest of the day?" She waved a hand toward the window and the relentless rain pouring down outside. "Well, as much as you can enjoy a wet rainy freezing cold day, I guess."

"That would be good." Cade stretched and then slid his coat from the back of his chair. "We'll eat junk food and watch Netflix when we get home. We'd planned on going hiking over spring break but the rain ruined our plans."

"How are the roads out there?" Piper looked past her and out onto Main. "Any local flooding? Will we be able to get home okay?"

"Yeah, you're good to go." Rio walked up to the counter. "I checked the weather conditions five minutes ago and the highway to our place is clear. Drive safe."

"I always do." Cade smiled at him. "See you at dinner." He led the way out of the office, with Piper close on his heels.

Flicking through the notes, Jenna could almost see a pattern. There'd been a number of people concerned about the missing college students and remembered the incident clearly, even after twelve years had passed. She headed up the stairs as Kane was walking down with Duke. She waved the notes at him. "We have a result. Head up to the conference room when you get back. We'll spread these out on the table and work through them together. She leaned over the railing. "Rio, grab Rowley and come up to the conference room. Bring any notes you have about what you've been doing all day."

Once inside the conference room, she went about filling the coffee pots and kettle to make herself a cup of hot chocolate. She turned and smiled at Rowley as he arrived carrying a box of takeout. Being out in the rain and cold all day, she would appreciate a hot drink and a pastry. "Oh, can I smell donuts?"

"Yeah, Susie told me that Aunt Betty's has purchased a new donut fryer. She has been selling them as fast as they can cook them." Rowley slid the box across the table toward her. "Eat them while they're hot. I'll make you a cup of hot chocolate. I'll even thrown in a few marshmallows."

"Do you want a rundown of what we've been doing or do you want to go through the hotline calls first?" Rio dropped into a chair and yawned. "I can't imagine why Kalo enjoys hunting down people. I've scanned so many images of college students over the last few hours my head is spinning."

"What did I miss?" Kane walked into the room with Duke close behind. He peered into the box of takeout and then went to the counter to pour a cup of coffee. "Mmm, hot cinnamon donuts."

Savoring the bite of the delicious sugary treat, Jenna licked her fingers and then, after pulling a legal pad from a drawer, picked up her pen. "Okay, Rio, what have you got for me?"

"We compiled a list of everyone in that year at the college and added kids from the year before as Wolfe is convinced that both the killer and Cole were part of the football team. We separated the players from the others but kept all the girls' names from two years previously as well. Mainly because guys date girls younger than they are some of the time." He blew out a long sigh. "Then we went through those students who were in social clubs together. We found most of this information from the yearbooks and put them into groups."

"Yeah, we found the majority of the football players dated the cheerleaders, going on the prom photographs we found in the archives of the local newspaper. We made a separate list of them." Rowley handed Jenna a cup and slid one across the table to Rio. "The newspapers covered the missing students as well."

"Hmm." Kane licked sugar from his fingers. "All these responses from the public, the media, and yet the sheriff didn't make so much as a note about it in his daybook. That's very strange."

Unable to comprehend why such an important thing had been overlooked by the local sheriff, Jenna sorted the hotline information into four separate piles and handed three to the others. "We'll need to follow up on every one of these." She glanced at her watch. "However, as we don't have a killer roaming around murdering anyone at the moment, we will finish at five and take this up again first thing in the morning. I figure we just call each of these people and try to get them to expand a little more on their information." She moved her attention to Rio and then Rowley. "Did you get the name of the local reporter at the time, or find anything that might assist with the case?"

"I did." Rowley smiled. "They still work at the local newspaper and they have a very good memory. Main problem is that when the local sheriff and the media interviewed the kids, they all came up with the same story. A group of them read the flyer and a large group camped alongside the river. Where they stopped was a long way from the Whispering Caves. It was bitterly cold at that time of the year and none of them wanted to go that high up the mountain and camp out overnight. Many broke away from the main group and left before midnight, saying they'd decided to drop by the Old Mitcham Ranch to see if they could see any ghosts. A couple of the kids mentioned that they noticed Cole and Abby heading up the mountain trail toward the Whispering Caves. Nobody took any notice as cheerleader Abby had been getting the attention of Cole for some time. None of them stayed there overnight. It was so cold that by a little after one, without any sight of the Whispering Caves Axman's ghost, people had started wandering away. Nobody knew anything about Cole and Abby going missing until one or two days later."

"That's just about the same story we got from Josie Grady, now Josie Campbell." Kane reached for another donut. "This is going to take some detective work. Someone out there knows the names of the close group of friends who hung out with Cole and Abby."

Sipping her drink, Jenna looked from one to the other. "When we do, we'll split this case wide open."

ELEVEN

The Old Mitcham Ranch

Head bent against the rain, Wyatt Twotrees used bolt cutters to break the chain securing the gate to the Old Mitcham Ranch and pushed it wide open. It had been a very long time since he'd been at the haunted ranch house. After more than one mass murder had happened in the exact same place, he figured it wasn't only Mitcham, who'd murdered his wife and then hanged himself, who haunted the place now. The old place was dangerous and anyone could be waiting in the shadows. The hairs on the back of his neck stood to attention as he looked out across the shadowed driveway. The haze from the rain had been enhanced by the swirling mist rising from the river and in the moonlight the old ranch house, with its peeling paint and empty windows, radiated a warning not to enter. He looked toward the barn, where Mitcham had hung himself from the rafters. The legend was that on Halloween he could be heard swinging back and forth, the rope creaking with each sway of his decaying body.

Wyatt wasn't sure if he believed in ghosts, but over the

years, he had sure seen a few weird things happening in Black Rock Falls, so anything could be possible. He stood to one side as vehicles drove into the driveway forming a circle, their headlights highlighting the downfall of rain and making the perimeter outside dark and foreboding.

Over the last twelve years since the incident at the Whispering Caves everyone involved had taken a low profile, going their separate ways and meeting only at college reunions. They all had close friends within the group, figuring that was normal as they'd spent so long together in college. He'd married and divorced and worked in the spare automobile parts industry, and his close friend Clint Wasser worked in sales. He was still single, saying he liked to play the field on his sales trips. Both his other college buddies Jess Hallon and Dustin Crawley worked on their parents' cattle ranches. Dustin was often away on the rodeo circuit and had never married, but Jess had a son and a wife. The girls in the group he didn't make contact with at all. Josie had married Bob Campbell. Marissa, a tax accountant, was still the little scared mouse he'd known at college, and Lily was a hairstylist. They did talk but kept it on the down-low. In all, they'd hid their secret from the world very well.

He climbed into his truck and headed for the other vehicles. He buzzed down his window. "I'm not standing out in the rain. Drive into the barn." He grinned at them. "Unless you're chicken."

"I don't know why you dragged us all out here in the middle of a flood, Marissa." Wasser shook rain from his baseball cap and glared at her. "No one is going to know we're talking. Why do you figure the cops believe we're involved?"

"It's been a very long time, Clint." Marissa stared at him from under her hood. "Haven't you watched the news? The sheriff is hunting down friends of Cole and Abby. They found their bodies floating in the river. I wanted to make sure we all understood the implications of what was happening and to ensure that after all this time, our stories were the same."

"I agree." Hallon shrugged and removed his hat to shake out the rain. "You know the law. Murder doesn't come under the statute of limitations. We covered this up and I'm not blaming anyone because most of us would have done the same thing in the circumstances, so we're all equally guilty. If the truth comes out, we'll all go to prison for murder one."

"I still find it hard to believe Cole murdered Abby." Lily pushed both hands into her coat pockets. "Why would he? They got along real well and she was really nice. I know she loved him. I wonder what really happened. Did they argue?"

Rolling his eyes, Wyatt Twotrees gaped at her. "That's water under the bridge now, Lily. Why he did it is irrelevant. All we need to remember is he murdered Abby and needed to be stopped. You all know it was the right thing to do and any one of us would have done the same. We all agreed to bury the bodies that night and nothing has changed."

"If we'd let him go, he'd have murdered us in our sleep." Dustin Crawley, rugged and strong, rested both hands on his belt and his buckle glistened in the headlights. "It's too late now to have second thoughts. We go over the story and stick to it." His gaze swung to Josie. "I hope you didn't spill your guts." His gaze shifted to the other women. "Y'all are weak links and we're trusting our lives to you. One slip and y'all become liabilities. Us guys are solid. Look what happened today. Who did they question first? Josie, and they'll get to the rest of y'all and try and make you talk. You know the sheriff's reputation: she can read a lie and she will hunt us down like a dog after a bone."

"It doesn't matter who killed Cole." Clint Wasser folded his arms across his chest and his gaze moved around the group. "We're all equally to blame. We have never spoken about it since that night, and Josie calls Marissa the second the cops leave. How stupid is that? Don't you figure they'll check the phone records?"

"Yeah, and what does Marissa do?" Jess Hallon stood feet apart and back straight. He pointed a finger at Marissa. "Within seconds of disconnecting, she contacts Lily." He shook his head. "Didn't you think it through before you acted? You'll get us all life in prison." He threw his arms up in the air and glared at them. "My dog's got more brains than you two."

Twotrees held up a hand. "Calm down, everyone. Arguing about what's already done will get us nowhere. All we need to do is get our stories straight, is all." He looked at Josie. "Tell us from the beginning what happened today. Don't leave out a single detail."

He listened as Josie recounted the sheriff's visit. He looked around the group. "The one thing we need to make clear is we didn't go near the caves. As we moved into the other group's camp down the mountain making a noise, everyone will recall we arrived late. I built the fire with Jess and we made a point of talking to everyone so people there would remember us being there. As us guys were all wearing our college jackets and identical Halloween masks, I doubt anyone noticed Cole and Abby were missing. They'd have seen a group of Alpha Pi guys, is all."

"I recall Bella Crooke asking me if I'd seen Abby." Lily looked at him with haunted eyes. "We were all cheerleaders, if you recall. I told her she'd headed up the mountain with Cole. So if the cops get to her, she might remember our conversation."

"I had a similar conversation with Valerie Janecki but she was asking about Cole." Wasser grinned. "I told her he'd headed into the forest with his girlfriend." He laughed. "She wasn't happy. Seems she had a message for him from his mom. They were neighbors."

Nodding, Twotrees stared out into the rain and then back to the others. "Anything else specific you can recall about that night?"

"Yeah." Jess Hallon's brow wrinkled into a frown. "Cory got into a fight with Birch over some girl. Remember they stumbled through the fire and we had to stamp it out?"

Twotrees nodded. "Yeah. So we can add that information." He looked around. "Only tell the story of who you spoke to, not ours, or it will sound rehearsed. We're not kids. We can handle the cops as long as we give them the same information about Abby and Cole." He looked around the group. "They left and we never saw them again that night. We figured they'd gone somewhere to be alone and then left."

"We were all too busy toasting marshmallows and telling ghost stories to notice they didn't return." Wasser shrugged. "That's what we were doing. Just do a time shift in your memories."

"Just remember." Hallon stared at the three women. "If one of you chickens out, we'll fall like a house of cards. Think before you do anything else stupid, Josie."

"Okay." Josie's cheeks reddened and her fingers trembled as she pushed a strand of wet hair from her eyes. "I'm just wondering who pointed them in my direction in the first place?"

"They know we were Abby's friends. They'd only need to ask our folks or look in a darn yearbook." Marissa shrugged and gave him the stink eye. "It was just bad luck they decided to speak to her first, is all." She blew out a long breath like smoke from a cigarette. "I need to get home. We done here?"

Twotrees had a bad feeling someone in the group would talk. Everyone would go to prison for life and he had no plans to ruin his life for a slip of the tongue. He nodded slowly and looked at the others. "Keep the contact between us to an absolute minimum and don't call everyone. Call one of us using the burners and get them to pass on the message and so on. Let's get out of here, one at a time, not in a darn convoy. I'll shut the gate." He went to his truck and watched everyone drive away in intervals. Nothing had convinced him that they'd get through this unscathed. Not now that the sheriff was making waves. He shook his head as they left one by one and stared at the red taillights vanishing into the darkness. A cold breeze tainted with rain brushed over him and all around him the old barn moaned. The sound might have bothered some people, with the tales of the dead rising and haunting the old barn and ranch house, but not him. The dead were dead. It was the living he needed to worry about. He headed for his truck and climbed inside. The faces of his friends hadn't changed and most looked almost the same as on that Halloween night. He let out a long sigh. "Which one of you will fold first?"

TWELVE

TUESDAY

Gray storm clouds rolled across the mountains to join the mist-covered pine trees, and it was as if the forest was living under a cloak of fog. The continuous rain was getting monotonous, and Jenna and Kane spent two hours driving from one place to another to inspect the flooding. The updates were coming in regularly from the Montana Department of Transportation, and Jenna expected the governor to declare a state of emergency as the flooding became widespread. After flooding a year or so previously, the drainage throughout the town and much of the surrounding county had been updated, but nothing could stop the constant flow of water. Swollen rivers were breaking their banks at a rapid rate. The melt was always a problem, but no one had expected it to rain for a month.

As Jenna sat in the Beast her phone buzzed. She checked the caller ID as it lit up the screen in the truck. It was Johnny Raven. Raven had agreed to join their team as a consultant. He had a trained K-9 that would take on dangerous work that wasn't suitable for Duke. Raven served in the Medical Corps and after an injury spent his rehabilitation learning how to become a K-9 trainer. So he offered double value to the team.

He was an extra doctor, a pilot, and, at six-five and two hundred fifty pounds, a good person to have for extra backup should the need arise. When not needed, Raven trained rescue dogs for self-protection and in general was a dog guy, finding forever homes for strays he'd used for his dogsled and offering medical services to the off-the-grid folks in the mountains.

Jenna glanced at Kane and gave him a surprised expression. Raven rarely called the office. "Good morning. How are you, Dr. Raven?"

"Oh, come now, Sheriff. No one calls me Dr. Raven." He chuckled. *"I'm Raven. The folks around here like that just fine. Are we on speaker? I can hear the Beast's engine."*

"Morning, Raven." Kane smiled at Jenna. "What's happening in the mountains? We have no idea. You've been blanketed in mist and rain for so long we've forgotten the mountain is there."

"Conditions are not good, I'm afraid, but I do have some good news." Raven blew out a long breath. *"I've spent a long time clearing an old trail that leads from my cabin to the fire road. It means I can now drive my truck into town and get to you at short notice. That's the good news."*

Jenna nodded. "That's great and much safer for you. What's the bad news?"

"You'll recall the avalanches we had over winter. Well, it seems they've done more damage than we first anticipated. Trees have been ripped out by the roots. Fine if you need a good supply of firewood or need to build something but real bad with this rain." Raven cleared his throat. *"I'm no expert but I figure you need to get someone to check out the avalanche areas. They look too darn unstable to me and we're still getting rumbles through the mountain. It's only a matter of time before we'll get mudslides."* He sucked in a breath and let it out in a huff. *"You know there's people living all over up here. Many don't want to*

be found but we need to at least warn them if there's a chance of mudslides."

Frowning, Jenna stared at the screen. "Yeah, I'll call it in and see if they can get a team up there to check it out. I'm not sure what they can do to stop it." She pushed hair behind one ear, thinking. "Last time we had a bad slide, the forestry planted a ton of new trees and undergrowth, but that's impossible in this weather."

"If there's a chance of mudslides, I can contact people over the CB radio, and messages get passed along. You could get warnings out over the media." Raven paused for a beat. *"There are many old cabins people could move into out of the danger areas. They just need to know the threat is there."*

Trying to consider whom she needed to contact, Jenna nodded. "Okay, I'll get things moving and keep you in the loop. Thanks for letting me know."

"I appreciate it." Raven disconnected.

Jenna made the necessary calls and nodded slowly as she repeated the same request. Disconnecting, she turned to Kane. "Everyone I called is going to coordinate a team to check the state of the mountain in the avalanche areas. It's a matter of organizing the right people. I guess we wait and see."

"I'm sure they can see that this is a matter of urgency." Kane pulled into a parking space out back of the office. "I'll be interested to see what Rowley and Rio have come up with this morning. We need more details on the college friends of Josie Campbell. The person she mentioned, Marissa something, is someone we can hunt down today."

Working on a cold case was always difficult because people had short memories and details were overlooked. It usually entailed a ton of grunt work and interviewing people who couldn't remember what they had for breakfast the previous morning. For Norrell, it was something to get her teeth into.

Her work with Wolfe would no doubt bring to light more details to assist with the case. Jenna nodded. "Yeah, I'd like to hear what she has to say." She met his gaze. "You might believe I'm losing my mind but have you ever felt as if you're in a mystery novel? I mean this case is throwing us tiny morsels of clues as if they're being fed to us via an author."

"Hmm, I guess that's one way of looking at it." Kane burst out laughing. "Do you figure they would let us have a peek at the end of the book? It would save time and we could go home and cuddle in front of the fire."

Smiling, Jenna shook her head. "Wouldn't that be nice?"

"I figure it's the nature of a cold case." Kane slipped out of the door and unclipped Duke from his harness. "Small fragments of information come to light as we move along. To be honest, I'm enjoying hunting down a murderer without someone trying to kill us. I would imagine that the killer is long gone from this area by now." He smiled at her, his eyes dancing with mischief. "And for the record, I do love a good mystery."

Stepping out into the cold damp air, Jenna hurried inside the office, glad to see Rio and Rowley working at their desks. "Morning, everyone. Can you bring all your information upstairs to my office, please?" She sailed past them and headed for the front counter. "Morning, Maggie. Is there anything interesting for me today?"

"I've already given all the information from the calls on the hotline to the deputies." Maggie stared over her shoulder at Cade and Piper, who were sitting in front of the TV. "They've been here since seven and they're having a break at the moment. I must say they've been a great help. The calls come in after each news bulletin and it gets a little chaotic, then nothing happens for hours. There are quite a few people who recall the kids going missing in Stanton Forest. We've had a couple of calls from the group of students who were in the forest that night when Abby and Cole went missing. They have information about that night but are not clear on exactly what you need. They might be people you could put on your list to interview."

Waving at Cade and Piper, Jenna moved her attention back to Maggie. "That sounds like a plan and at least we have some leads. I was getting to the point where if I hadn't seen the victims' bodies, I'd have assumed they didn't exist at all. There's too much mystery around this murder, as if it's been a giant cover-up. I'm wondering if the old sheriff had anything to do with it."

"As he's long gone, I doubt we'll ever know for sure." Maggie rested both hands on the counter. "The deputies have been working hard all morning as well and I'm sure they'll have more information for you."

Nodding, Jenna smiled at her. "I guess I should go and find out." She indicated toward Cade and Piper. "Make sure they get something to eat. They can order takeout and put it on the account or do the same at Aunt Betty's or the pizzeria."

"I'll make sure they put in an order when I do mine." Maggie held up one hand when the phone beside her rang. "Gotta go."

The smell of fresh coffee drifted toward Jenna as she headed upstairs to her office. Kane had gotten everything organized in her absence. Two pots of coffee, one regular and one decaffeinated, dripped from the machines. Rio was working industriously in front of the whiteboard. With his retentive memory, he made short work of listing all the information that he and Rowley had accumulated earlier. She removed her slicker, hung it on the peg beside the door, and changed her footwear. After giving Duke a pat on the head, she headed for the whiteboard and looked at Rio. "What have you got for me?"

"The information coming in over the hotline is just about identical." Rio lifted one shoulder in a half shrug. "Two kids went missing. They can't remember their names but one was the college quarterback. People were saying that they ran away together—until they found Cole's truck. It was Abby's father who got the search parties together and some of them mentioned the forest rangers were involved as well. They found the campsite where everyone had stayed that night but no trace of Cole or Abby."

"The local newspaper gave us a write-up of the story, and it has pictures of the students who went missing. There was one follow-up story saying that no trace of them had been found and they believed they'd run away together." Rowley shrugged. "So the media reports are absolutely useless, much like the records in this office from that time."

"What else did you discover about the women involved?" Kane glanced at them over one shoulder.

"Josie Grady, Marissa Kendrick, Abby Jaye, and Lily Jones are all friends from college." Rio added the names of them to the whiteboard. "We discovered numerous images of them in yearbooks, and in high school as well, so they go back a long way. As you've already interviewed Josie Campbell, that is her married name, I believe, do you want us to move on to Marissa Kendrick and Lily Jones?"

"I figure women are more likely to talk to each other about what happened during their college years. They would likely recall who was dating who and the like." Rowley looked up from his tablet. "We forgot to mention that they all knew Abby and Cole. They're in a group photograph at a prom along with a few other people who we've yet to track down. We have names but that's all for now. Unfortunately, there's nothing to prove that any of them were together on the night that Abby and Cole went missing."

Jenna frowned. "This is what makes cold cases so frustrating, there isn't anything shared on their social media profiles.

We don't have phones to look at and I doubt anyone would still own a computer from twelve years previously, but I guess we can check it out."

"I have a laptop from twelve years ago." Rowley glanced up from his tablet. "It still works okay, although it's a little slow compared to today's models. So don't count that idea out. College kids would have had phones at that time."

"Maybe, but most of them would have been useless in the mountains, apart from taking photographs and using the flashlight." Kane poured coffee and handed the cups around. "I don't recall college kids being able to afford satellite sleeves back then —or now. Not many college kids would own a satellite phone, even now."

Trying hard to think outside the box, Jenna stared out the window and into the dull gray morning. "There were no phones with the two bodies. You could assume that Abby was carrying one in her hand when she was murdered. We could have found one in Cole's back pocket, unless he left it in his truck or it washed out in the river. We'd need to interview his parents again to discover if there was any evidence left in the truck." She glanced from one deputy to the other as she took her seat behind the desk. "If we could find one of their phones, we would have a contact list. What about social media? Have you hunted down the list of names and seen who they have as friends?"

"That was one of the first things we did after finding them in the yearbooks. We found images of ten or so men who were photographed with one or all of the women, and all the guys were on the football team. Five of them were in Alpha Pi." Rio sat in front of the desk and reached for a cup of coffee. "The guys might have been friends in college but they're certainly not friends on social media."

Adding cream and sugar to her cup of decaffeinated coffee, Jenna stirred slowly as she considered the implications of what

Rio had said. "Don't you think that's a little unusual? Most people, especially frat brothers, keep in contact with their close friends from college. It doesn't make sense that this group of guys, who knew the three women and Cole, were close friends back then and now avoid each other like the plague."

"Do they all still live in Black Rock Falls?" Kane sat down and sipped his coffee. "It's easy to lose track of people when they leave town."

Interested, Jenna leaned forward in her seat and stared at Rio. "Do you have any names?"

"Yeah. Four of the men live in Black Rock Falls, as do three of the women. You already know the women's names." Rio stood and went to the whiteboard. "Wyatt Twotrees, Jess Hallon, Clint Wasser, and Dustin Crawley." He added the names to the whiteboard and turned back and took his seat. "We haven't had time to hunt down what they do for a living or where they live. We'll check the MVD and get that information for you as soon as possible. You already have the details of the women, and Lily is a stylist at the beauty parlor."

Pleased by their results, Jenna nodded as she munched on a cookie from the jar on the desk. "Okay, we'll leave you to keep hunting down those guys' information and we'll head out to speak to Cole's parents again. If he did have a cell phone, it wouldn't be something that a parent would throw away, especially if it held images of their son."

"Maybe they've left his room intact." Kane collected the cups and placed them in the sink. "Some parents never give up the hope their kids will return home someday. Maybe we'll be able to find something there to connect the dots."

Pushing to her feet, Jenna looked at her deputies. "Okay, we'll leave you to it and go and speak to Cole's mom again and then we'll drop by and see if we can find Marissa Kendrick. Can you update my files when you discover anything new?"

"Yes, ma'am." Rowley stood and headed out the door.

It was good having Rio as her chief deputy. He'd keep working without orders. His promotion had taken a ton of worry from her shoulders. She grabbed her slicker, shuddered, and looked at Kane. "Back out into the cold soup. Let's hope we get a positive result."

THIRTEEN

Duke hated storms, so when the weather was unpredictable Kane preferred to leave him at the office dozing in his basket. He made sure the dog had a good supply of food and water. He gave Duke's head a rub, pulled the blanket over him, and listened to his contented sigh before following Jenna downstairs. He figured they'd get two more interviews out of the way before lunch. He smiled at Jenna as he slid behind the wheel. "Mrs. Peters first?"

"Yeah." Jenna fastened her seatbelt and arranged her things in the center console. "It's been a long time, but as you said, parents could be keeping things as a shrine to their son. I'm hoping they have, and we'll find evidence inside the truck or his bedroom to help us find out who killed him."

Starting the engine, with rain pouring down the windshield and the wipers increasing speed to cope with the deluge, Kane turned the Beast toward Main. "It's a longshot but it's all we've got right now. Although most parents see their kids in a different light to what they really are."

"How so?" Jenna turned to look at him.

Kane slowed down to negotiate a large puddle of water

across the blacktop. He smiled as a three-year-old wearing bright yellow rubber boots and a red raincoat ran along the sidewalk in front of their mother, jumping in the puddles. The child looked completely oblivious to the fact that he was soaked through. The bedraggled mother pushing a stroller hurried after him. The scene brought back memories of times with him and his sister when they did the exact same thing and got themselves into trouble.

They stopped outside Mrs. Peters' home and dashed through the pouring rain to the front porch. The driveway squelched under foot. Changing his boots for a pair of thick lined rubber boots and two pairs of thermal socks had been a good idea. Splashing through puddles, Kane followed Jenna up the steps. The door flew open and Mrs. Peters stared at them, her mouth hanging open.

"Have the DNA tests come back yet? Is it my Cole?" Mrs. Peters looked from one to the other, a terrified but expectant look in her eyes.

Kane exchange a meaningful glance with Jenna and reached for his phone. "They hadn't when we left the office, but I'll see if they've been uploaded onto the server."

"The medical examiner does require a positive DNA sample to identify Cole, but from all the evidence that we have already, I am certain that it's him." Jenna moved closer to Mrs. Peters. "My aim is to discover who did this to him and I need your help."

"How can I help you? I don't know anything." Mrs. Peters stepped back into the passageway and waved them inside. "I spoke to my husband last night and we tried to recall every detail, but we haven't come up with anything new."

After scanning the files and the positive ID that Wolfe had uploaded earlier that morning, Kane gave Jenna a slight nod and pushed his phone back inside his pocket. "I'm afraid that the sample you gave us came back as a positive match to the victim. I'm very sorry for your loss."

"We've always hoped he'd come back one day, but deep down inside I knew that was false hope. Whatever the reason he left, he would never have given up football. When he didn't show after the draft pick, we believed he was gone." Mrs. Peters' eyes filled with tears. "This makes it so final, but at least now we can lay him to rest." She straightened as if gathering herself. "Now what can I do to help you find this monster who killed my son?"

"Did you by any chance keep his room intact?" Jenna's expression was hopeful. "And what about his truck? Did you sell that or do you still own it?"

"His room is exactly the same as when he walked out on that Halloween night to meet Abby." Mrs. Peters looked from one to the other. "I always expected him to walk back through the front door. Same with his truck. It's in the garage and hasn't been touched since we found it in the parking lot near the forest ranger's station."

This might be the breakthrough they wanted, but they couldn't rush into this as they needed more information about Cole. "Before we take a look, can you give me more information about his relationship with Abby? Did they get along or did they fight a lot?"

"He was infatuated with her and what young man wouldn't be? She was a beautiful girl." Mrs. Peters went to the mantel in the family room and beckoned them inside. "Look at all these photographs of them together. They made a perfect couple. Abby was a delight and never had a bad bone in her body. She doted on Cole and planned to move to wherever the draft sent him. To be honest, from what Cole said to me, I honestly envisaged him asking her to marry him once they knew he was literally set for life." She shook her head. "I don't recall them ever fighting. They started off as friends in high school and that blossomed when she joined the cheerleading squad. I can't imagine why anyone would have wanted to kill them. They minded their own business and did nothing to hurt or annoy anyone."

"There are people on this earth who are jealous of others' happiness." Jenna met the woman's gaze. "Then there are others who just kill when the opportunity arises. You'd be aware of the murders that happened in this town over the last few years. None of them actually make any sense. They were all part of the killer's deluded fantasies."

"Well, go upstairs. His room is the third on the left." Mrs. Peters sighed. "I keep the door closed now because it brings back too many sad memories. His laptop is there and also his phone. We found that in the center console of his truck, so he must have left it behind that night." She tapped her chin, thinking for a beat. "I recall him taking the flashlight from the kitchen before he left that night, and we didn't find it in the truck. You will know it if you find it because it's metal and has the name Peters engraved on the side. It used to be in my husband's toolbox and was forever being borrowed by one person or another."

Kane added that information to his notebook and followed Jenna up the stairs.

FOURTEEN

A knot tightened in Kane's belly. He found it disturbing, almost intrusive, to walk into a dead person's room, more so when it was a young person whose life was cut off midstride. He scanned the room, taking in the football posters from twelve years previously. Pennants and images of him and Abby were plastered everywhere. Trophies crammed three sets of shelves. This young man was not only good at football, he excelled across many sports. He played baseball, won trophies in track and field, and was proficient in swimming as well. Kane's attention was drawn to a collection of gun trophies and he discovered Cole was at competition level in rifle. He turned to look at Jenna. "What a terrible waste of life. This young man had everything going for him, didn't he? I wonder who took it into their head to kill him. If this was a serial killer, surely there would be others going missing around the same time. Was this an opportunistic thrill kill?"

"As the sheriff didn't bother to keep his files up to date, we have no idea." Jenna made a beeline for the laptop, pulling on gloves along the way. "I guess we should avoid contaminating the room, even though it isn't technically a crime scene." She followed the power cord and turned it on at the wall. "Let's see if this boots up after all this time." She pointed to the phone sitting on the desk. "Can you hunt down a charger? Maybe it's in one of the drawers."

For a college student, Cole was incredibly tidy, unless his mother had cleaned the room after he'd left. The bed was made and there was not a speck of dust to be seen anywhere. He gathered that Cole spent a good deal of his time in the fraternity house and maybe came home on weekends. Halloween that year just happened to fall on a Friday. Kane opened drawers and found the phone charger. He attached the phone and plugged it in. It was an old phone and would likely take over an hour or maybe more to recharge. It seemed that the laptop was in good shape. It was slow to boot up but hummed along nicely and opened up using *Alpha Pi* as the password. "That was a good guess." He leaned over Jenna's shoulder, staring at the old screen.

"Ah, emails." Jenna slowly scrolled through them one at a time. "I'll take a quick look, but we'll need to take these back to the office and go through them. We need to spend time searching the room."

Kane straightened. "Although it's so clean it's hard to imagine he even lived here."

He opened closet doors to find a variety of normal gear. Dumped in one corner of the closet was a duffel bag and he hauled it out to take a look inside. The bag was filled with dirty laundry. This would be the reason the room was so clean. No doubt his mother would have come in and dusted but Cole must have dropped in before he left to pick up Abby. He dumped his bag in the closet and likely forgot to tell his mother. If she had found it after he'd gone missing, perhaps she was reluctant to open it or destroy the last few things her son had touched. He recalled asking Wolfe about what had happened to his things as he didn't have even one small reminder of his wife. Wolfe told him that, as he'd reportedly been killed in the accident, all his belongings had been moved into storage. It was a military storage unit and the items would be there for at least ten years before he would be able to access them if necessary. One thing that always bothered him was the fact that he had never been able to speak to his father or mother before they died. His going dark had been absolute, much the same as Jenna's, but she didn't have any family that he knew about to care where she'd ended up. Her parents died before she became an FBI agent.

He scanned the walls, his gaze moving over the photographs. It seemed that he printed many from his phone. One in particular caught his eye. It was a group of six young men. Cole was the center, with both arms resting on the other young men's shoulders. All were wearing football jerseys, and the Alpha Pi fraternity pins were evident on everyone's chest. He took the photograph from the wall and placed it on the desk beside Jenna. "I do believe I found the group of friends that went up the mountain on Halloween. This image doesn't denote anything particularly special apart from a group of friends out having fun. This might be the clue we've been looking for."

"There's not much to and fro in the emails, mainly college stuff and information from various places offering Cole work over the breaks." Jenna blew out a long breath. "There's too much here to go through. He has hundreds of emails piled up. My bet is anything interesting will be on his phone. Not many people email their friends and that's who we need to speak to—and Abby's. It's a shame we were never able to find her phone. My bet it would be in the cave where they were buried or some-where close by, although were phones water resistant those days? I have no recollection of smartphone functionality twelve years ago. It's not something I worry about too much."

Kane chuckled. "Me neither. I'm usually just impressed how many things the phone can do these days. It seems every new model has something I desire greatly and need to buy right away. Often during my missions I was literally a guinea pig for some of the new technology in weapons and armor. I never minded and enjoyed giving anything they gave me a thorough workout. I figure Wolfe is much the same as me. He has every possible innovation in his laboratory that POTUS offers to send him. He has things there that are usually sent out only to military doctors for evaluation. This is how he had the special laser to alter my fingerprints." He sighed. "I haven't found anything of interest apart from the photograph and the duffel full of unwashed clothes in the corner of the closet. I didn't believe this room looked lived in by a college student, and seeing the duffel would mean he came home to say hello to his folks, dumped his dirty washing, and took off to meet Abby."

"I would agree because his mom would have cleaned his room while he was away for the week at college." Jenna stood slowly and placed one hand on her rounded belly. "The baby is very active today, especially when I sit down. I'm coming to the conclusion it has very large feet." She gave him a long stare and then chuckled. "I do believe big feet come from your side of the family."

Kane collected the laptop and phone. "Only on the male side. My mother was dainty."

"That's good to know." Jenna pulled a receipt book out of her pocket and made a list of the items they had taken. "We should show the picture to Mrs. Peters and ask her if she can identify the others in the photograph with Cole. I wouldn't mind betting that they're the same men who Rowley and Rio hunted down."

They headed downstairs, and Mrs. Peters came out of the kitchen to greet them. Kane handed her the photograph. "Do you recognize any of these young men with Cole?"

"I do. They were his best friends in college." She pointed to each of them in turn. "Wyatt Twotrees, Jess Hallon, Clint

Wasser, and Dustin Crawley." She smiled. "We used to enjoy watching them play football together."

"Do you recall if Cole mentioned going with them as a group to the forest on Halloween?" Jenna leaned forward. "It would be a great help if we knew who was with him on that evening so we can talk to them."

"No, he never mentioned it to me." Mrs. Peters' eyes filled with tears again. "I'm sure if they had been with him, he would have been okay, but as far as I know, that evening he was going out with Abby. He didn't even mention the forest, so I assumed they were going through town like everyone else does on Halloween. I know he'd purchased a Halloween mask, but at the last minute he left it behind."

Kane straightened. "You wouldn't by any chance still have it, would you?"

"Yes, in fact I do. Do you believe it will make any difference?" Mrs. Peters hurried off and returned a few minutes later with a horrific Halloween mask. "I recall, he believed it was too scary for Abby as she really wasn't into all the graphic Halloween costumes."

Kane held out his hand. "It might make a whole lot of difference. Do you mind if we add it to the list of things that we need to take with us?"

"If it would help find my son's killer, you can take the entire house." Mrs. Peters folded her arms across her ample chest. "When will we be able to bury our boy?"

"The medical examiner, Dr. Shane Wolfe, will contact you." Jenna handed Mrs. Peters the receipt. "You must understand that because it's been twelve years, these things take time, but I can assure you that Dr. Wolfe's team gives everyone who goes through his hands the utmost care and dignity. His fiancée, Norrell, is the forensic anthropologist working on the case with her entire team and Emily his daughter is a medical examiner in training. Cole and Abby couldn't be in more caring or better hands. You have my word."

"Thank you, that eases my mind some." Mrs. Peters took the receipt and followed them to the mudroom. "Are you going to search his truck? It's unlocked."

They pushed their feet back into their boots and pulled on their slickers. Kane had the phone and laptop along with the photograph and mask in one large plastic evidence bag. He turned to Mrs. Peters. "Yes, we'll go and check out his truck and then leave. We'll keep you up to date with the investigation, and as before, if you can think of anything unusual about that night or if you heard anything that people were saying that might be of interest, please give us a call."

FIFTEEN

Heart sore for Mrs. Peters and her husband, Jenna stood in the garage and waited for Kane to search Cole's truck. Hunger gnawed at her, and she wished she could have a nice cup of hot chocolate overloaded with marshmallows. The thought made her stomach rumble just as Kane backed out of the truck. She smiled at him. "If my stomach is making noises along with yours by the time we get to Aunt Betty's Café, we'll sound like a choir."

"We can delay dropping by Marissa Kendrick's until after lunch if you would prefer." Kane shut the door of the truck and shrugged. "There's nothing of interest in there. I'd say his parents cleaned it out, or someone did. There's only the license and registration in the glove box. Nothing to indicate it belonged to a kid in college at all. If it wasn't for the college parking sticker on the windshield, I'd say it belonged to someone else."

Frowning, Jenna shook her head. "How strange." She headed back to the Beast, splashing through the deepening puddles. "We need to keep moving. As much as I'd like to go and eat lunch now, I'd rather go and see Marissa Kendrick and get it out of the way so that we can spend the rest of the afternoon in the office. I'm exhausted. I had no idea being pregnant used so much energy."

"You'll need to use the footstool I placed under your desk." Kane headed out of the driveway and along Main to Maple. "Walking around is fine but resting is good too, and keeping your feet up will prevent swollen ankles."

Jenna smiled at him. "So will rubbing my toes when we snuggle in front of the fire. The other day, I rubbed Pumpkin's toes. She purred like mad and stretched out her paws. She's a lovely cat. I'm so glad she found us, and she keeps Duke company as well."

"I like her too." Kane slowed outside a log-built house with a large porch, turned into the driveway, and stopped out front. "I hope she's home. It will save time if we don't need to keep coming back here."

Pulling her slicker over her head, Jenna dashed to the porch with the rain hammering on her hood and pounded on the front door. The net curtain beside the window moved and she caught sight of a shadow looking out at them. As Jenna's slicker had SHERIFF across the front and back, the hesitancy of the woman coming to open the door wasn't because she didn't know who was waiting outside. It never ceased to amaze her how people didn't recognize her even when they voted for her in the last election. They were a prominent couple around town, easily approachable, and yet she still found townsfolk reluctant to speak to her. The door opened slowly, restricted by a heavy chain, and a woman with dark straight hair wearing a thick sweater and jeans peered at them with wide-open brown eyes. Jenna met her gaze with a pleasant expression. "I'm Sheriff Alton. I'm here to speak to Marissa Kendrick."

"I'm Marissa." The woman hadn't moved to open the door. "Why do you want to speak to me? Has someone died?"

"No, we're investigating the murders of two of your friends

from twelve years past." Kane removed his hat and shook off the raindrops. "Do you figure we could come inside and speak to you. It's wet and cold out here."

"I guess. You'll need to leave your slickers and boots in the mudroom. I don't want you tracking dirt all through my house." Marissa closed the door to unhook the chain and then opened it wide and waved a hand toward a small vestibule on the left. "Through there." She waited for them to remove their things and then led the way along a passageway and into a typical country kitchen. "It's warmer in here than any other room. Please take a seat and tell me what this is all about."

Jenna took out her notebook and placed it on the table alongside her pen. The woman sat at the table with an agitated expression on her face and it was obvious that she didn't want to speak to them about her old friends. Jenna needed to take a different approach with this woman by letting her know they had information about that evening. It might push her into telling the truth. "We are aware that you were close friends with Abby Jaye and Cole Peters during your time at college. We also believe you were with them the night they went missing, on Halloween twelve years ago. What I'd like you to tell us is your recollection of that night and who were the other people on the mountain."

"There would have been over twenty students from Black Rock Falls College, maybe more, spread out all over as it was set up as a dare. You recall the legend of the Whispering Caves Axman? Well, the dare was to stay on the mountain by the caves past midnight to see his ghost. It was really just a party, nobody camped near the caves. I couldn't possibly tell you everybody's names because I don't know. Yes, I was there with Abby and Cole, but I don't recall seeing them for very long. They were there when we were sitting around the fire toasting marshmallows and then they got up and walked away. That was the last time I saw them."

"Who else was in your group around the fire that night?" Kane leaned on the table and gave her a direct stare. "It was a memorable night as your friends never returned."

"I'm not exactly sure. There were people coming and going all the time." Marissa's eyes shifted from side to side and she refused to make direct eye contact.

It was obvious to Jenna that Marissa had something to hide. She tapped her pen on her notebook and sighed. "I have a few names that might jog your memory. Do the names Wyatt Twotrees, Clint Wasser, Dustin Crawley, and Jess Hallon ring a bell?"

"We have numerous photographs from yearbooks and other sources that put you all together as a group of friends, so please don't deny that you know these people." Kane leaned back in his chair and folded his arms across his chest.

"It's a lifetime ago, Deputy. I recall them, yes, but there were a ton of other kids on the mountain that night." Marissa looked aghast. "You don't think we had anything to do with them disappearing, do you? Heck, I didn't even know that they'd died until I watched it on the news."

"We aren't chasing down these people for a murder charge. We just want to know who was on the mountain that night and if anyone suspicious was hanging around." Kane huffed out a sigh. "It's a cold case and we don't expect the murderer to be in the forest now, but that doesn't mean we'll stop investigating their deaths. Cole and Abby deserve to have their killer brought to justice and we aim to do it." His gaze became almost predatory. "No matter how long it takes."

Jenna dragged her attention away from Kane's face. It was obvious that he had the same impression as she had about Marissa. The woman was fidgeting in her chair, couldn't look at them, and was thinking before she spoke, and the long pauses within the conversation were getting annoying. "Marissa, what I would like you to do is just tell me everything you can recall about that night. What the weather was like is a good place to start. Did you go there with a special friend or did you go with a group of friends?"

"It was cold like it is most Halloweens. Mist was rising up from the river and spilling through the forest." Marissa stared into space. "There were students everywhere, following each other up the trail and heading toward the river. Some were wearing Halloween costumes. Many were wearing masks of one sort or another. I remember the group of boys that were with us as we walked up the mountain. They are all about the same size and wearing their college jackets with identical Halloween masks, so no, I don't know exactly who was there."

"Yet you recognized Cole and Abby. How so?" Kane's hard gaze was relentless. "What made him different from everyone else in the pack?"

"They were walking in front of me." Marissa gripped her hands tight on the table, making her knuckles go white. "Cole was slightly smaller than some of the other boys on the football team and he wasn't wearing a mask. He was holding Abby's hand and carrying her backpack over one shoulder. Abby had a flashlight and was using it to show the way along the trail." She chewed on her bottom lip as if she was trying to think up another lie. "We all ended up alongside the river. It was cold and very damp. The boys went about making a fire and the girls collected rocks to make a fire circle. We dragged some old stumps to the edge of the fire and sat around telling ghost stories and toasting marshmallows. As I said before, I recall seeing Abby whisper in Cole's ear and then stand up. He followed her up the trail toward the Whispering Caves. They were consenting adults and what they did when they left the group is none of my business. I didn't even have a thought about it. I just recall it happening. I didn't watch out to see if they returned."

Jenna made a few notes. "Who did you come to the forest

with that night? Did you drive yourself or get a ride with someone?"

"I went with Josie Campbell. She used to be Grady back then." Marissa lifted her head slowly and looked at Jenna. "I gave her a ride. My parents had supplied me with a truck for college. We were friends then and we still are now. I call her maybe once or twice a week but she's always busy working."

Nodding, Jenna made a couple more notes. "Did she happen to mention that we dropped by to speak to her?"

"Yes, it did come up in a conversation we had after we saw the news report about the deaths of Abby and Cole." Marissa pressed a hand to her chest. "It was such a shock to find that they had died and been left in the mountains all this time. To think that I've hiked to the river many times since that night. Do you know where they were found? When I was speaking to Josie, she figured they must have gone down the mountain or walked along the river and maybe fallen in."

"Nope." Kane unfolded his arms and leaned on the table. "Somebody buried them in a cave. It must have been deep inside the mountain away from water because the bodies are mummified, which means they are exactly the same as when they were buried. At this point in time the medical examiner is going over every inch of their bodies looking for clues. Their clothes were intact. This is how they were so easily identified."

"Oh, I see." Marissa's gaze hit the table again and she picked at her fingernails restlessly. "Well, I don't have anything else to tell you. We sat around the fire after Cole and Abby left, listened to everyone telling ghost stories, waited until midnight, and then everyone just sort of drifted off. I walked down the mountain with Josie and we went home. Of course, we knew by the following Monday that Cole and Abby had gone missing. Search parties were organized, but the sheriff who came and spoke to us intimated that he believed they'd run away together. None of us thought that was true because Cole had gone into the draft and would have made a professional football team. That's not something he would have run away from with Abby or anyone else." She sighed. "After the search was called off, we sort of went back to normal. We all graduated and went about our lives. I'm sorry there's not anything else I can tell you."

"How often do you see the group of men that you were with that night?" Kane scrutinized her face. "They all live in town as far as I'm aware, so surely you'd run into them from time to time."

"Me?" Marissa snorted a laugh. "No, not all of them. Most of them have gone their separate ways. I'm a tax agent and Clint Wasser is a client, but none of the others have contacted me since graduation. I might nod to them in passing but they're not close friends. I haven't had too much luck when it comes to romance. In our group at college, I was just along for the ride. Josie got plenty of attention, but none of the boys were interested in me."

Folding her notebook and pushing it inside her pocket along with her pen, Jenna stood. She handed a card to Marissa. "If you think of anything else, give me a call. It's obvious you didn't hear a noise or see any strangers hanging around, which puts the blame directly on the group of students that were on the mountain that night. Try and bring back that evening by going over what happened from the time you got dressed to the time you went home and see if you can recall any strange vehicles or people wandering around that evening. If you do remember anything at all, no matter how small, you can call me anytime."

"I'll give that some thought." Marissa followed them down the passageway and stood staring at them as they put on their boots and slickers.

The moment Jenna stepped out onto the porch, the chain slid into position on the front door. It seemed that Marissa wasn't taking any chances of an intruder getting into the house.

As she jogged back to the Beast, she turned to Kane. "What do you make of her?"

"She's hiding something." Kane swung into the truck. "That story she told us is almost the same as Josie's. As everyone's memories are slightly different, I find that a little bit hard to believe." He started the engine and turned the truck around before heading back along Main. "I figure that she's spoken to Josie about our visit and they decided to get their stories straight. Another thing I find hard to believe is that college students who live in the same town are practically strangers after being close friends for many years in college and probably high school as well. Unless they all argued about something between themselves, it doesn't make much sense."

Running the interview through her mind, Jenna nodded. "Yeah, I kept in contact with many of my college buddies. I knew where they'd started work and where they were living. Many of us would get together and go out for coffee or drinks. Then there were the reunions—the five-year and the ten-year reunion—that these people would have attended, no doubt. You're correct, maybe what's keeping them apart is the fact they're all involved in two murders." She rubbed her hands together. "Now can we have lunch?"

"Not a problem." Kane smiled at her.

Happiness surrounded Jenna like a warm hug when she walked inside Aunt Betty's Café. The wonderful aromas of food cooking and freshly ground coffee made her stomach growl with appreciation. It had been a long time since breakfast and suddenly she understood exactly how Kane felt most of the time. Being ravenous was unusual for her, but of late she couldn't seem to get enough food to fill her for more than a couple of hours. She stared at the specials list—barbecue pork ribs with all the trimmings. It was something she'd usually have for dinner, but as the delicious smell crawled up her nostrils, she grinned at Wendy behind the counter. "I'll have the ribs with all the trimmings, including the sweet corn. Peach pie and ice cream and a tall glass of milk."

"I'll have the same, but forget the milk. I'll just have coffee." Kane snorted a laugh behind her. "I never thought I'd see the day you'd come in here and order the entire specials menu."

Removing her slicker as she strolled through the restaurant, Jenna glanced over one shoulder at him. "It's not my fault. Our baby is obviously favoring you. Big feet and a voracious appetite are a clue I can't ignore." She hung her slicker over the back of the chair beside her and smiled at him. "At least now I can be sympathetic when your stomach growls with hunger. I know just how it feels."

SIXTEEN

Why couldn't the cops just leave it the heck alone? No one even mentions Cole and Abby anymore. We'd all forgotten about them long ago and now they have to rise up from the dead like avenging angels to cause problems for everyone. There's only one person who can keep everyone under control, and that's me. The problem is right now anything can happen, and I can't trust anyone. The phone calls started happening the moment the sheriff and her deputy left Marissa's home. They at least stuck to the rules on getting a call and passing on the information to another, but it doesn't take a genius to know that Marissa is close to breaking and that can't be allowed to happen. From the call I received from Lily, Marissa had divulged or acknowledged the fact that all of us guys were with those girls that night. From what Lily had mentioned, Marissa had tried to cover up who we were by saying we were all wearing Halloween masks. This was true, but she shouldn't have agreed that we were all there on that evening. How much longer will it be before she starts divulging more details?

Nervousness had come down the line when Lily spoke to me. As a very outgoing woman who deals with people all day as a hairstylist, I've rarely seen her upset with anyone and yet she was fuming when she called me. She figured that Marissa could have covered up our names by just saying it was a long time ago and she'd forgotten who was there, but no, she had to agree with the deputy when he read out a list of names. It's obvious that Marissa is easily intimidated. Heck, when I was speaking to her out at the Old Mitcham Ranch, she was practically shaking in her boots. I could imagine Deputy Kane staring her down would have been enough to make her talk. This doesn't mean that they have any evidence against us. Just saying we were there doesn't make us guilty as there were many more people on the mountain that evening.

Things keep piling up against me and I need to take action to protect myself. Friendships might last a long time, but I can't trust anyone right now. I noticed a newsflash on the TV at lunchtime saying that the medical examiner and the forensic anthropologist would be doing a media conference to discuss the bodies they found in the river. The broadcast mentioned that new clues had been uncovered. Right now, the group of us is in danger of being discovered, and Marissa is a loose cannon. As I stare out into the pouring rain, I slowly shake my head as I formulate a plan. Taking Marissa out is my only option of silencing her, but it will be a huge risk. I've kept my killing sprees out of Black Rock Falls since that night and settled into a life where people have no idea what I do for recreation. Living in a town renowned for hunting and coming back from a trip spattered in blood doesn't raise an eyebrow, and oh boy, I've done that so many times now I've lost count.

That night in the mountains, I needed to kill so bad my hands were shaking, and then Abby and Cole headed my way. I didn't choose them. The first person to walk by would have satisfied my need and doing two at once was an extra thrill, but hiding the bodies and explaining the blood to the others was a problem. Not for my folks. When I arrived home that night, I told my mom I had fake blood all over from a Halloween prank and she made it vanish without a trace. I still recall the expressions on the faces of Lily and Marissa as I walked back into the camp blood-splattered and excited. You see, it's very difficult to come down from a kill. My heart pounds so fast and my muscles quiver. I need time to walk around and become normal again.

I gathered them all together and even managed to shed a tear or two to show how terribly upset I was. How I've done the most terrible thing and I needed their help. The lies had come easily. I told them I'd decided to go and see if anyone had had the guts to go up to the Whispering Caves, but when I got there I heard someone cry out, but the sound was muffled. I ran into the cave and found Cole standing over Abby with an ax. There was blood everywhere and I attacked Cole and got the ax away from him, but he pulled a knife on me. I said Abby was still alive, and she was because I killed her last. I told them I heard Abby moan, and Cole turned to stab her in the chest. At this point I faked sobbing and leaned heavily on Marissa for a time.

When they asked what had happened, I recall looking at them one at a time and asking them what they would have done. They all said that I should have stopped him. When I told them that as he turned his back, I hit him with the ax and figured I'd killed him. Instead of being horrified, they all nodded in agreement. It didn't take too much to convince them to come back up the mountain with me and bury them in the cave. We used the ax and our hands to dig the hole. Once we had them buried, I threw the ax into the river, along with the knife and Abby's phone. We all washed up and then cleaned our camp. We headed down a different trail and then returned as if we just arrived and joined the others alongside the river. That evening was the last time I'd had a single thought about Abby and Cole. As we were all in it together, I had no worries that anyone would run to the cops.

I now have a dilemma. I have too many skeletons in the

closet for the law to look at me. If they even suspect me and get my DNA, it won't just be Abby and Cole. They will tie me into all the others across the state. I can't allow this to happen. If my friends become my enemies, then the Whispering Caves Axman will need to strike again.

SEVENTEEN

As she pushed her empty pie plate away from her, Jenna's phone buzzed. It was Norrell. She passed one of her earbuds to Kane to join the conversation. "Hey, Norrell, have you discovered anything new?"

"*Shane has organized a press conference in half an hour to discuss our findings in the bodies-in-the-river case. He mentioned he discussed it with you earlier about trying to flush out anyone involved by giving out small snippets of information to make them believe that we are onto them.*" The sound of sugar being added to a cup of coffee and a spoon stirring the brew came through the speaker. "*We do have more information than previously. I did find a few snippets of skin under Abby's fingernails. The problem is, without a DNA specimen for comparison, it is practically useless. It doesn't belong to Cole Peters. There's something else that's extremely unusual when you're looking at a double homicide: Although Abby was likely positioned under Cole, as there are imprints of his outline on her skin, she isn't soaked in his blood.*"

Jenna shot a glance at Kane and raised one eyebrow. "What does Shane say about this?"

"He figures that it indicates that Cole Peters was attacked first, because he has Abby's blood on the front of his jacket. If he'd died second, it would have made sense that he would have bled all over her. Shane also believes Cole Peters was moved, likely dragged some distance, as there are deep grazes to the flesh on his torso, which would indicate that his shirt was pulled up as he was dragged over a rough surface. There are no such injuries on Abby, which would make him believe that she was carried to her final resting place."

"So this is a clear indication that more than two people were involved." Kane rubbed his chin. "From what you are describing, Cole was dragged over rough ground by his feet. This would pull up his jacket and expose his back to the ground, whereas Abby was carried probably by two people holding her arms and legs. As her throat was cut, she would have been bleeding profusely. We know she was still alive, so her blood would have still been pumping from the wound. I believe this would have been the reason not to carry her any other way."

"Then we have the Alpha Pi fraternity pin she was clutching in her hand. I know it's hard to believe, but we actually took prints from that pin. There is half of a thumbprint on the front. Shane is running it through all the databases as we speak, but again, just like the DNA, it's useless if we can't get a match."

Jenna listened intently, turning over the information in her mind. "The thumbprint could belong to anyone. Someone could have handed the pin to him just before he went out, or it belongs to the owner. I do think that Abby tore that pin from him to prove who was trying to kill her. She likely scratched him as well, but after twelve years we're never going to discover who had scratches on them from that long ago."

"There is something else of significance." Norrell paused a beat. *"The sand samples that we retrieved from Abby's lungs are consistent with samples taken from the Whispering Caves. As you recall, Atohi Blackhawk is on my payroll, and I sent him to*

the mountains to hunt down anywhere where there's been seismic activity that could have caused a cave to wash out. He found a group of caves with large new fissures above them where water had washed down into the caves and down the mountain. One of the caves he discovered forms part of a new river system that runs into Black Rock Falls. He considers that particular area is the most likely place where bodies could have been washed from caves and into the river. As the melt is almost over in that area, as soon as the rain stops I'll be heading to the Whispering Caves to check out the area and see if there's anything we can use to determine if that's where the bodies were buried. The only problem I can envisage is that, for water to dig out enough sand to move the bodies into the river, it likely hasn't left anything for us to discover. However, sand being heavy, and this particular sand carries a lot of gravel, there is a chance that there might be things left behind. Personal items, for instance. It's worth the trouble to go and check it out."

Jenna considered the risk. "Let me know when you're going, and if Wolfe isn't going with you, I'll arrange for one of my deputies to escort you. Even though it's been twelve years, you should never assume it's safe in the mountains. It's not only murderers you need to worry about. The bears will be waking up very hungry, so an escort or going armed in a group is essential."

"I've been moving around the forest with my team since I arrived. I know they're aware of the dangers. Three of them attend the dojo with Rowley four times a week. I'm now surrounded by very fit young men. I'm sure we'll be fine, but I will inform you when we are heading up that way."

"That's good to know." Kane wiggled his eyebrows at Jenna. "I'm glad my little talk with them about fitness gained results."

Jenna smiled at him as they bent over the phone. "Do you want us at the press conference?"

"Yes, and the reason I'm calling is to discuss with you how

much we're actually going to reveal to the press. Shane suggested that we have reason to believe that Cole was murdered first. If it is a group of people, as you suggested, it might throw the cat among the pigeons. Whoever was with them would be only an accomplice, and maybe that is something you can use to get them to come forward and give information about the killer."

Pushing her hair behind one ear, Jenna considered all the information. "Yeah, I figure that's a good idea, especially as we're homing in on a group of friends that were together that night and they all know the victims. Maybe you could mention that you have other evidence that you're waiting to be confirmed and that you'll be going to visit the crime scene in the next week." She stared into space for a beat. "Tell them that we know they were buried in the Whispering Caves, and as they are fully preserved, all the evidence is intact. Maybe that will cause a ripple?"

"I hope so. Head on down. The press conference is being held in the medical examiner's foyer. It's too wet to hold it outside. It will be a squeeze, but Shane suggested we stay behind the counter."

Nodding, Jenna glanced at Kane, who shrugged. "Okay, we'll be by in a few minutes. We're just finishing up at Aunt Betty's. We'll park round back and avoid the crush. Catch you later." She disconnected. "This will be interesting. Wolfe has CCTV, doesn't he? We need to have a record of who was there. The media conference was given out on the local news. Our killer might just show up to see if we have any evidence." She stood and pulled on her slicker. "Let's go. This is getting interesting."

EIGHTEEN

Stomach churning, Marissa sat down in front of the TV waiting for the news conference to begin. After the visit from the sheriff and the phone calls received from the others, she'd started to wonder whether keeping silent was a good idea after all. She stared at the TV and listened in interest as the medical examiner and the forensic anthropologist explained all the details about the bodies they'd found. They'd discovered their identities and exactly when they went missing. The fact they had found evidence on the bodies disturbed her. What evidence had they found? She allowed her mind to drift back to that terrible night. The images of Cole and Abby pale and lifeless always sat in the recesses of her mind. Seeing her best friends dead wasn't something she could forget. They'd all been around Cole and Abby that evening. Earlier that night she'd given Abby a hug. This would mean her DNA was probably all over her, some of her hair perhaps as she used to wear it long and flowing those days. It would be the same for the others. Every one of them touched the bodies. It was Josie and her who grabbed an arm each and helped two of the boys carry her deeper into the cave. They wanted to keep them as far away from the entrance as possible so no one would ever find them.

Her phone buzzed and she looked at the caller ID, surprised to see Josie on the line. They'd decided to cool their conversations of late rather than make it look like that they were discussing the murders. "I'm watching the press conference, are you?"

"*Yes, of course I am. I want to know what's going on.*" Josie was breathing heavily down the line as if she'd been running a distance. "*The medical examiner is going to speak now. Maybe he'll let us know what he's discovered.*"

Dr. Shane Wolfe's voice boomed out from the TV, and Marissa held her breath in anticipation.

"*This is a very heinous crime. Not only were two young people slaughtered, but we have evidence to prove that they were buried alive. Whoever attacked these two young people in the Whispering Caves over Halloween twelve years ago needs to be brought to justice. I can assure you that my department will go to every length possible to determine who is responsible for this crime.*"

"*Do you have any suspects?*" A reporter thrust a microphone into the sheriff's face.

"*We do have a list of possible suspects and we'll be working through them over the coming weeks.*" Sheriff Alton stared down the camera. "*This may be a cold case, but for me it's brand new. We were very fortunate that the bodies were mummified and so they carry a great deal of evidence. I do believe that we'll have an arrest in this case very soon.*"

"*Dr. Wolfe, what type of evidence have you retrieved from the bodies so far?*" A reporter moved their microphone back to the medical examiner.

"*A great deal of evidence, and my colleague Dr. Norrell Lawson will be examining the gravesites as soon as the rain eases and it's safe to go to the Whispering Caves. From the evidence we have discovered on the bodies, we believe we have located the gravesites. We'll be looking for any personal items or other evidence we can use to prosecute the killer of these young people."* Dr. Wolfe held up a hand. *"That's all we have for you today. We'll keep you updated as the information comes to hand."*

Marissa's hand shook so hard the phone slipped from her palm. She grabbed it up and pressed it to her ear. "We didn't kill anyone. I'm not going to prison for the rest of my life. We should tell them the truth so they know it wasn't murder. It was self-defense."

"It's murder now." Josie sucked in a deep breath and let it out slowly. *"We thought they were dead, didn't we? The problem is they now have proof they were buried alive, and we buried them alive. So we're all equally to blame for their deaths. Even though Cole injured Abby, what it really comes down to is the fact that it was us that dug the grave and us that buried them alive. We're all murderers. Our only chance is if we stick together and don't say anything to anyone."*

Horrified at what they had done, Marissa ran a hand down her face. "If we explained the situation, it might be okay. He was only stopping Cole from killing her, wasn't he? What else could he have done? It was self-defense and we've kept his secret all these years because it was the right thing to do, but now we might have to consider saving our own necks. I know if someone is implicated in a crime, they can seek immunity for giving information. I figure we should think long and hard about what we're going to do. Maybe we should speak to Lily as well? If we went in to see the sheriff as a united force, we might be able to broach a deal with the DA."

"Are you batshit crazy?" Josie was pacing up and down, her feet audible on the polished wooden floors of her home. *"Can you imagine what Bob would say if he knew I was involved in two murders? Unlike you, I have a family to consider. Abby and*

Cole are dead and there's nothing we can do about it. There's no use wasting the rest of our lives on a stupid mistake. It wasn't our fault. Cole attacked Abby with an ax. That's the truth. He got what he deserved, and we owe it to our friend to keep his secret."

With trembling fingers, Marissa lifted the remote to turn off the TV. "Okay, I understand what you're saying." She drew in long deep breaths and blew them out slowly to try and calm her nerves. The report on the TV had brought every second back to her in a rush of blood and horror. Now she had to carry the burden of knowing that she buried her best friends alive. "I don't believe we should stop calling each other or going out for coffee. I figure staying away from each other would attract more attention. I'm sure if the sheriff is suspicious, she'll be looking for any change in behavior."

"Yeah, sure, I can do lunch tomorrow at Aunt Betty's Café. I'll be there at one." Josie tapped her nails on the phone. *"Don't forget to smile and act normal when you arrive. There are CCTV cameras everywhere. If anyone is watching us, we'll need to appear like we have nothing to hide. The news report was as disturbing to us as everyone else, but as we were not involved, it doesn't concern us. Our only interest is in the fact that they were friends a long time ago at college."*

Marissa nodded even though her friend couldn't see her. "Okay, I'll see you tomorrow at one." She disconnected and dropped her phone onto the plush velvet sofa.

Her home had taken so long to perfect. She walked around the room, fingering the furnishings, saved for and purchased with the hope that someone would share them with her one day. Did she deserve to be living with hope of a better future when Cole and Abby had been cut down so young? Had the story told on the mountain that night been the truth? The series of events had happened so fast. She hadn't had time to think it through. In fact, she'd just gone along like a sheep and followed the others. The faces of her dead friends haunted her and now would fill her nightmares knowing they hadn't been dead after all. Cold shivers slid up her spine. What if they'd regained consciousness in the grave? The thought was too horrific to consider. It was her worst nightmare and she could almost feel damp soil pressing against her face.

Mind spinning, she'd need to face her problems alone. Speaking to the others about her misgivings would send shockwaves of mistrust through the group. There must be an option, a way out of this mess. Keeping silent could mean years in prison, but could she tell on her friends? It would be the greatest form of betrayal, but how could she cope being restricted to a small area and never being able to see the mountains again? She would die in prison. Knees trembling, she headed for the kitchen and pulled out a bottle of red wine from the cabinet. She drank long and hard from the bottle and swiped her hand over her mouth, breathing hard. Deep down inside, the awful truth was eating at her conscience. She doubted she would ever sleep again.

NINETEEN

The foul weather was making Clint Wasser's life a misery. Being in the automotive industry and responsible for making sure replacement parts were available on demand was getting more difficult by the hour. When the call came from Dustin Crawley, he leaned back in his seat and watched the rain pour down his windshield. "Heck, Dustin, I really don't need to deal with this right now. Maybe you need to drop by and see Lily and settle her down?"

"Lily's not the problem. It's Marissa. From what Lily said to me during our conversation, the woman is freaking out over the news conference." Dustin was speaking from inside his truck. Wasser could hear the engine roaring in the background. *"Josie called Lily and she called me. I needed to pass on to you what's going on and you can tell Wyatt. That was the deal, wasn't it?"*

How Wyatt Twotrees had become the leader of their group he had no idea. They were equal partners in the dealership, selling popular new cars and servicing them as well. Wasser heaved a sigh. "Okay, what's the emergency this time? What did Lily tell you, and don't leave anything out or embellish any of the information because when we're passing things back and forth important information gets lost."

He listened with interest to what Josie had told Lily about her conversation with Marissa. It was obvious that the news about Cole and Abby had hit Marissa hard. She'd always been a mousy little girl from grade school. He'd often wondered how she'd become friends with the other girls because she just didn't fit into the group. Having her around all the time made it difficult for the guys if they wanted to pursue a romance with any of the others because she was always hanging around. In the end it had only been Cole and Abby who had gotten together. The others just hung out. It had been fortunate that the incident with Cole and Abby had happened over Halloween as they'd graduated the following December and gone their separate ways—until now.

Rain hammered down on the roof of his truck, sounding like buckshot. Alongside the curb, water rose up halfway to his hubcaps. The vehicle parked ahead of him had clumps of debris piled up to its grill. It seemed that not only bodies were being washed down from the mountainside. It would be like a quagmire up there with no pine needles covering the forest floor. Rain and flooding left all the trails covered in slimy mud and it sometimes took a complete year before the vegetation repaired the damage. "You know we wouldn't be the only people who buried bodies up in the mountains. I figure it goes on all the time with the number of serial killers that end up in town. I'm surprised the river isn't filled with zombies floating by. It won't be too long before people will be getting used to seeing them."

"This is the point. Most bodies decay." Crawley didn't sound amused. *"They should have been bones by now and not almost perfectly preserved with all the evidence intact. This is the problem. We can all keep our mouths shut and hope it goes away. I can't imagine that there's any evidence on the bodies that would point to us at all. It was cold that night and everyone was*

wearing gloves. We know the bodies have been in the river for heck knows how long, so I figure if we happen to have dropped a few hairs here and there, the chances of them being on the bodies would be remote. Personally, I don't believe we have a thing to worry about provided we stick to the same story. We were never at the Whispering Caves that night. I figure if we insist this is the case, they'll leave us alone. With the number of serial killings going on over the last few years, surely the sheriff has more on her plate than worrying about a twelve-year-old accident. We all know it was self-defense, but now with a few more years under my belt, I figure I would have called the cops and explained what had happened but that's too late now. We'll just hope that no one cracks."

Wasser rubbed the back of his neck, thinking. "Do you figure us guys are solid?" He listened intently as Crawley sucked in a breath. "Women are so emotional when it comes to things like this. On second thought, we should have handled it ourselves and not risked bringing them into it at the time, but I figure they would have got suspicious of us rushing around to move camp and all and then making like we just arrived."

"Yeah, I don't figure we have any problems with the guys and I don't think Josie would risk getting the cops involved when she's happily married. That's not the sort of thing you'd want to divulge to your husband, is it? Especially now that we are technically all murderers. I hope you caught the part of the media conference where they said they were buried alive. This makes us all equally responsible for their deaths."

Staring at the roof of his truck, Wasser grimaced. "Yeah, I heard that, but we still need to keep the women on track. I'll pass the information on to Twotrees and he'll contact Jess."

"Lily mentioned that Josie and Marissa are having lunch at Aunt Betty's Café tomorrow at one. I'm wondering if one of us should drop by, make it look like a casual meeting, maybe have a cup of coffee with them. We need to make sure that they are still

on the same page." Crawley turned off his engine, and rain could be heard pounding the roof of his truck. *"It would have to be you or Twotrees, as Clint and me rarely drop by Aunt Betty's Café for a cup of coffee."*

Starting his engine, Wasser stared at his reflection in the rearview mirror. "I can't go. I'll be in a meeting at one, but I'll relay the information to Wyatt. When we work something out, I'll give you a call and you can pass it on." He disconnected and headed his truck along Main. "One thing's for darn sure, they always say that bad deeds come back to kick you in the ass. Seems like that's true."

TWENTY

After the media conference Jenna gathered her deputies in her office. With the hotline buzzing for most of the day, Rowley and Rio had been rushed off their feet collecting information from the callers. Piper and Cade had made great notes and sorted out the best potential witnesses for that weekend twelve years previous. Her deputies' jobs had been to call back the most interesting leads and try to form a timeline of what happened that night. In the meantime, Jenna had enrolled the assistance of Kalo to complete background checks on their list of possible suspects.

Although experienced with media conferences, the constant bombardment of questions had left Jenna exhausted. It would have been fine if she had the answers, but this early into an investigation of a cold case her reply of "no comment at this time" didn't appease the press. She'd literally turned the entire thing over to Wolfe and Norrell, and both had given clear and precise information. It had been just enough to hopefully bring the killer out of the woodwork. The media conference had at least jogged a few people's memories and information was flowing into the office at a rapid rate. She looked at her deputies.

"Just out of interest, have any of the potential suspects called the hotline to tell us about being with Abby and Cole the night they went missing?"

"Not as far as we are aware." Rio leaned back in his chair and stared at his tablet. "I specifically asked Cade and Piper to keep an eye out for any information from the people on our list." He sighed. "I guess it's early days yet, but this is a hot topic in town and I'm starting to find it very suspicious that none of the people who were actually with the victims bothered to call the office."

"Unless the women that we interviewed have already contacted them." Kane rested one boot on his opposite knee and stared at Jenna. "If this is the case, maybe they figure they have an excuse for not calling the hotline or dropping by the office. They know we're aware they were with them that evening. Maybe they've discussed it and believed that's enough. Or that we'll get in contact with them if we figure it's necessary."

Jenna sipped a cup of decaffeinated coffee, wishing it were their normal rich aromatic brew. She sure missed her coffee. "Has Kalo called in with any background information on our potential suspects?"

"Yeah, and they're all clean." Rowley ran a hand through his dark curls, making them stick up in all directions. "Twotrees and Wasser are partners in the automotive dealership in town. They started that business straight out of college. Dustin Crawley and Jess Hallon have worked on their family's cattle ranches since leaving college. Crawley is quite the rodeo star and follows the circuit, so he's not around as much as the others." He glanced down at his notes on his tablet and then lifted his gaze back to Jenna. "I figure you know about the women, but Kalo ran them through the system anyway. Lily has worked at the beauty parlor since leaving college. She is now part owner. Josie is married to a guy by the name of Bob Camp-bell, and Marissa is a tax accountant who works from home.

They're all squeaky clean, apart from Crawley, who has a few minor misdemeanors against him for roughhousing in the bars all along the rodeo circuit. Mainly a few fines for busting up the place along with a few of his friends. He seems to settle down once he returns home, and Kalo couldn't find anything, not even a speeding ticket, in Black Rock Falls."

Chewing on her bottom lip, Jenna stared at the ceiling for a few moments. "This gives us nothing to use as leverage. If they'd had a few misdemeanors along the way, we'd have a reason to pull them in for questioning. Being on the mountain that night along with another twenty or so students isn't good enough as many of those students were also friends with Abby and Cole. It's inconceivable to believe that they had only these few friends in college. Most of them would have taken different classes and would have had a wide variety of acquaintances. We can go and talk to them, but in all honesty, they really don't have to speak to us at all because we have absolutely nothing on any of them."

"All I can suggest is we keep going through the hotline information as it comes in." Kane leaned forward in his chair and took his cup of coffee from the desk. "There's a chance that somebody saw something or remembered something unusual happening that night. You would be surprised that sometimes it's the smallest things that end up leading to the conviction of a killer."

"I'm still not convinced any of the kids who were on the mountain that night were necessarily responsible." Rio drummed his fingers on the arm of his chair. "As far as we are aware, no other murders happened around that time, which wouldn't indicate a serial killer. Abby's and Cole's murders could have been a random thrill kill or a jealous lover attack. I figure we need to delve deeper into the relationships in this group. It wouldn't be too difficult to find out who was in the same classes at college. We could interview those people and find out if there had been any problems between the friends in that small group."

"The brutal attack when Cole's back was turned could indicate the killer was making a point, as in 'this guy stabbed me in the back, so I'm giving him the same treatment.'" Kane sipped his coffee and eyed Jenna across the rim of the cup. "It could have been a spur-of-the-moment act fueled by rage at seeing Cole with Abby. We have no idea if they were making out in the caves before they died. If Abby had been involved with one of the others in the group or had rejected one of her classmates, it might be a motive for a single kill. Jealousy is a very strong motive for killing. We know that Cole was murdered first and attacked from behind. I'd like to know where Abby was at this time. Did she witness the murder? If she did, wouldn't her first reaction be to scream at the killer for killing the person she loved?"

Nodding, Jenna pictured the scene in her head. "Maybe she tried to push the killer away and that's how she grabbed his pin."

"Exactly." Kane reached for a cookie from the jar on the table. "If she was screaming and hitting him, it would provoke an attack just to shut her up. It's a logical solution, and as Rio said, as there were no follow-up murders, I believe we can assume this is the case. He may have suffered remorse after killing Abby and moved away from town." He sighed. "We can't be sure we have the entire group of close friends as no one is talking."

Jenna nodded in agreement. "Yeah, it seems very strange that there weren't any more murders. We've dealt with serial killers so many times over the last six or so years, I guess we expect every murderer to be a serial killer, when in fact, crimes of passion, domestic violence, and accidental homicide do account for many murders in other towns. I figure we need to look outside the box with this one. It may never be solved. The person responsible could be long gone or even dead."

"I figure when Norrell mentioned her team would be going to the crime scene to hunt down evidence, it would have shaken the tree. If the killer is still in town, it might cause a panic reaction." Rowley's mouth twitched into a smile. "Wouldn't it be good if they returned to the scene of the crime?"

Laughing, Jenna nodded. "Yeah, well, I guess stranger things have happened in this town."

After spending a very pleasant hour with Josie in Aunt Betty's Café, Marissa purchased a few groceries and climbed into her truck. Before she had time to start the engine her burner phone chimed. She had no idea who was calling her and nervously pressed the phone to her ear. "This is Marissa."

"We've called an urgent meeting out at the Old Mitcham Ranch in half an hour. Same place as before. Drive into the barn and we won't get wet. We're staggering the arrivals or someone will notice a convoy heading there. You leave now and you'll get there second." The male voice at the other end was muffled by the noise of the rain. *"Josie has voiced her concern about what's happening with the medical examiner's office. We need to know where everyone stands. She mentioned that you're worried as well and she suggested maybe we should all take ourselves down to the sheriff's office and explain what really happened that night. If we plan on doing this, we need to make sure that we all have the same story because the moment we get into the sheriff's office they'll split us up and start asking us questions. If we make a mistake, rather than one of us trying to prove it was self-defense, we'll all end up going to court for murder."*

Swallowing the bile crawling up the back of her throat, Marissa stared into space. This was what she wanted, and surely, they would all be cleared if they came clean about what really happened that night. "Yeah, I figure we should go and speak to the sheriff. She seems to be a very levelheaded woman. I honestly believe she'll listen to what we've got to say and be sympathetic. We were just frightened college kids."

"So your vote would be to go to the sheriff and give ourselves up?"

Marissa nodded. "Yes, I figure it would solve the problem and maybe put our minds at rest."

"I guess we'll see what everyone else has to say. I'll see you in a few." He disconnected.

Marissa checked her watch. She'd need to leave now to get to the Old Mitcham Ranch. It would be slow going with the flooding hampering most of the roads. Perhaps she would see Josie along the way. If she did, she'd hang back some and keep distance between them. She waited for a few vehicles to pass by and then turned her truck and headed along Main. Nerves cramped her belly, but the idea of lifting this terrible burden from her mind once and for all made her a little lightheaded. She wanted to be able to convince the others that it was the right thing to do and went over a few ideas to persuade them. Satisfied, she turned on the radio and tried to calm the rising panic by singing along to the tunes.

Traveling out of town in the rain with so much water across the roads disturbed her more than she'd like to admit. In truth, she rarely went out, preferring to stay home and tend her garden when she wasn't working. The lonely drive to the Old Mitcham Ranch made her wish that she had called Josie and asked her to go with her. She must still be in town and it would have been safer if the two of them had traveled together. She glanced around at the wide-open spaces. Everything was so wet, with large brown expanses of water spreading out as far as the eye could see. She couldn't imagine why they wanted to meet up at the Old Mitcham Ranch again, other than the fact it was so remote that nobody came by. It became a tourist attraction over Halloween but the rest of the time it didn't attract any interest.

Marissa turned onto the driveway of the Old Mitcham Ranch and crawled her truck along the overgrown track. The gate was hanging open at a jaunty angle, leaving just enough room for her to squeeze through. She eased her truck inside and drove past the old ranch house and headed for the barn. She spotted a truck and pulled up a short distance away, leaving plenty of space for everyone else to park. The barn didn't creep her out in the daylight. It just resembled any old barn, but rain had blown through the open doors, wetting the floor. Cobwebs hung from rafters piled high with bird droppings and the ground was littered with tumbleweeds. It was hard to believe so many people had died here. The wife of the original owner had been murdered in the house. Her husband had hung himself from the rafters in this barn. That had been many years ago, but since then, more murders had occurred inside the house. A massacre of a group of people less than four years ago had made world news. She recalled reading that there was so much blood it was running down the steps.

A shiver skittered down her back as she scanned the over-grown yard. It just looked like an old ranch house. Dilapidated and uncared for, with plants growing out of the gutters. Most of the windows were broken. She imagined that at one time it had been a beautiful place to live, with views of the mountains and lowlands.

In her peripheral, something moved and the door to the vehicle beside her opened slowly and a familiar face smiled at her. She clambered out of her truck and walked around to meet him. "It's just you and me right now. I figured I'd see someone following me along the way, but I guess it's slow going with the weather being so bad and all."

"They're not coming." He leaned inside his truck and pulled out an ax. "They sent me to talk to you. Nobody wants to go to the sheriff and we've all decided that you need to be silenced."

Horrified as light sparkled on the sharp blade, Marissa backed away from him. She needed to get away and turned to run to her truck, but a strong hand grabbed her by the back of her jacket and spun her around. She stared into ice-cold eyes and swallowed hard. "I won't say anything. I've kept the secret all these years. Why should I say something now?"

"We can't trust you to keep your mouth shut." He shoved her hard against the hood of her truck. "This is the only way."

Unable to believe what was happening, Marissa gaped at him. "You can't just kill me in cold blood. People will report me missing and the sheriff will soon find out you're to blame. They'll find my body. There'll be evidence and you'll be in more trouble than you are already. It will be much better for us to all go to the sheriff and explain what happened that night. Think what you're doing. Killing me will get you nowhere."

"Killing you will be something I'll enjoy." He rolled his shoulders and then swung the ax back and forth. His intent expression fixed on her, like a cat watching a mouse.

Allowing his words to resonate in her brain, she gaped at him. "What do you mean, you enjoy killing?"

"Do you believe that Cole and Abby were my first kills?" His lips spread into a grin. "Yeah, for the record, I killed Abby, but she wasn't my first."

Aghast and shaky, Marissa shook her head, not believing what he was saying. "You said Cole was killing Abby and then turned on you. We all believed you."

"I guess I owe you the truth as you're gonna die." He

shrugged and his eyes darkened. "Cole was my best friend until Abby got her hooks into him and he became her lapdog. I killed him, but I wanted her to watch so she knew it was her fault." He stared over her shoulder into space. "She just stood there babbling as I hacked into his back." He swung his emotionless gaze back to her. "She was no fun at all. I wanted her to run but she just stood there beating on my chest. I pushed her away and finished her. Then I dragged Cole's body over her and went back to camp." He snickered. "You all believed me. It was incredible."

Horrified, Marissa took another backward step. "You won't get away with killing me. The sheriff will find you. It's not like back then. They have a ton of ways to find killers. Look at their record—no one gets away with murder in Black Rock Falls."

"Until now. I'm smarter than the others and no one will know I've been here. I'm not carrying my regular phone nor driving my own truck. This one is a loner from a friend who is establishing an alibi for where he is right now. In fact, he is at the sheriff's office giving them information about seeing a mountain man hanging around that night. It's all lies, of course, but it would only take one of us to collaborate his story."

Trembling in disbelief, Marissa could only stare into a face she'd trusted for so long. Maybe she could keep him talking and convince him she'd remain silent. She needed to move away and kept taking tiny steps backward, holding up her hands to ward him off. He seemed so relaxed, calm and not angry. To anyone watching, he'd appear normal and almost nice. Could this be some type of sick joke just to frighten her? What if it wasn't and he fully intended to end her life? Panic tightened her throat, but she must try to reason with him. "Look, this is just a silly mistake. I won't say anything and what happened here will be our little secret. You don't want my blood on your hands."

"Ah, but I do." His eyes never left her face. "I fantasize about killing. I crave the smell of blood and dream about watching the life leave my victims. The killing never lasts long enough. They always go and die just as I start to enjoy myself."

Heart racing like a freight train, Marissa stared into the face of a madman. "You're sick."

"No, this is me being nice." He wet his lips. "I can be nasty, but as we're friends, I'm giving you my good side."

Gasping for breath as terror seized her lungs, Marissa forced out her words. "If I'm a friend, why kill me?"

"I needed a distraction on a miserable day, is all." He took a step closer and then laughed as she flinched. "You can't get away from me, Marissa. I'm bigger and faster than you and no one will hear you scream. This was a perfect place to kill someone years ago and nothing's changed. You're gonna die and it's gonna hurt. I can't make it fast even for you because that wouldn't be any fun at all, would it?" He ran his thumb along the blade. "I sharpened this just for you."

Terrified, Marissa turned and ran, stumbling over the uneven ground and deeper into the dim interior. At one end was a stable containing a bank of old stalls. She ran to the end and ducked down, hoping he couldn't see her in the gloom, but his footsteps, slow and deliberate, echoed in the barn. Each step louder than the one before, each second closer to finding her. As he came around the corner and smiled at her, she let out a long scream. "Please... don't. *Please.*"

"That's better." He lifted the ax high and stepped closer. "Screaming is so satisfying and I'm so gonna make you scream."

TWENTY-TWO

THURSDAY

Jenna stood at her office window staring at the mountains. It had stopped raining, but a thick mist hung across the forest as if the clouds had slipped down from the sky. Dense green pines filled the bottom slopes of the mountain range, the color fresh and still soaked from the rain. The blacktop still bore the scars of the flooding. Brown patches of soil spilled across the road and large dirty puddles were still evident as the water drained away. Everything smelled damp, and outside there was a strange putrid odor on the wind. The usual fresh pine and alpine fragrance was missing. High above, a small patch of blue sky was trying to push its way through the cloud cover and a stream of sunshine was making rainbows. It would be an artist's dream to paint a picture of that minuscule moment in time, the exact second when the seasons changed and new life emerged from the forest.

She turned at the sound of footsteps on the stairs and Kane looked up from his laptop as expert tracker Atohi Blackhawk knocked on the door. She smiled. "What brings you into town? It must have been difficult driving down from the res in this weather."

"The highway from the mountain is clear, although the drive from the res to the highway was difficult." Blackhawk's eyes narrowed. "The mudslides throughout the mountain are extensive, many usual trails are blocked. One of the fire roads is almost impassable. When I get home, I'll make a map and send it to you. I figure you'll need to convince the mayor to get a crew up there to clear the fire road before summer." He sighed. "I came into town to see Norrell. She gave me the task of hunting down which one of the Whispering Caves flooded. As they cover a mile across one side of the mountain range, I hunted down those close to the river."

"Did you discover anything interesting?" Kane leaned back in his chair, twirling a pen in his fingers.

"I assume you're aware of the seismic activity that occurred during winter and the avalanches?" Blackhawk rested one hip on the edge of Jenna's desk. "From what I observed, the seismic activity has caused fissures in the side of the mountain above the caves in one area. During the melt and the subsequent rain, a new water channel was opened up. A small river is evident. It comes down the mountainside through the caves and runs into the river. I believe this would be the most probable place for the bodies to have been buried as there are mounds of sand and debris. I discovered very old animal bones usually found deep in caves spread alongside the new riverbank." He smiled. "It's far too wet for Norrell and her team to risk the mountain at this time. I figure give it a few days to dry out, or we'll have search and rescue out there digging them out of the mud. I don't figure the evidence will be going anywhere." He pulled out his phone and scanned through some images before handing it to Jenna. "As you can see, when the debris initially burst out of the cave it was spread over the forest floor. Since then, the water flow would have been slower and now it's little more than a trickle. Unless we get some more heavy rain, I don't think it will be an issue."

"The bodies were dehydrated, so very light." Kane walked over to the kitchenette and filled the coffee pots. "I figure once the top layer of sand was washed away, they'd have been picked up like dead leaves and floated down the river. Even after being in the water for a time, they were still emaciated. The only thing that was bogging them down was their clothes."

Interested, Jenna leaned back in her chair and stared at the images. "There seems to be debris all over. Did you happen to notice anything out of place or interesting?"

"Norrell made it clear that I was not to disturb any evidence." Blackhawk raised his eyebrows, and a smile lit up his face. "I did mention I'd assisted you at many crime scenes, but she insisted I take only photographs and GPS coordinates. I used crime scene tape to mark the area. I also took coordinates of all the mudslides, trail blockages, and the fire road I mentioned. I'll send all the information to you as soon as I get home."

"Coffee?" Kane pulled cups from the cabinet and laid them on the table next to the fixings.

"Thanks, it's been a long morning." Blackhawk dropped into a chair in front of Jenna's desk. "I must apologize for not dropping by to see Tauri. The flooding has been a problem for everyone, I believe. I seemed to have been spending all my time moving horses to high ground. How is he and how are you, Jenna? You're looking very well."

Jenna smiled. "Tauri is great. If you get time, you should drop by the kindergarten to see him. He would love a visit. He talks about you all the time." Unconsciously, she rubbed a hand over her belly. "I'm doing really well. The moment I stopped spewing, everything seemed to return to normal, apart from a ferocious appetite."

"That has to be a good sign, not that I'm an expert on pregnancy, but when my dogs are in whelp they eat like crazy." Blackhawk chuckled. "Not that I'm comparing you to a bloodhound." He took the cup of coffee that Kane offered and added the fixings. "I'll be sure to drop by the kindergarten on my way to Aunt Betty's Café. Now the rain has stopped, I'll have more time to spend with Tauri after kindergarten." He looked at Kane. "Is he still practicing his languages? He told me you were teaching him Spanish as well."

"He has a thirst for languages, so I'll take it slow and give him a good basic knowledge as we go through." Kane handed Jenna a cup of coffee and sat down beside Atohi. "He needs you and your family in his life. We don't want him to lose touch with his cultural heritage. We both figure it's essential that he walks on both sides of the path."

"In the end it's his choice." Blackhawk opened his hands. "We can only offer him guidance along the way. Whatever he decides, we all know in our hearts that he's been raised with love, and that is all that really matters."

Jenna's computer pinged to announce an incoming video call, and she turned her screen around. "It's Kalo." She accepted the call. "Hey, Bobby. Did you find anything interesting?"

"Well, Cole Peters' laptop and phone arrived this morning. I didn't have a problem getting into them, but there isn't really anything interesting to report. The laptop is mainly filled with college assignments and a few downloaded images of various things. His phone has images of him, Abby, his parents, and his dog. The only message of interest I discovered contained his plans to drop by Abby's place on Halloween. They'd planned to walk down Main and look at the Halloween attractions in town and then head up the mountain to meet their friends. He only mentions the friends as 'the guys.' His phone calls are back and forth between the group of men that we know about and Abby. There are a few calls to his parents, the pizzeria, and various other takeout places, but overall, it's just a typical record of a young man's life in college. I'll work on it for a couple of days just in case there's anything that I've missed, but to be perfectly

honest, I don't think there's anything on his laptop or his phone that we can use to pin his murder on anyone."

Disappointed, Jenna leaned back in her chair and sighed deeply. "I had hoped we'd find some useful information. From the people we've spoken to about him, Cole was a nice guy, an incredible sportsman, and a loyal friend. Whoever decided to end his life might remain a mystery because we can't find a motive for his death."

"Well, if you do come up with any interesting suspects, send them my way and I'll put them through the wringer." Kalo smiled at her. *"If there's any dirt on any of them, I'll find it. Catch you later."* He disconnected and his image vanished from the screen.

Jenna reached for her coffee. "One dead end after another. I'm starting to believe this one will slip through the net."

TWENTY-THREE

Worried, Lily's gaze slid back to the clock. She'd watched it since five after ten this morning. It was now two-fifteen and Marissa was a no-show for her appointment at the beauty parlor. She'd called her repeatedly for four hours without getting a reply and that just wasn't like Marissa. Since she started her tax advice company, she'd been available twenty-four/seven and taking on as many clients as possible. She grabbed her burner phone from her purse and headed into the break room. She tried calling her again, wondering if she'd gone somewhere that she didn't want anyone to know about. After discovering her concern about the revelations in the medical examiner's media conference, perhaps she'd sought out one of the guys to get some advice.

The call just rang and rang, and she disconnected before calling Josie. "Hey, have you seen Marissa? She was a no-show for her hair appointment today and that's just not like her. I've been trying to reach her for hours without any luck."

"We had lunch yesterday at Aunt Betty's Café and she mentioned her hair appointment, so she hasn't forgotten it." Josie paused for a beat as if thinking. *"The media conference has*

upset all of us. I've been worried sick since listening to what they had to say. I know Marissa was feeling the same and I figure she made some good points about giving ourselves up to the sheriff. Maybe she's gone to speak to one of the guys and hasn't got back yet? She could just roll up to where they work or one of the ranches to meet them. Maybe that's where she is because we all agreed if we moved around between each other, we'd leave our phones behind so they couldn't be traced."

Although worry gripped Lily for her friend's welfare, she needed to be at the beauty parlor as her assistant manager was sick. "Yeah, but I called the burner and she's not picking that up either. You're not too far from where she lives. Can you drop by and see if her truck is out front? If it is, maybe go and see if she's okay. She could have taken a fall and I just don't feel right not knowing what's happened to her."

"Sure, I'll drive by and see if she's there." Josie was obviously not enthusiastic about going out. *"Knowing Marissa as I do, she probably turned off her phone for some reason and forgot to turn it back on. I'll go now and take a look and give you a call when I get back."*

Relief flooded over Lily. "Thanks, I appreciate it. Chat later." She disconnected and went back to work.

Less than half an hour later, her phone vibrated in her pocket. When the caller ID lit up Josie's name, she excused herself from her customer and headed into the break room to answer the call. "Did you find her?"

"Nope. No sign of her truck." The noise from Josie's engine rattled through the earpiece. *"There's no smoke coming out of the chimney, and I don't figure she's in the house. The one thing I know about Marissa is that she hates the cold and always has that fire piled high with logs. I looked through the window into the family room, and the grate is cold and filled with ashes as if it's being left to burn overnight. There's no way she lit a fire there this morning. I wonder where the heck she is."*

Lily's stomach dropped. "Did you check out back in case she'd had a fall?"

"Yeah, I looked all around the place, including her sheds and the old garage. I felt like a Peeping Tom. The kitchen is neat and tidy as if she just walked out. No dishes in the sink. I could clearly see into the mudroom and the coat that she always wears is missing. She is not in the house. What do you want me to do? Is she legally a missing person or do we need to wait twenty-four hours or whatever?"

Chewing on her bottom lip, Lily stared out of the beauty parlor window and along to the pizzeria. She noticed Jess Hallon slipping inside. "I see Jess. I'll go and speak to him and see if he's heard anything. She might have contacted one of the guys about her concerns with the media conference. He's in the pizzeria, no one will notice me in there. People are coming and going all day."

"Okay, find out what he knows and get back to me." Josie cleared her throat. *"If we can't find her, we'll need to report her missing."* She disconnected.

TWENTY-FOUR

Lily went to speak to her client and arranged for one of the other stylists to finish blow-drying her hair. She smiled at her stylists as they drifted into the break room. "I figure we can take a break at three as we don't have any more clients this afternoon until four. I'm going to get us some pizza." She hurried out the door and headed for the pizzeria.

She put in an order and then turned around slowly, scanning the booths alongside the wall. She spotted Hallon, wearing a dark brown sheepskin jacket with his cowboy hat pulled down low over his eyes. She wandered up to the booth and then slid inside and sat down. He glanced up, holding a piece of garlic bread in front of his lips and his eyes widened with shock. "Don't make a fuss. I need to ask you something."

"You know darn well we made an agreement not to meet up in town where people could see us." He kept his voice to just above a whisper. "What the heck do you want and why is it so important that you couldn't have called? That's why we bought those darn burners in the first place, wasn't it?"

Running a hand casually through her hair, Lily tipped back her head and laughed. "Maybe looking at me like we are friends rather than enemies would cause less suspicion. It's not unusual for old friends to chat while they're waiting for a pizza. I chat to everyone in here, even people I don't know just to pass the time. It's no secret that we were all at college together. What are you doing in town anyway? Shouldn't you be out on the ranch riding the plains or something?"

"There's not too much to do right now. When it dries up some, I'm guessing I'll be repairing fences from sunup to sundown." Hallon sipped a glass of soda and nodded slowly. "Once we've taken out feed to the cattle, I only spend a short time doing chores. When you live on a ranch, coming to town and buying pizza is a luxury."

Lily smiled at the handsome cowboy. "How's your wife, and you have a son, don't you?"

"Yeah, I dropped Dawn by her mom's for the day. They don't want me around, so I'm just hanging. Although, if one of her friends sees us together and Dawn gets some crazy notion I came here to meet up with you, things will change real fast. She's the jealous type." He sighed. "So what's so important you came here to speak to me?"

Lily leaned forward on the table, to make sure no one could overhear their conversation. "Marissa is missing. No one has been able to get in contact with her since she left Aunt Betty's Café yesterday at lunchtime. Josie dropped by her place and her truck is gone. She looked through the windows and the fire has been out for a long time, so we figure she didn't get home last night."

"Maybe she went to visit someone?" Hallon leaned back in his seat as the server came with his pizza. Without waiting, he picked up a slice, folded it over, and bit into it.

Shaking her head, Lily stared at him. He wasn't concerned at all. "She had lunch with Josie yesterday and she would have mentioned if she was going to visit somebody else. They're very close friends and discuss everything. Another thing, Marissa is very reluctant to go anywhere alone. It's not as if she would visit a client's home, for instance. She always insists that they come to her office, and she always keeps her weapon in the drawer just in case there's a problem."

"So you figure something happened to her on the way home from Aunt Betty's Café at lunchtime yesterday?" Hallon shook his head slowly. "That would be difficult as she only lives a few blocks away and it was in the middle of the day. There would be people around. Her vehicle would have been abandoned on the side of the road or something. I'm sure if Josie drove to her house, she'd have noticed if her vehicle had been left somewhere along the road. In any case, why would anyone want to abduct Marissa? It's not as if she has anyone who could offer a ransom for her recovery."

Lily bristled at his attitude. "It's not anyone we're worried about. Are you sure it wasn't one of the guys putting the fear of God into her because she wanted to go to the sheriff?"

"I haven't heard anything, and if there'd been some sort of plan, they'd have involved me." He bit into another slice of pizza and chewed slowly. "In case you've forgotten, we're all involved. Any decisions that we make must be as a group. If one of us breaks the silence, it makes all of us look worse, and the sheriff will never believe the truth of what really happened."

Of course, what he was saying was true. They'd stuck together all these years and perhaps they could ride out this current investigation. "I agree with you, but I can see the merit of what Marissa was suggesting. She figured it would be easier on us if we gave ourselves up before they discovered who we are. You know darn well the sheriff has an incredible team of investigators around her and it won't be long before they discover the truth. Back when it happened, the old sheriff didn't know what day it was. He just told everyone they'd run away together and that was the end of it. Now that they've both surfaced and a new investigation has been opened, you know as well as I do that this sheriff will never give up before she discovers what really happened."

"I'll talk to the guys about your concerns and get someone to give you a call." He sipped at his drink and glanced at the counter and then tapped the number she'd placed on the table. "Your number just came up." His eyes moved back to her face. "Unless I contact you, forget I exist. No more dropping by for a chat. Got it?"

Surprised by his attitude as they'd dated a couple of times in the past and she'd found him to be a very nice and respectful guy. Time changed many people, and the man sitting in front of her was no longer her friend. "Sure. Same goes for me." She stood and went to collect her pizzas.

As she left the pizzeria, she glanced back at his booth to see him on the phone with a sour expression on his face. He was calling the guys to explain the situation. Talking to him hadn't gained any information or assistance for finding Marissa. When she got back to the beauty parlor, she dumped the pizzas in the break room and headed outside into the street. She called Josie. "I've spoken to Jess and he was absolutely no help whatsoever. He doesn't give a darn Marissa is missing. I'm tied up here at work. Can you get down to the sheriff's office and report her missing? If we leave it any longer, she could be lying somewhere in a wrecked car on the side of the road. Did she even mention going anywhere else when she left you?"

"Nope and I drove around on the way home, looking for her vehicle just in case she had broken down somewhere and walked. It wouldn't be too difficult to fall into the rushing water alongside the road and drown. Stranger things have happened, but I couldn't find her truck anywhere. Something's happened to her, and she wouldn't be offline for so long. I've been calling her every hour." Josie sucked in a long shuddering breath. "I'll head out now and report her missing. Maybe the sheriff will be able to track her car?"

A wave of panic hit Lily's stomach. "You'll need to be very careful what you say. Don't mention anything about Cole and Abby. Jess turned quite hostile when I told him that Marissa wanted to go to speak to the sheriff before this all blows up in our faces. He knows you feel the same way and he's going to call the guys to discuss what we should do as a group. He suggested we don't go in and speak to the sheriff alone. It has to be all of us at the same time if it's going to work."

"*My lips are sealed as always.*" Josie cleared her throat. "*I'll drop by the sheriff's office now and don't be surprised if you get a call from her as you're one of Marissa's close friends. I'll call later and tell you what happened, but I'd say it would be just paperwork. They'll take a few details and maybe drop by her place to make sure she's not there. I wouldn't expect too much to happen right away.*" She sighed. "*Catch you later.*" She disconnected.

Despondent, Lily dragged heavy legs back into the beauty parlor and headed into the break room. Deep down inside, the terrible feeling that something bad had happened to her friend just wouldn't go away. She needed a gallon of coffee right now to stay alert. After speaking to Jess, her nerves were shot. Where the heck was Marissa? If something bad had happened to her, they'd be coming for her next. A shiver ran down her spine. Her group of friends had been so close, and now she couldn't trust anyone. Maybe she shouldn't have told Josie she intended to talk to the sheriff. Dread dropped over her as she peered around the break room door and out into Main. Someone was watching her. She could almost feel their eyes boring into her. She pushed open the door and, looking both ways, dashed into the street. She hurried toward the sheriff's office. Fear had her by the throat as she scanned the way ahead. If they saw her speaking to the sheriff, would she make it home alive?

TWENTY-FIVE

Jenna put down the phone and looked at Kane. "Maggie is sending up a woman who's reported a friend missing since yesterday lunchtime. I figured it would be better if we spoke to her, in case it's a problem."

"That makes a lot of sense." Kane swiveled around in his office chair and watched the door as footsteps sounded up the stairs.

Jenna was surprised to see Josie Campbell, the woman they'd interviewed previously peering hesitantly through the door. It seemed very coincidental that a person on her potential suspects list in a cold-case homicide would walk into her office. She stood and waved her to a seat. "You have a missing friend? Can you give me more details, please?" She sat down and took a legal pad out of her drawer. "Let's start with her name." She lifted her pen and looked at Josie expectantly.

"I believe you've met her. Her name is Marissa Kendrick." As she sat on the edge of her chair, Josie fiddled with the clasp of her purse. It was obvious she didn't want to be here.

Well, well, well, Marissa, another person on their potential suspects list, had gone missing. She already had Marissa

Kendrick's details and background information on file. She looked up at Josie. "What makes you believe she's missing?"

"I had lunch with her yesterday at Aunt Betty's Café and she hasn't been seen since." Josie lifted her chin. "I've been calling her for hours and went by her house. Her truck is missing and when I looked through the windows, her family room fire is dead. She'd never allow that fire to go out in winter. I've driven around the streets, searching for her truck in case she had a wreck or was washed away in the flood, but I can't find any trace of it." She searched Jenna's face with a concerned expression. "Marissa very rarely travels far from home. She'd never go anywhere in this kind of weather unless it was an emergency. I've called all our friends and no one has heard from her. I didn't know what else to do, so I came by to talk to you."

"When was the last time you saw her?" Kane leaned forward in his chair. "Did she mention going anywhere when you spoke to her over lunch?"

"We met at Aunt Betty's at one, and I don't recall the exact time we left but she never mentioned going anywhere and was heading home." Josie turned back to look at Jenna. "I know it was broad daylight and there were people everywhere, but that doesn't explain why she's missing."

"I'll call the hospital." Kane made the call.

Jenna ran down her mental list of questions she needed to ask. "Has she had any problems in her life recently? Is she depressed?"

"I figure we're all a little concerned after discovering the bodies of Abby and Cole had washed up in the river after being missing for twelve years." Josie hugged her purse to her chest as if it were a life preserver. "We talked about them over lunch and how shocking it was to discover they hadn't just run away and someone had murdered them. The press conference was very disturbing for all of their friends." She let out a long sigh. "If you believe that Marissa would take her own life because of what happened that night, you're mistaken. It was such a long time ago. To be honest, I can't even remember their faces."

"No one of that name has been taken to the hospital." Kane placed his phone on the desk. "Are you sure there's no one she might visit? Does she have friends in another town? If she drove to Blackwater, for instance, as the roads are flooding, she might have gotten into trouble. We wouldn't know unless somebody called it in. In that case, surely she'd call one of her friends to tell them?"

"Like I said before, Marissa doesn't like to drive long distances." Josie shook her head. "There's no more information I can give you."

Watching her intently and seeing her agitation, Jenna moved down her mental list of questions. "If she was feeling depressed about Abby and Cole, would she have gone to church?"

"No, I'm sure she'd have mentioned it if she'd wanted to speak to Father Derry, and it's unlikely she'd stay there overnight." Josie shook her head. "Is the next question 'has she got a boyfriend?' because the answer is no. I gave a list of our friends to the receptionist and filled out all Marissa's details, even what she was wearing." She stared at Jenna. "Are you going to help me or not?"

Nodding, Jenna met the woman's gaze. "Of course. Do you know the make and model of her truck?"

"Yeah, she has a white GMC Sierra." Josie leaned back in her seat with an exhausted expression on her face. "I don't know the plate number but it's easily recognizable. She has a sticker on her bumper. It's bright red with white lettering advertising her tax consultancy company. As you know, she works from home and has an office out back. I checked the office. She'd be safe there because she keeps a Glock in her drawer. Her desk faces the door, so no one is going to sneak in behind her and snatch her away—and why would they? She helps people resolve their tax problems. She is just about the kindest, gentlest person I know."

Jenna pushed to her feet. "That's good to know. We'll get onto this right away. As her vehicle is a late model, it will have GPS and there might be a way of tracking it. As she doesn't have any close relatives and we believe her life to be in danger, we don't need a search warrant to hunt down her location. I'll get our tech guy on it now. Leave this with us and I'll be in touch with you as soon as we discover where she is. Make sure you leave your contact details with Maggie at the desk."

"I already have, and I'm sure you have them anyway." Josie stood, looking irritated, or was she scared? "Thank you."

"If you hear from her in the meantime, don't forget to let us know." Kane stood as she left the room and closed the door behind her. He went to Jenna's desk and leaned on it, looking at her. "Well, this is weird. The two people we interviewed are suddenly involved in another missing persons case. Do you figure there's a connection?"

Jenna shrugged. "If you mean that Marissa was involved in the deaths of Cole and Abby and decided to skip town before we discovered her connection, we'll need proof that she packed a bag and ran. I figure we go and drop by her house. We have due cause to enter on a welfare check after a missing person's report has been filed."

"That sounds like a plan." Kane grabbed his coat from a peg behind the door. "If you give Kalo her details, he'll be able to hunt down her plate number via the MVD and maybe track her GPS. I'll go and tell the others where we're going and give them an update. Honestly, Jenna, I figure there's more to this than meets the eye. It's too much of a coincidence that one of these people goes missing as soon as we start investigating the cold case. Someone is hiding something."

TWENTY-SIX

Kane made short work of getting inside Marissa's house. She had security set up on the front door but had neglected to include the office at the back. The locked internal door between the house and the office was insufficient to slow down anyone who could pick a lock. They cleared the house, carefully moving from room to room, but it had that empty feeling a house does when it's unoccupied. There was no smell of death but rather a hint of stale coffee drifting through the neat home. Although there were three bedrooms, the main bedroom where she slept was easy to distinguish by the colorful throws on the bed and a wide-screen TV at one end. Inside the closets, clothes hung neatly with shoes in lines beneath. They found two suitcases under the bed and both were empty. In the attached bathroom, cosmetics, lotions, and a toothbrush and paste had been left as if she'd just finished using them. There was absolutely no sign whatsoever that she'd decided to make a run for it. He followed Jenna down the stairs and back to the office.

"There's a list of her clients on the desk." Jenna took out her phone and copied each page. "I'll get Maggie to call them and ask if they've seen her. Maybe we'll be able to discover if she goes to their offices or works strictly from here."

Kane nodded. "That sounds like a plan."

He locked the doors again as they left the office. As he turned to head back to the Beast, Jenna paused to answer her phone. When she turned and gave him an incredulous look, he went to her side. "What is it? You've gone sheet white."

"That was Kalo. He traced Marissa's truck to the Old Mitcham Ranch." Jenna gripped Kane's arm. "She went from here to Aunt Betty's Café, did a J-turn on Main, and drove to the Old Mitcham Ranch, and her truck is still there."

The Old Mitcham Ranch held so many bad memories and Jenna had almost been killed there. One of the first murders he encountered after arriving in Black Rock Falls was the horrific homicide of a young woman whom he found mutilated in the root cellar. It had been particularly gruesome, and memorable as the young woman resembled his sister. It hadn't been something he could easily forget. A year later over Halloween, they discovered an entire group of workers slaughtered by a maniac. That had been the day their cat, Pumpkin, arrived on their doorstep splattered with blood and insisting they follow her to the crime scene.

During his time on the battlefield, Kane had seen many gruesome injuries but nothing had prepared him for walking into a dark root cellar and finding a young woman brutally murdered. The idea of history repeating itself knotted his stomach, and from Jenna's expression, she had the same concern. He sucked in a deep breath. Dealing with death and destruction was part of the job, but everything about the Old Mitcham Ranch posed a danger and he did not intend to walk into a trap. "Oh, that can't be good."

"I'll call it in and get Rio and Rowley for backup." Jenna reached for her phone and made the call. She spoke to Rio. "Wear your Kevlar vests. We have no idea what's waiting for us out there. Marissa Kendrick's disappearance could tie in with the current cold case, and we can't take any chances. Holding the press conferences might have flushed out the killer, so we need to be on our guard. This could be a setup. We'll meet you at the end of Main in ten minutes." She clicked off and stared at Kane, resting her hands on hips. "If there's one place I'd prefer to avoid at all costs, it's the Old Mitcham Ranch. I wish they'd razed it to the ground like they wanted to years ago. Why the local council stepped in and said it was of historical importance, I'll never understand, but I guess they make their bucks out of the visitors who go there over Halloween."

Kane slipped an arm around her shoulder as they walked back to the Beast. "There is one redeeming feature about the Old Mitcham Ranch, Jenna. It was Halloween when Pumpkin came to our door to alert us about what had happened there. You have to admit that cat chose to live with us, and since she's arrived, she couldn't be a more loving and devoted companion. Even Duke loves her and he isn't a fan of cats at all. So hang on to that one positive about the place."

"Yeah, and when I see her, I don't get flashbacks about that time at all." Jenna leaned into him. "She has become part of the family now, and I think I would miss the little purring bump curled up at my feet each night."

Kane smiled down at her. "Me too." He opened the back door of the truck and handed Jenna her Kevlar vest. "Keep that happy thought in your mind when we go back to the Old Mitcham Ranch. It might help."

"I'll do my best." Jenna pulled the liquid Kevlar vest over her head and put her jacket over the top. "It's just that that place gives me the creeps."

Sunlight peeped through the clouds in long streams, giving the blacktop ahead the appearance of being under spotlights. Shafts of sun lit up patches of grass and reflected in the pools of muddy water still lingering in the fields. If the rain held off for a time, the land would dry and the awful smell that floods left behind would be blown away in the wind from the mountains. As they drove onto the highway, Rio's truck fell in behind them and they proceeded to the Old Mitcham Ranch. The notorious ranch was situated on the same road as their home and maybe a couple of miles closer to the river. They drove by their ranch and the snowplow guy's place. Twenty minutes or so after they'd left town, Kane took the driveway that led to the heavy metal gates that barred the way to the ranch. The gates had been installed by the company that had taken over the place as a Halloween attraction. He slowed the Beast and came to a stop at the open gate. He glanced at Jenna. "Wait here for a second. I'll go and check how they got into this place."

Outside the gate, Kane searched through the undergrowth for the length of chain and padlock that usually secured the gates. He found the damaged padlock. It had been cut using bolt cutters and casually tossed to one side. The length of chain still hung on a gate pressed hard into the bushes alongside the driveway. No distinguishing tire tracks showed on the over-grown gravel driveway. The only sign that anyone had been there was the bent-over vegetation along the center. He opened the heavy gates wide before heading back to the truck and climbing behind the wheel. "They used bolt cutters and that's a very strong lock. It wouldn't have been easy to cut through. The gate is heavy as well and rusted on the hinges, so I doubt Marissa opened the gate herself. She must have been meeting someone here."

"That's kinda obvious, going on what her friends say about not liking to travel anywhere alone." Jenna frowned. "It also tells us that she met someone she could trust. No one in their right mind would come out here to meet a stranger." She looked at him, her eyes filled with concern as she tapped her mic to relay a message to the deputies. "Keep scanning the property. We don't know who might be out there."

"Copy that." Rio's voice came through their earpieces.

Safe inside the Beast, nothing could touch them. Designed to protect Kane, the vehicle was virtually bombproof, but the second they stepped outside they'd be vulnerable. The Old Mitcham Ranch had a number of outbuildings and was surrounded by hillside, which a sniper could utilize. As they drove in, Kane considered every possible scenario. "The barn doors are open, and I don't see a truck anywhere. That would be the logical place to park, especially if it had been raining when she arrived yesterday. I recall what it's like inside. It has a wide-open space and stables along one end. In the middle is a trapdoor that leads down to a root cellar. The hayloft was in pieces the last time we came by, so I would doubt anyone would risk climbing up there to take a shot at us."

"So inside the barn would be the safest place?" Jenna's head swiveled from side to side as she scanned every angle as they drove past the ranch house.

Kane nodded and, flicking on his headlights, moved the truck into the huge barn. The powerful beams lit up a white truck on the far side, and as he swung the truck around, turning it to face the opening, the headlights picked up a line of red on the dusty floor. The long smear led from the stables to an open trapdoor. He turned to look at Jenna. "I see a blood trail from the stables to the root cellar."

"Okay, let's take a look." Jenna rested one hand on the door handle and flicked him a glance. "Are you getting a feeling of déjà vu? Because I sure am."

Pushing the memories to the back of his mind of the day he found the body in the root cellar, he climbed from the truck, constantly scanning the area for any movement but found nothing. As he led Jenna to the parked white truck, Rio and Rowley parked in the barn and waited for instructions. He turned and looked at them. "Clear the barn and watch your backs."

He peered inside the truck and, using his phone, took pictures of a bag of groceries and a purse sitting on the passenger seat beside a phone. The keys hung in the ignition and he found no sign of any disturbance. "It looks like she arrived here and climbed out of the vehicle. I figure you're correct. She did know the person she met here. She didn't even bother to take her phone with her."

"There's nothing of interest on this side of the vehicle. The dust has been disturbed but there are no distinguishing footprints." Jenna pulled on examination gloves before opening the door. "Now this is interesting. Look what I found in the console." She held up a cheap burner phone. "Why would a tax accountant require a burner phone? This case is getting more mysterious by the second."

"We followed the blood trail and one of the stables is a bloodbath. There are footprints all over." Rowley moved to Kane's side. "Whatever happened here occurred in the stables, and from the blood trail, I figure we'll find Marissa Kendrick at the bottom of the steps leading to the root cellar."

TWENTY-SEVEN

Sick to her stomach, Jenna grabbed a flashlight from the Beast. The last thing she wanted to do was to go into a root cellar to hunt down a body. A cold wind blew across her face, making the hairs on the back of her neck rise. It was as if someone was watching them. She glanced at Kane. "Ready?" She turned to Rio and Rowley. "Watch our backs. Keep under cover. We could easily have a sniper out there. In this barn we're sitting ducks."

"Yes, ma'am." Rio nodded. "Do you want me to call Wolfe? I figure there are body parts in the stables. They could be fingertips. If they belong to Marissa Kendrick, she fought for her life."

A sickening wave rushed over Jenna at the terror the victim must have endured, and she swallowed hard. *What will we find in the cellar?* "Yeah, we'll need him. Explain the dangers surrounding the situation and ask him to take precautions."

Trying to gather her courage to follow Kane into the dark root cellar, Jenna took out a face mask from her pocket and pressed it to her nose. She looked into Kane's suddenly unemotional expression and realized he'd fallen into the zone to protect his mind against what horrific sight he was going to encounter in the root cellar. She'd tried many times to emulate him but memories of the dead they'd found over the years never left her. Although the flashbacks she'd suffered after her time as DEA Agent Avril Parker had subsided, the memories of murder scenes often played in her mind like a horror movie. Some very bad memories came back, triggered by similar events, and she couldn't turn them off, and even flooding her head with happy thoughts didn't distract them from tormenting her.

Following Kane down debris-strewn steps and into complete darkness took every ounce of her courage. She wrapped her fingers around a flashlight, the beam was powerful but didn't deter the encroaching shadows trying to smother her. Making an effort to ignore the strong metallic scent of blood and the stale smell that arrives just before a body turns putrid, Jenna pushed down the need to run away. She sucked in a breath behind her face mask and nodded to Kane. "Let's go."

Drips of congealed blood coated the stairs down to the root cellar. No attempt had been made to disguise the footprints, although they were unremarkable in size and had the typical pattern of any rubber boots purchased from a number of stores in town. In fact, they could belong to anyone in the county and beyond, as everyone owned a pair of rubber boots and wore them frequently during wet weather. Ahead of her, Kane moved his powerful flashlight in a wide arc as he descended the steps. She followed in his footsteps, keeping to the outside to avoid the blood spatter and ducking away from the dead roots hanging down to clutch at her clothes and grab at her hair. When he stopped suddenly in front of her, she bumped into his back. "What is it?"

"What's left of Marissa Kendrick." Kane turned slowly to look at her, his wide frame shielding her from the sight. "Are you sure you want to see this? It's what nightmares are made of."

Of course, Jenna wanted to say no. Her heart pounded so

hard in her chest she could hardly breathe as she moved the flashlight in a slow arc ahead of her. Old dusty cobwebs torn from their moorings hung like filthy lace curtains around the entrance. Thick grime covered the floor and animal skat, likely from the thousands of rats that roamed the property, crunched under her boots. She gave Kane a slight nod and he moved to one side to reveal the horror before him. Breath caught in her throat.

Her chest tightened and she wanted to turn and run away. The body of Marissa Kendrick resembled a broken storefront dummy, although nothing could disguise the open red lacerations covering her entire body. She hadn't just been murdered. A monster had slowly dissected her and from the amount of blood, she'd lived through every second. Dizzy, Jenna swayed and put out one arm to steady herself against the brick wall. "How could anyone do that to a person?"

"Someone with absolutely no empathy whatsoever." Kane's hand wrapped around her arm as he urged her back up the steps. "There's nothing we can do for her. We should leave the processing of the scene to Wolfe and his team. Just being down here is contaminating the evidence. It looks to me like this guy wasn't too careful by the number of footprints he's left behind. It's likely there's trace evidence all over."

Nauseous, Jenna moved slowly up the steps and staggered out into the barn. Scanning the immediate area, she aimed her flashlight across the ground in front of the trapdoor. "Look here." She moved the beam over an unusual circular patch of blood on the ground. "What do you make of that?"

"The killer came up the steps and removed his clothes here." Kane pointed to the bloody footprints of rubber boots beside an unusual wrinkled pattern on the floor. "Looking at this, after killing her, he stripped off. The marks on the floor are where he dropped his blood-soaked clothing. See the very fine drops of blood heading toward the white truck? I figure he bundled up all his blood-soaked clothes, removed his boots, and carried them over to where he parked his truck. If he planned this murder, it would make sense that he laid out something close by like a large plastic bag or similar to place his clothes in so he wouldn't carry any trace evidence to his vehicle."

Heartsore for the poor woman, Jenna nodded. She turned away and stared into the anxious faces of her deputies. She realized the horror from the root cellar must be reflected in her expression. Keeping moving on the investigation would clear her mind. Sticking to procedure helped and she had a list in her head to work through. That small modicum of rational thought helped her get through some of the most terrible crimes. She lifted her chin and composed her thoughts. "So I imagine Marissa arrived to meet an acquaintance and climbed out of her truck. Things took a turn for the worse, she tried to get away, and her killer chased her down in the stables. The initial attack must have occurred there."

"Yeah, from what I can see, he was swinging an ax or a long-blade knife, maybe a machete." Rio led the way toward the stables, carefully avoiding the drag marks on the floor. When they reached a blood-splattered stall right at the end of the line, he pointed out the chips of wood gouged out from the side of the stall. "That looks like ax marks to me, and look down here. I'm not one hundred percent sure but that looks like fingertips."

Scanning the area, Jenna noticed clumps of hair. "So he incapacitated her here and then dragged her by her hair to the root cellar. I wonder why he didn't just kill her and leave her here?"

"I'd say it was for the fear factor." Kane folded his arms across his chest. "It's dark, filthy, and disgusting down there. He wanted to make it as bad as possible, as if he planned to teach her a lesson. This is a very twisted individual. Just from the brief moment I looked at the victim, I could see he wanted to give her a slow death. This is a monster enjoying the thrill of the kill. His aim was to inflict as much pain as possible. If this is one of her friends, I'd hate to meet her enemies."

Mind racing with the implications of another monster roaming Black Rock Falls, Jenna scanned the faces of her deputies. "It seems we have stirred up a wasps' nest by investigating the cold case. We must be getting closer to the killer of those kids than we imagined. I figure the killer was concerned that Marissa was going to inform us about what really happened on the mountain that night. He's sending a message to everyone involved to make sure they all keep their mouths shut."

TWENTY-EIGHT

The moment Wolfe got the call about a murder at the Old Mitcham Ranch, he grabbed a generator and portable lights. Without his daughter Emily, who usually assisted him and was currently completing her residency at Black Rock Falls General, he only had his assistant Colt Webber. He called on his fiancée, Norrell, and her team to assist. Although Norrell and her team were forensic anthropologists, they were well versed in crime scenes since arriving in town. With everything packed into his van, they headed to the Old Mitcham Ranch. He'd worked on all the previous murders that had occurred at the cursed place and was fully aware of the dangers. He made sure every member of the team wore a liquid Kevlar vest and carried weapons.

As he arrived, Kane and Rio were in the process of moving their vehicles out of the barn. When Kane jumped out of his truck and waved him inside, he headed into the dim interior. Immediately the smell of blood and putrid flesh crawled up his nose. He jumped down and went over to where Jenna was leaning against a post. Her bleak expression spoke volumes. "What have we got?"

"Mutilation." Jenna shuddered and wrapped her arms around her chest. "It's not the worst I've seen but it comes close."

Wolfe squeezed her shoulder. "I can take it from here if you like."

"I would like to say yes, but I'm not leaving you or your team here without backup." Jenna met his gaze. "When you see what happened to Marissa Kendrick, you'll understand why we need to hang around."

Nodding, Wolfe waited for Kane to walk over and raised his eyebrows. "Rio mentioned there were two crime scenes and we have only one body. Where do you want me to start?"

He listened as Kane explained what they'd discovered. He turned to Norrell, who had joined the group. "Can you process the scene in the stables and I'll go down into the root cellar with Webber?"

"Not a problem." Norrell turned to Jenna. "Do you have any suspects? I gather this is involved with the cold-case crime we are investigating. Marissa Kendrick was one of the people you spoke to recently, wasn't she?"

"Yes, and now she's dead." Jenna's brow wrinkled into a frown. "I have a list of possible suspects and I can assure you I'll be hunting them down to find out exactly where they were when Marissa was murdered." She straightened. "I'll be in the Beast while you're processing the scene. I've everything I need there to start the investigation."

Once Wolfe had set up the lights, he sent Webber to video the entire scene and then take photographs. He stood to one side to absorb the scene in front of him. This murder had started in the barn and progressed to the root cellar. From the blood spatter and the angle of the incisions on the body, including the shattered bones, he identified the murder weapon as a long-handled ax. The swing from the ax had sent streams of blood spatter in arcs from the body across the ceiling and down the wall. The bloody arcs crisscrossed, which proved that the victim moved as the killer stalked her across the floor. The victim had extensive defense wounds on her arms and legs. Marissa Kendrick hadn't died easily.

Once Webber had finished taking the images of the scene and every footprint that they discovered, Wolfe bent to look more closely at the remains. To his surprise the face and neck had not been injured. Although blood matted the woman's hair and covered one side of her face, the killer had avoided striking her head. He shook his head slowly, wondering if there'd been a conversation between the killer and the victim. From the precise pattern of injuries, the killer was making a statement. One thing for sure, this wasn't a crime of passion. In those cases, men would often attack a woman's face or breasts. He straightened and sighed. "Okay, I believe we have everything we need. I don't see any fingerprints anywhere, so it's obvious he was wearing gloves. We can only hope he's left some trace evidence on the body. Let's get her bagged up and back to the lab."

When they finally carried the body up the narrow steps and loaded it into his van, he went to the Beast and removed his gloves and face mask. When Jenna buzzed down the window, he met her troubled gaze. "We're done here. There are no fingerprints to process. I'll be doing the autopsy tomorrow morning at ten as usual, if y'all want to drop by, but I figure I'll be looking for trace evidence more than anything. At this point, I don't have a cause of death, and with multiple injuries, it could be difficult to determine. When people are injured to this degree, they usually die from blood loss." He gave her a long look as a doctor rather than a friend. "You need to get back to the office and put your feet up for half an hour or so. I know you're tough, Jenna, but we all need to take a break sometimes and I figure the time is now." He slapped a hand on her door. "Doctor's orders."

TWENTY-NINE

Josie's heart pounded as the big black truck rolled into her yard and Sheriff Jenna Alton climbed out followed by Deputy Kane. After the call from Lily about her encounter with Jess, her mind had been reeling. She'd expected phone calls from some of the others, either offering support or giving her guidance about what she should do next. The guys seem to have everything under control and none of them appears to be particularly worried about what was going on. The idea of ignoring everything and just keeping their heads down seems to be working for them, but now Marissa was missing and the sheriff was heading for her front door. Panic gripped her as she stood in the passageway waiting for the knock on the door. She tried hard to compose herself as she reached for the door handle. "Is there any news about Marissa?"

"Yes, can we come inside and speak to you?" Sheriff Alton looked at her. Her face was pale and drawn.

Standing to one side, Josie allowed them to pass. "The family room is on the left. It's warmer in there." She followed them inside, but nobody took a seat. They just stood there looking at her. "Have you found her? Where is she? Is she okay?"

"Maybe you'd better sit down." Deputy Kane took her arm and led her to the sofa. "It's not good news, I'm afraid."

Josie swallowed hard. "What's happened?"

"We found the body of who we believe is Marissa Kendrick out at the Old Mitcham Ranch. We traced her truck there." Sheriff Alton perched on the edge of the sofa beside her. "I'm sorry for your loss."

Overwhelmed with grief, Josie wrapped her arms around her stomach and rocked back and forth. Tears streamed down her face and moments later, Deputy Kane was pressing a glass of water into her hands. She stared at the water as it trembled, unable to comprehend what had happened. "How did she die?"

"The cause of death is unknown at this time but we're treating the matter as a homicide." Deputy Kane looked at her. "You might have information that will help us catch her killer."

"We checked her vehicle GPS, and after she left you at Aunt Betty's Café, she went by the ranch." Sheriff Alton leaned forward, looking at her. "Did she mention anything about meeting someone at the ranch over lunch?"

Unable to control her sobs, Josie shook her head and looked from one to the other. "No, she mentioned buying groceries and I watched her heading in that direction when I went to my vehicle. We talked about general things, friends, and her work and clients. There was absolutely no mention about meeting anyone. I couldn't possibly imagine why she'd go anywhere like the Old Mitcham Ranch. She is reluctant even to leave town to visit old friends in a group of people. She would never go somewhere like that on her own."

"I see you were close friends." Deputy Kane pulled a large plastic bag from inside his coat pocket and held it up to display two phones. "Did she ever mention why she needed a burner phone? It seems very strange for someone who doesn't socialize very much."

Josie stared at the phones in disbelief. How could Marissa have been so stupid as to have carried them both at the same time? She took a deep breath and tried to compose herself and then indicated to the light blue smartphone. "I recognize that one. Marissa carried it around all the time. I can only imagine that she kept the other one for work. She is a very private person and perhaps she liked to keep her clients separate." She pulled a tissue from her pocket and dabbed at her eyes.

"Hmm, that's very interesting." Sheriff Alton tapped her bottom lip as if considering what she'd said. "Would you mind calling her phone, please? I would be interested to know if she's using the burner phone for her friends. It would be very unusual for a business to use a burner phone unless it was corrupt, and as she is a tax agent it might be something we need to look into."

Desperately torn between keeping quiet and telling the sheriff everything she knew, Josie stood and went to the kitchen to collect her phone. If she called the burner, then would she be admitting she knew it existed, and if she didn't, would it make Marissa look as if she were a corrupt tax agent? She sucked in a steadying breath, not knowing what to do for the best. Fingers trembling, she made the decision. Marissa was dead and she had herself and the others to protect now. She called Marissa's smartphone. When it rang, she hurried back to the family room.

"You can disconnect now." Deputy Kane was looking at the smartphone. "You came up on the caller ID."

"Okay, that's all we need for now." Sheriff Alton stood and handed her a card. "I'd like you to run through the conversation you had with Marissa at Aunt Betty's. If you can recall anything at all that might lead us to who did this to your friend, it doesn't matter how small or seemingly insignificant." She sighed. "Also, if you can recall any living relatives she might have, we'll need to contact them. Do you know if she had a lawyer?"

Feeling numb from shock, Josie nodded. "Sam Cross does just about everything in town. We talked about making wills some time ago and his name came up. I don't recall any names of her relatives, but he might know. I remember when her folks died, no one came to the funeral."

"That information is very useful." Sheriff Alton headed for the door. "Thank you for your assistance."

Josie sat down hard on the sofa, staring at the phone in her hand. She needed to call Lily but hesitated, not sure if it was the right thing to do. Confusion gripped her. Everyone should be told about Marissa but she needed to follow the rules. Taking a deep breath, she made the call. "Lily, you need to get away from everyone for a second. I have some terrible news to give you."

"Okay, I'll go into the break room." The music from the beauty parlor was muted as she shut the door. *"I'm all alone. What's happened?"*

Trying hard not to break down and cry, Josie pressed the phone against her ear. "Marissa's dead. Someone murdered her out at the Old Mitcham Ranch sometime after we had lunch at Aunt Betty's Café yesterday. The sheriff was just here asking me questions. As far as they're concerned, I'm the last person to see her alive."

"Oh, sweet Jesus, no. Marissa's dead? Why did they head straight to you? They can't possibly believe that you murdered her, can they?" Lily let out a sob, fighting back tears. *"Who would do such a thing? Marissa never hurt anyone and what was she doing out at that horrible old ranch? No one in their right mind would go there alone."*

Trying to stay calm, Josie sipped the water Deputy Kane had given her. "No, she wouldn't go there alone but everything points to the fact she did. The sheriff has her truck's GPS records and it showed that she left Aunt Betty's Café and headed out to the Old Mitcham Ranch. They also have her burner phone."

"They what?" A chair screeched as metal legs tore across tile and Lily let out a long breath as she sat down. *"Now you know why Wyatt insisted that we keep only one number on each phone. If we'd had everyone's numbers, it wouldn't take them too long to discover our identities. You have his burner number, don't you? If so, I suggest you contact him immediately and let him know what's going on. I'll call Dustin Crawley—he'll pass it on and get back to me. It's not suspicious, us talking, because we always do and now with what's happened to Marissa it would be normal."* She blew her nose and cleared her throat. *"This is terrible. I can't think straight. Do you figure she was killed because she wanted to go to the cops? Heck, I agreed with her. What if one of the guys killed her to shut her up? Do you figure any of them are capable of murder? If so, maybe we should risk it and tell the sheriff. I'm not planning on being murdered anytime soon."*

One slip of the tongue and they'd all go to prison. Pulling on her inner strength, Josie shook her head. "She was my best friend, but we can't fall to pieces and start blaming each other." She stared at the wood burning in the fire and the dancing orange flames. "We live in a town known for serial killers. Her murder could be a random act of violence, and no, after all these years, if one of us was a killer, we'd know long before now. Get the word out and I'll do the same. For heaven's sake, act normal. Our friend has been murdered, so it's okay to be upset." She disconnected and stood to retrieve her burner. The phones would be running hot tonight.

THIRTY

As Dustin Crawley rode the fence line checking for breaks, he received a frantic call from Lily. At home, he'd turned off his burner phone the moment he'd heard the news about finding the body of Marissa Kendrick out at the Old Mitcham Ranch. The discovery would have the women in their secret group on edge—and rightly so. Living with his parents had its drawbacks, and a phone going off every five minutes would cause undue attention. His pa believed that smartphones were a time-wasting curse, and he'd turned on the burner only once he'd ridden out of earshot.

He'd wanted to leave home to forge a life for himself years ago, but his parents needed him to run the ranch as they weren't getting any younger. The time he spent away on the rodeo circuit meant that his father had to hire someone to take his place, but it was the only respite he got, as living with his folks was anything but easy.

He listened in silence as Lily raved on about Marissa's death. He understood that she was upset and caught her underlying concern that it was one of them who had murdered her. The idea of her going to the cops with this notion would undo years of careful planning to keep all of them safe. "Nothing has changed, Lily. What happened to Marissa was tragic and can't possibly be related to what happened twelve years ago. Don't you figure if one of us was a serial killer, we'd have all been murdered by now?"

"It just seems very strange." Tunes from Lily's car radio came through his earpiece. "Nothing happens for twelve years and then their bodies turn up and now Marissa is murdered."

Pulling up his horse and dismounting to go and check the fence line, Crawley shook his head. "Nope, it's just a coincidence. This is the problem with you women: you start panicking the moment a small thing goes wrong. Us guys just keep on doing what we're doing, keeping our heads down and not interacting with each other. You have to admit that you, Josie, and Marissa have been acting like idiots this week. The moment those bodies showed up in the river, suddenly there's a conspiracy between us. I'll contact Clint and pass on your concerns but if you've already been seen in town with Jess, you could have caused irreparable damage. You know what people are like in this town. The sheriff asks for information and people love to gossip. The pizzeria has CCTV cameras, so meeting him isn't something you can deny. Trust me I don't want to go to prison because you're making stupid mistakes."

"I made it look like normal." Lily sucked in a breath. "It was more like 'well fancy seeing you here after all these years,' rather than a planned meeting. We spoke for a few seconds and then I picked up my pizzas and left. Jess was more concerned about his wife discovering that he'd met another woman in town than what I was telling him."

Taking a pair of pliers from his tool belt, Crawley twisted the wire to repair the fence. "Really? You come on about Marissa wanting to go to the cops about what happened twelve years ago, and you don't figure it's going to cause a problem? Have you considered the implications if she'd blabbed? The fact that you believed it was a good idea sent shockwaves through us guys. It's just not about you girls, you know. We have responsibilities and people who rely on us. You just can't make up your minds to do something stupid without due consideration of what might happen to everyone else."

"Do you figure any of the guys are capable of murder?"

Suddenly glad that Lily couldn't see him, Crawley bit back a laugh. That night on the mountain, all the guys knew that Cole and Abby were still alive. They would die from their injuries and there was little hope that they would survive, but they all knew. Anyone of them could have stopped the burial but none of them wanted to risk the implications of what had happened. They'd all covered up a crime and were equally responsible. Maybe it was time to make Lily fully aware of the truth. "That night on the mountain, when we buried Cole and Abby, we knew they were still alive. Josie knew they were still alive as well. Do you recall when we went over to the bushes and talked in a huddle? You and Marissa were sitting on the rocks bawling your eyes out. We all agreed that Cole deserved to die and Abby would be better off dead than living with the injuries that she'd sustained. We did what was best for everyone. The moment you pushed dirt into that grave, you were as guilty as the rest of us. So if the question is 'which one of us might be capable of murder?' the answer would be 'all of us.'"

"Oh, my God. You knew?" Lily sucked in panicked breaths. *"I had no idea. Look, I've gotta go. I'm late for work."* She disconnected.

Crawley stared at the phone for a few moments. Marissa's death had absolutely no effect on him whatsoever, but her threat to go to the cops had been a problem. He thought for a beat and then called Clint Wasser. After bringing him up to speed about the phone call from Lily, he climbed on his horse and headed back to the ranch house. "I figure Lily is losing her mind. She doesn't seem to be coping and right now she's a loose cannon. I've tried talking to her and explaining what would happen to all of us if she went to the cops."

"*So she has it in her mind that Marissa's death is tied in with what happened before?*" Wasser gave a strangled laugh. "*Don't they understand that if we hadn't trusted them, in a town like Black Rock Falls, any one of us could have murdered them and no one would have known it was us? We don't have a motive to kill them, well, as far as the cops are concerned. Maybe we were naïve to trust them.*"

Heading into the stables, Crawley dismounted. "Well, I'm guessing it's too late to change things now. Contact the others and then get back to me. I still believe if we stick together, we'll be okay. There's no evidence to prove we were on the mountain near those caves that night. We've gone over it a thousand times. What we did on that night gave us a watertight alibi. Others saw us arriving at the campsite by the river, we all left together after midnight and there were many more walking down the mountain with us. Unless one of the girls spills, no one will ever know what really happened that night." He hauled off his saddle and dumped it onto the rack. "The only thing that concerns me at the moment is if any of us left any evidence at the Old Mitcham Ranch when we had our meeting. It was a very safe place to meet and the perfect place to murder someone."

"*Yeah, but we can't risk meeting there again. The sheriff will be all over that place, but I doubt they'll discover we've been there. It's unlikely there'd be any tire tracks. That old gravel track is thick and hard even after all the rain. Everyone was freezing cold and wearing gloves. It's not as if anyone could have left fingerprints anywhere. I figure we're safe enough.*" Wasser paused a beat. "*Now that you've made the situation clear to Lily, when I speak to Twotrees I'll make sure he reads the riot act to Josie. She has a lot to lose being married and all. I can't imagine Bob staying with her if he discovers her dark past. Maybe she needs to be reminded of that before she goes flapping her lips."* He sighed. *"Leave it with me. I'll get back to you."* He disconnected.

Crawley removed the bridle from his horse and commenced brushing it. He looked into the bright brown eyes and smiled. "I wish people were as uncomplicated as horses."

THIRTY-ONE

That morning at the kindergarten Jenna and Kane spent time admiring their son's artwork. The theme this week in the class had been spring, and Tauri proudly described each painting in the display of his work. The little boy had proved to be talented in many ways. At five he could read and speak three languages and had an awe-inspiring intuition. In fact, Jenna's son never ceased to amaze her. She'd been told being a mother would be difficult, especially raising a child who wasn't her own. There would be things in Tauri's past they would need to get through, but this didn't seem to be the case. It seemed he'd been one of the lucky ones when it came to foster care. The little boy had always insisted that he'd been waiting for them to come for him, and the moment they'd arrived at Blackhawk's ranch he'd recognized them as being his parents. The feeling had been mutual, and they had become an immediate family.

Tauri was tall and robust, and now five-and-a-half years old, he was head and shoulders above the other children of his age. There'd been no mistake about his date of birth or his heritage. His mother had died but had left as much information as she could gather with the baby as if she'd known the end was close.

The only thing they didn't know was his father's name. The entire time he was in foster care, not one person had come forward to claim him until a DNA match had put him as a close relative to a Atohi Blackhawk and, way back on his mother's side, a distant relative to Kane's dead wife, Annie. Blackhawk had become his guardian and it was only fate that had brought them all together one day on the res. As if the planets had aligned, Tauri had completed Jenna and Kane's world.

Impressed by the scenes of forest wildflowers and bright blue skies, Jenna hugged Tauri. "These are wonderful. I hope you'll be able to bring them home so we can put them up in your room." She pointed to a picture of the three of them outside their ranch house. "This one would look really good in the passageway beside the front door."

"I'd like that." Tauri beamed at her. "I'll make sure not to crease it when I bring it home." He looked at Kane. "See I made you bigger than all the other daddies in the class."

"You included the motorcycle." Kane bent to peer at the painting. "These are very good. I'm so proud of you." He ruffled Tauri's hair. "I wish we could stay a little longer but we must go to work now. You have fun and we'll see you later."

After a quick hug, Jenna reluctantly followed Kane to the door, turning to give Tauri a quick wave. The ache of leaving him at the kindergarten had eased since the first few weeks. Her little boy enjoyed the company of the other children and thrived with the input of knowledge. The school was very progressive and the curriculum covered a wide range of subjects. With the added security and Nanny Raya on hand, it assured that when they were working, Tauri had the best possible care available.

They headed to the office to find Rio and Rowley hard at work. After returning from the crime scene, they'd divided the list of potential suspects to hunt down their exact location. Kane had unlocked Marissa's phones but found absolutely no reason why she went to the Old Mitcham Ranch after lunch at Aunt

Betty's Café. Jenna had refused to believe her death was a random act of violence. Someone had lured Marissa to the ranch and it must be someone she knew. The idea of an angry client did enter her mind, but as far as she could ascertain, Marissa's clientele was more than happy with her work. In fact, when she'd called her client list, they all sang her praises.

The main problem Jenna faced was they didn't have a valid reason to question the suspects. She might believe there were possible links to the death of Marissa Kendrick, but she had no proof or motive whatsoever. As everything had occurred since the discovery of Cole's and Abby's bodies, the probability that the cold case and Marissa's murder were entwined had become more than coincidental. If the group with Cole and Abby on the night they'd died had something to hide, she'd do everything in her power to uncover the truth.

She scanned the whiteboard. Rio had painstakingly added all the information possible on the suspects and was currently adding photographs. She turned and looked at Rowley. "Do you have their current locations?"

"I have where they should be." Rowley stared at his tablet. "Clint Wasser and Wyatt Twotrees own the vehicle dealership in town and both should be there, although Wasser does move around. He works in sales, so moves between franchises. Twotrees works mainly from the office, as far as I know." He scrolled through the page on his tablet. "Dustin Crawley should be at his parents' ranch. He is single and works the rodeo circuit every year, but the weather has held up everything this year so he should be at home. Jess Hallon is married to Dawn and they have a son. He works on his parents' ranch and lives in a separate house on the property."

Jenna made notes and then looked at her deputies. "Okay, we need to establish the men's whereabouts when Marissa was murdered. I don't have a time of death, so we'll take it from when she had lunch with Josie Campbell and when we discovered her body. Rio and Rowley, you hunt down Crawley and Hallon. We have an autopsy at ten, so we'll do the local suspects. It's imperative we discover who fits into Marissa Kendrick's timeline."

"Copy that." Rowley stood and gathered his things. He looked at Rio. "I'll drive. I know where they live." He headed out of the door.

Thinking ahead, Jenna stood and took her coat from Kane. "I figure I'll start the questioning with what happened twelve years ago and then move on to their whereabouts when Marissa was murdered. It will be interesting to see their reaction."

"That should work." Kane pushed on his hat and zipped up his jacket. "The main problem I see is that if they've been keeping a secret for twelve years, they'll be hard to break. After time a lie becomes the truth. I've seen people trick polygraphs with much the same."

Jenna smiled at him. "It will work. You'll be watching him and you don't miss a thing."

THIRTY-TWO

Blue-and-white bunting fluttered in the breeze around the dealership. The lot out front was filled with highly polished vehicles of all descriptions. Jenna headed toward the glass-fronted building. Inside, an array of prestige vehicles spread out, all tastefully arranged with large advertising boards beside them listing their many attributes. She weaved her way through the vehicles to the main counter with a bright red sign across the top that read SPARE PARTS. The area was surprisingly busy, with customers required to take a number and wait in line to be served. They went right to the counter and received a few disgruntled looks from people in the line. She waited for someone to come out from the back and got his attention. "Can you direct me to Mr. Wasser and Mr. Twotrees offices, please?"

"Do you have an appointment?" The server looked from one to the other and raised his eyebrows. "You'll need to go to the administration office and speak to them there. It's down the passageway to the left."

Jenna nodded. "Thanks."

They found the administration office without any problems. The door was open and Jenna walked right in and leaned on the counter. The sign on the counter read NATALIE GANNON. As a woman came into the office, Jenna smiled. "Ms. Gannon. I'm Sheriff Alton, I need to speak to Mr. Twotrees and Mr. Wasser right away. Can you show me to their offices, please?"

"I'm not sure if that's possible. They're very busy." Ms. Gannon straightened and reached for the phone. "I'll see if Mr. Twotrees will see you." She made the call. "Very well, I'll send them in." She pointed to the door. "Down the passageway to the right. His office is the first one you come to."

Jenna exchanged a meaningful glance with Kane, turned on her heel, and headed along the passageway. She knocked on the door and walked in without waiting for a reply. The man behind the desk would have been in his mid-thirties, and as he stood his athletic appearance was enhanced by his wide white smile and pleasant features. Jenna made the introductions and took the chair he offered in front of his desk. She took out her notebook and pen and then leveled her gaze on him. "I'll come straight to the point. You'll be aware that the bodies of your friends from college washed up in the river this week. We've spoken to Josie Campbell, Marissa Kendrick, and Lily Jones about that night over Halloween. What do you recall about that night?"

The story that Twotrees recounted was exactly the same as they'd heard from the women—verbatim. Jenna nodded and made a few unnecessary notes. "I feel like this is Groundhog Day, every one of you tells me exactly the same story without any deviation whatsoever. I find it hard to believe that all your recollections of that evening are exactly the same down to the time and the people that you saw around you that night. Everyone has different memories especially after twelve years." She tapped her pen on his desk, showing agitation toward his replies. "I know you were on the football team with Cole. From the yearbook photographs, the group of you were close friends.

Did he ever mention any problems with his relationship with Abby?"

"Nope." Twotrees rested his elbows on the desk and towered his fingers. "As far as I'm aware, they were happy little lovebirds. The last time I saw them they were walking away from the campsite up the trail hand in hand. I didn't take too much notice because they were always going off alone. That's what kids did in college, as I'm sure you can remember."

"You didn't think to raise the alarm when they didn't return?" Kane leaned back in his chair observing him with interest.

"Nope, why would I do that? I had no idea what they were doing." Twotrees' mouth twitched into a grin. "Well, I did have some idea, but it wasn't for me to go and disturb them or hunt them down to find out where they were. As consenting adults, it was none of my business. They drove to the mountain in Cole's truck, as far as I'm aware, so I guess I figured they'd just left. I know that Abby wasn't happy about going into the mountains over Halloween. She wouldn't allow Cole to wear his Halloween mask either because it frightened her."

Jenna made a few quick notes and then lifted her head to look at him. "Did that cause a problem between them? Did you hear this disagreement and how was Abby when she came to the mountain? Did she seem upset at all?"

"No, no, and no." Twotrees rolled his eyes. "Cole mentioned it before we went to the mountain. I believe it was in the dressing room after practice but I can't be sure. It was a long time ago. Trust me, he would have done anything for that girl— not wearing a Halloween mask wasn't an issue between them. When we walked up the mountain together, they acted normal. There's nothing else I can say. I didn't see anything. I didn't hear anything. We were all just out having a good time. It was a big shock to discover that someone murdered them."

Unconvinced, Jenna kept her expression neutral. "Can you

account for your whereabouts between two on Wednesday afternoon and eleven on Thursday morning?"

"Why would you want to know that?" Twotrees' eyes narrowed and he placed his hands flat on the table.

"That would be the estimated time of death of Marissa Kendrick, and as a friend of hers, we need to know where you were and who can collaborate your movements around that time." Kane leaned forward eyeballing him. "I'm sure as a businessman you would be able to account for your movements during the day."

"Let me see." Twotrees' fingers ran over his keyboard. I believe I was in the office on Wednesday. I don't recall doing anything else but going home on Wednesday night and coming back to work on Thursday morning. I had orders to process. I don't have a personal secretary. We all use the same administrative assistant."

"So if I check the GPS system on your vehicle, it will confirm that you remained in the office all day, or did you go out for a bite to eat for lunch?" Kane's attention hadn't moved from Twotrees' face.

"It's very possible. I went out for lunch. I go out for lunch most of the time." Twotrees' mouth formed a straight line. "It's not something I plan and it depends on what I've decided to eat." Annoyance shimmered off him. "I don't remember because it wasn't significant. Now, if that's all, I've got work to do."

Jenna slowly took a card from her pocket and slid it across the table toward him. "If you do have any memories of the night Cole and Abby went missing, or if you remember where you were on Wednesday, I would advise you strongly to contact me."

"Okay, I will but I can't remember anything now and I don't think that's going to change." Twotrees ran a hand down his face. "It's terrible what happened to Marissa but I haven't seen her for many years. I don't even recall seeing her in the street and whatever happened to Cole and Abby is a mystery I've struggled with for many years. Cole was my best friend and he never mentioned running away with Abby, and that was the general consensus when they didn't show. As time went by, I stopped thinking about them, until this week when their faces were all over the news. I believe that trying to tie in the two incidents is a mistake because we rarely see each other now. In fact, I don't ever recall any of us getting together apart from the college reunions. The only person I speak to from back then is my business partner, Clint Wasser. His office is next door and he's in today. Feel free to go and speak to him, but you'll get the same information as I gave you." He waved a hand toward the door.

Unable to think of anything else to ask, Jenna stood and leaned on the table to stare into his eyes. "Unlike the sheriff who was in charge when Abby and Cole went missing, I will get to the bottom of this. We have evidence that will lead to the person who murdered Abby and Cole. We've discovered the burial site and have a leading forensic anthropologist on the case. She will find evidence to convict. There's no statute of limitations for murder and I don't believe it's a coincidence that Marissa was murdered the same week as their bodies were found in the river. I figure she was planning on letting me know what had happened that night in the mountains and someone murdered her to keep her quiet."

Pausing long enough to take in the surprise expression on Twotrees' face, Jenna straightened and headed out of the door. As Kane came up beside her, she turned and smiled at him. "I figure I got his attention."

"Yeah, you sure shook his tree." He indicated to a room farther down the passageway with Wasser's name on a metallic strip on the door. He knocked and pushed it open. "Mr. Wasser? The sheriff would like a word with you."

THIRTY-THREE

Heading into an interview with a person who could be a violent criminal was never easy. Keeping a casual and unthreatening attitude was pivotal to getting information from people. After witnessing what had happened in the root cellar at the Old Mitcham Ranch, any of the men they were interviewing could be a monster. After speaking with Twotrees, the hairs on the back of Jenna's neck had stood to attention. She'd interviewed so many nice serial killers hiding in plain sight that she often relied on her own intuition to bring these people to justice. Both these men were close friends and up until this moment she'd never considered the possibility of two monsters.

Her attention moved to the man behind the desk. Steel-gray eyes met her gaze from a sharp face. He had a pencil tucked behind one ear and in front of him was a legal pad covered with notes and numbers. Long shirt sleeves had been rolled up to display muscular arms that ran to wide shoulders. Both men had a familiarity about them in their build, and she had no doubt they'd been a force to be recognized when playing football. She introduced herself and Kane, and Wasser surprised her by smiling good-naturedly and waving her to a seat.

"You both look very serious. May I offer you a cup of coffee or a soda?" Wasser moved to get up.

"We're good, thanks." Kane waited for Jenna to sit down and then took the seat beside her.

Jenna set her things out on the table. "Mr. Wasser, you'll be aware that the bodies of your friends Cole and Abby were discovered in the river this week."

"Yeah, it's a terrible thing. I saw it on the news." He clasped his hands on the table, covering the notes on the legal pad. "We always wondered what had happened to them. Did they get lost in the caves or something?"

Jenna shook her head. "No, they were murdered and now we're investigating the case. I'm conducting interviews with the members of the group of friends who went to the mountain on the night they went missing. We've already interviewed Josie and Marissa, as well as your business partner, Mr. Twotrees. If you could start from the beginning, as in when you arrived at the mountain, and go on until you returned to your vehicles, I would appreciate it."

When Wasser gave a facsimile of Twotrees' account of the night, Jenna looked at Kane and rolled her eyes. The story was so well rehearsed he even chuckled in the same place. "That story is word for word from everyone we've spoken to so far. Surely, there must have been something else that happened that night. A detail we can check up on. Right now we have only the group of you to prove you were together at the riverside camp. What I need are witnesses to confirm you were in a certain place at a certain time."

"Hmm." Wasser rubbed his chin thoughtfully. "It's such a long time ago but hearing about Abby and Cole has stirred a few memories. Two of the players on our football team got into a fight over a girl, they stumbled through our firepit, and we needed to stamp out the flames. Is that the type of thing you're looking for?"

Surprised by the extra information, Jenna lifted her pen and nodded. "Yeah, that's perfect. What were their names?"

"Cory Dunn and Alan Clarke. I don't recall the name of the girl they were fighting over. It was all over in a few seconds." Wasser stared into space for a beat. "I know Cory moved to LA with his parents just after he graduated, but Alan still lives in town here somewhere. I did see him at one of our last reunions."

Relieved to get more information about the night Cole and Abby were murdered, Jenna made notes and then lifted her head to look at him. "You'll be aware that Marissa Kendrick was found murdered on Thursday. Can you account for your movements from lunchtime on Wednesday to approximately eleven on Thursday morning?"

"I move around a fair bit in my job, making sure that consignments are sent and parts ordered. Many garages across the county rely on getting their parts without delay. I do believe I was in the office most of that day. I went home around seven o'clock that night. I stayed home and watched TV and then came back to work the following morning. I live alone, so I don't have anyone to corroborate my story, but I'll be happy to submit my GPS records in my vehicle and on my phone, if that's necessary. I have nothing to hide. My life is an open book."

"When did you last see Marissa Kendrick?" Kane leaned forward in his chair.

"Oh, last year around tax time." Wasser opened his hands wide. "It's no secret she was my tax agent. Someone from your office called me late on Wednesday to ask if I'd seen her and does she come to my office or do I go and see her, but you'd know that, right?" He sat back in his chair. "Marissa was very efficient. I'll miss her."

Jenna didn't know as Maggie had made most of the calls and his name must have slipped through the net, but then many of the townsfolk could have used Marissa's services. It didn't mean they'd murdered her. Although not convinced of his innocence, she would call his bluff. "To eliminate you from the investigation I would like those GPS records. She opened a new page on her notebook, wrote a permissions slip, detailing the information they required and his approval. She pushed the notepad across the desk to him. "If you don't mind signing and dating this? We won't need your phone or your vehicle, just the details: your phone number and carrier, your vehicle's plate number and make and model."

"Not a problem." Wasser wrote down the relevant information and handed the book back to her. "I hope you find Marissa's killer." He smiled at her.

Bodies of his old friends had been discovered and his tax agent had been murdered and he smiled at her as if he didn't have a care in the world. *Two can play at that game.* Jenna gave him a confident smile. "Oh, we'll catch him. The problem with killers like this one is they believe they're invincible, but even the best leave trace evidence behind and one skin flake is enough to identify them." She stood. "Thank you for your assistance. Have a nice day."

THIRTY-FOUR

Cold wind from the mountain whipped hair around Jenna's face as they walked back to the Beast. She inhaled and sighed in delight. It was the first time the alpine fragrance had returned since the floods. Raising her chin, she stared into the distance, absorbing the beauty of the bright green pines that at last had escaped the shroud of rain clouds. Wide patches of blue sky stretched across snowcapped mountain peaks. At last, the craziness of the last few months' bizarre weather was coming to an end. She checked her watch and pulled open the door of the truck. "We need to move it if we're going to get to the autopsy on time."

"What did you think of those two?" Kane started the engine and headed out of the parking lot at high speed.

Gripping the side of her seat as the truck flew around the corners, she flicked him a glance. "They made my hackles rise, as if they both had something to hide. They're close friends and have been for many years. When I was interviewing Wasser, I had the awful notion that they might both be involved." She allowed ideas to percolate through her mind and then took a deep breath. "My instinct tells me if they were involved in Abby's and Cole's murders, there's a good chance they were involved in Marissa's as well."

"It sounds logical, but without evidence, it will be difficult to prove." Kane flicked her a glance. "Circumstantially, all we have is they were on the mountain that Halloween. There's no obvious motive for them to murder Cole, Abby, or Marissa."

Determined to get answers, Jenna chewed on her bottom lip. "There's only one reason anyone would plan to murder Marissa and that would be if she threatened to reveal the truth of what really happened to Cole and Abby. I figure we need to speak to Lily Jones and see what she has to say. When Josie spoke to us it was because Lily was concerned that Marissa was missing. She'd been a no-show for an appointment at the beauty parlor and wasn't answering her phone. I believe Lily is part of the group that knows Cole's and Abby's killer. If she tells the exact same story, we'll know she colluded with the others about the night in the mountains. We have four on our list of suspects now. This leaves Crawley, Hallon, and Lily to interview. She was the other woman in all the photographs. Perhaps if we lean on her a little, she might break?"

"I guess it's worth a try, but it will be very difficult to break up a group that has stuck to their story for so many years." Kane pulled into the medical examiner's parking lot and stopped at the back door. "If they were involved in the murders of Cole and Abby, I doubt we'll be able to make any of them talk. They'd know if one of them breaks, they'll fall like a line of dominos."

After using the scanner, Jenna moved along the passageway searching the examination rooms for one with a red light. The red light indicated that Wolfe was conducting an autopsy. They slipped into the alcove, removed their coat and jacket, and then pulled on scrubs, face masks, and gloves. She waited for Kane to tap his ID on the card reader and then followed him. The distinctive smell of an autopsy suite accosted her nostrils as she stepped inside and the door whooshed shut behind her. Although Wolfe did everything in his power to keep the odors to a minimum, the stink of death hung around like an evil twin.

"There y'all are." Wolfe's gray gaze moved over them from beneath his face shield. "Right on time."

The idea there might be more than one killer circulated around in Jenna's mind. "We've been out all morning and I haven't seen what you've uploaded to the server. Do you have the crime scene images at hand?"

"Yeah." Wolfe moved to a control panel and in seconds the images were displayed across the screen array. "What's on your mind?"

Moving closer to search the images, Jenna gave her head a shake. "We've just interviewed Wasser and Twotrees. They're partners in the auto dealership in town. I don't know what it was about them, but they both made me feel uneasy. It was as if they were too cooperative. As it was so dark in the root cellar, I wanted to look at the crime scene images to determine if there could've been two people involved in the murder." She raised both hands and dropped them by her sides and then turned to look at him. "I can see there's only one set of footprints, so I can strike that idea off my list."

Wolfe nodded slowly. "The number of people involved in the Cole and Abby murders is yet to be established. Norrell is making great headway with that case and is very keen to head up the mountain to check out the potential crime scene. From the information that Blackhawk supplied, she'll be able to recreate what happened."

"I guess we should take it one murder at a time." Kane indicated to the body covered with the white sheet on the stainless-steel gurney. "At least we know her identity. We spoke to her the day before she died."

"To move things along, I conducted an initial autopsy to give you the results you needed in the fastest time possible. I collected samples from various skin areas and I'm running them through the DNA sequencer as we speak, although without someone to match them to, you won't be getting any answers in the short term." Wolfe pulled back the sheet to reveal a partially autopsied corpse. "As the time of death is imperative, apart from taking the body temperature at the scene, I checked the stomach contents the moment we got back to the lab. From the rate of digestion from her lunch, I can put the time of death within an hour of leaving Aunt Betty's Café. If you consider the time it took for her to drive from town to the Old Mitcham Ranch, she would have been murdered within minutes of arriving."

"So this was a planned cold-blooded murder?" Kane leaned back against the counter and folded his arms across his chest. "This woman was a very quiet tax agent who spent most of her time at home. I couldn't in my wildest dreams come up with a motive to kill her. She's not wealthy and she didn't have any love interests, so there must have been something significant to plan this murder and get her to go alone to the Old Mitcham Ranch." He swung his gaze to Jenna. "You must admit this murder was very well planned." He indicated to the image containing the marks outside the trapdoor to the root cellar. "That's a classic impression made by blood-soaked clothes and yet there's no evident trail of blood after he removes them. I did find a few spots but that could be spatter from his movements as he undressed. This tells me that he had a large bag of some description to use for his soiled clothes. From the way it was positioned, he planned to finish her in the root cellar."

The body on the gurney was horrendous and no longer looked like Marissa Kendrick. Compassion for what the woman had suffered flowed over Jenna. "You mentioned previously that he kept her alive for as long as possible. I'm struggling to find a motive for why he would do such a thing. If he was trying to teach her a lesson, it was a pointless exercise as he killed her in the end."

"Perhaps it was a warning to the others." Wolfe shrugged. "We're dealing with a deranged mind here, so I wouldn't go trying to rationalize what he did. This murder might not be anything to do with Cole and Abby. Although, it would be stretching the imagination to believe that this was a random thrill kill." He went to the body. "The person who did this took pains not to strike any vital arteries. He made a mistake by striking the ribs on the left side. Although you'd imagine that Marissa succumbed to blood loss from the many injuries he inflicted on her, her cause of death was due to asphyxiation. One of the blows fractured her ribs and punctured her lungs. Once that occurred, her lungs filled with blood and she suffocated. Although how long into the attack this happened is undetermined."

Swallowing hard to control the bile threatening to run up the back of her throat, Jenna looked at the defensive wounds on the woman's hands and legs. "We know the attack started in the stables, and she tried to defend herself. The tips of her fingers are missing on her right hand and she has suffered deep lacerations to both arms and the lower parts of her legs. She must have been fighting for her life."

"That's correct and the hematoma on her scalp would indicate that he dragged her by her hair from the stables to the root cellar. She has grazes containing dirt from the steps on her chin and palms. So we're talking about a strong, presumably male offender who was able to toss her around without effort." Wolfe indicated to the marks he was referring to and lifted his gaze back to Jenna. "If we roll her onto her back, you can see from the injuries she tried to get away from him. This is when the strike to the ribs occurred. If you look at the crime scene photographs, there's a pool of blood around her head. Although there are no injuries to her head or neck apart from where he pulled her hair. The blood you see came from her lungs and spilled from her mouth. Death would have occurred shortly after."

Jenna shook her head slowly. "What a terrible way to die."

THIRTY-FIVE

Discussing the case with Wolfe often gave Jenna different angles to attack crimes. He had a wealth of knowledge and great insight. All their suspects just happened to be big tough men, so again any one of them could be responsible. Determined to catch this killer, Jenna slammed a fist onto the counter. "We need to find this monster before he murders again. After a new taste of blood, he'll be finding it hard to control himself."

"What else have you discovered about Marissa Kendrick?" Wolfe gave her a direct stare.

"Not much. After speaking to her friends, we know she didn't like traveling any distance alone." Kane straightened from leaning against the counter. "Whoever did this to her was someone she trusted if they were able to lure her out to the Old Mitcham Ranch. The problem is she didn't trust many people. Since college she hasn't had any male friends and keeps only a close-knit group of women around her."

"Why would y'all figure the two cases are related?" Wolfe frowned. "It's not out of the realms of possibility that Marissa's murder could have been a thrill kill, and Abby's and Cole's were more like executions."

Jenna peered at him over her mask. "I've given this a lot of thought and always come back to the same conclusion. What if a group of college students were involved in Cole's and Abby's murders and kept the secret for all these years? When the bodies showed, Marissa was running scared. Maybe she threatened to speak to me. That would be a motive to kill her."

"Her brutal death would be a warning to the others to remain silent." Wolfe nodded. "That makes sense. What else have you got?"

"That's assuming that the person or persons responsible for Cole's and Abby's murders are involved." Kane adjusted his mask. "Since college, the group on the mountain that night has drifted apart. We know Marissa, Josie, and Lily kept in touch. Twotrees and Wasser became business partners. They did mention running into their old college buddies at reunions but that's it. It's as if they're consciously trying to avoid each other."

"If I recall, you mentioned that they were all members of the same fraternity." Wolfe covered the body and removed his gloves. "I'm sure y'all are aware a fraternity is a brotherhood and those guys usually remain close friends, especially if they live in the same town. Perhaps you should hunt down some of the other members. Maybe they can give you some insight into why these guys drifted apart?"

Nodding, Jenna removed her gloves and rolled them into a ball. "That's an angle I hadn't considered. Right now every time we ask about what happened that night on the mountain we get the same story. It's as if they've discussed it beforehand to make sure they all tell us exactly the same version. That's suspicious on its own and when you add the fact that they seem to be deliberately avoiding each other, it makes me believe they're hiding something."

"The avoidance and the verbatim stories point to collusion." Wolfe nodded.

"Agreed. Especially if the decision to take out Marissa was, as you said, a warning to the others." Kane narrowed his gaze. "We've seen how a psychopath can control people in other cases. It's not beyond the realms of possibility that this is the same type of situation." He looked at Wolfe. "If a close friend murdered Marissa and the killer is male, it certainly points to this group. Apart from Josie and Lily, she doesn't appear to have any other close friends at all. She was a loner."

Absorbing the information, Jenna thought for a beat. "So if this is a longtime conspiracy to cover up the murders of Cole and Abby, the group could be meeting in secret. This would account for the burner phone. In this case, Marissa would have trusted the others in the group and relied on them for years to keep their secret. Then the bodies show up and they all panic. They purchase burners to keep the group together and all on the same track."

"A psychopath would be influencing the others." Kane shrugged. "That wouldn't be too difficult, not when Norrell revealed Cole and Abby had been buried alive. Now it's not just the killer responsible for their deaths." He looked at Wolfe. "We have four possible suspects and they're all squeaky clean."

"I've gone over the body with a fine-tooth comb. If the killer left any trace evidence whatsoever, y'all know I'll find it." Wolfe led them to the door. "Norrell found traces of skin under the nails of Abby. We have only Cole's DNA to compare it to, and as the sample is degraded, it will take some time to process. There is also the fraternity pin. One of the people you're interviewing will be missing theirs. Likely that is the person who killed Abby. Who murdered Cole is a mystery, but after seeing the results of the attack on Marissa, the pattern of ax marks on her back are similar. The depth and angle change direction. They remind me of the way a wood chopper wields an ax during competition. They swing one way and then the other." He indicated with his hand as if chopping a V shape. It could be the same person, and I'd wager he has a woodcutting background."

Intrigued, Jenna stared at Wolfe in disbelief. "If it's the same person, it would certainly prove my theory that the killer murdered Marissa to prevent her from revealing who murdered Cole and Abby. Once their bodies were discovered and Norrell revealed we had leads, the killer needed to keep her quiet. Now we just have to untangle this group of friends and find him."

THIRTY-SIX

Rowley turned his truck into the Big H Ranch and headed along the impressive sweeping blacktop to the house set on the top of a hill. The ranch spread out in endless grasslands, and he recognized herds of Black Angus beef cattle. Safe from the wide areas of flooding, they grazed in lush green pastures on high ground. Well-maintained outbuildings, barns, and ranch hands' cabins made up part of a huge business. Another large ranch house sat at the end of a separate driveway with a massive garage on one side. He whistled and glanced at Rio. "Wow! This spread is impressive."

"This would be a beef cattle ranch?" Rio turned in his seat. "It's huge."

Grinning, Rowley headed for the barn with the OFFICE sign above a side door. "You're in Montana now."

"Hmm, well I figured the cattle ranches in Texas were big too until I visited Australia." Rio chuckled. "I'll give you a comparison. In Texas the biggest cattle ranch is 830,000 acres; in Australia it's 5,831,000 acres." He shrugged. "I guess they sure love their steaks Down Under."

Always amused by Rio's retentive memory and his wealth of useless information, Rowley swung out of the truck and headed to the office. The smell of cows washed over him, and flies buzzed around his head. The white painted office door stood open and a broad-shouldered man sat behind the desk working on a computer. He knocked and waited for him to look up. "Hi there. Deputy Rowley and Rio, we're looking for Jess Hallon."

"Oh, please don't tell me that one of our hands has gotten himself into trouble again?" The man leaned back in his office chair making it squeak. "I'm Jess Hallon and I run things around here."

Rowley shook his head. "I don't recall us having anyone in the cells overnight. We need to speak with you on a different matter."

"Do you own this spread?" Rio rested one hand on his weapon and waved his other one as if encompassing the entire ranch.

"I'm partners in the business with my pa." Hallon shrugged. "He's getting on in years. After a fall from his horse last spring, he's been taking it easy. So, what brings you here today?"

"If you'd watched the news over the last few days, you'd be aware that the bodies of two of your friends were discovered in the river." Rio was taking a casual pose. "We've hunted down who was with Cole and Abby over Halloween the night they went missing and your name came up. As there's no statute of limitations on murder and it's evident from the injuries on the bodies that we're looking at a homicide, Sheriff Alton has reopened the case. We're speaking to every member of the group who was with them on the night they died."

"Yeah, I have to admit it was quite a shock." Hallon leaned back in his chair crossing his legs to rest one boot on his opposite knee. "We all figured they'd run away together." He shook his head slowly. "One news report said they'd been buried alive. How so? I don't recall any landslides or anything that night. It was cold and clear with a heavy mist on the ground."

Surprised by the man's casual attitude, Rowley took out his phone. He needed to record this interview. He held up the phone. "Mind if I record the interview? If I forget to tell the boss something, I'll be back again tomorrow."

"Sure, I've got nothing to hide." Hallon's mouth twitched into a smile. "Ask away."

After hitting the record button, Rowley placed the phone on the desk. "Persons unknown attacked Cole and Abby with an ax and then buried them alive in a cave. We've established the location of this cave. The sand was washed out due to seismic activity, but the ensuing flood from the melt distributed the evidence in the same vicinity. Only the bodies were washed into the river and that's because they were mummified."

"Mummified, how on earth could that have happened?" A stunned expression crossed Hallon's face. "You mean like Egyptian mummies?"

"Yeah, much the same. When bodies are submerged in very dry sand, the normal decomposition process doesn't happen." Rio glanced at Rowley and gave him a "what the heck" shrug. "Most of the bugs that aid decomposition can't live in dry sand. The bodies just dehydrate. Without the weight of water in the tissues, they floated like dead leaves on top of the river."

"I see." Hallon cleared his throat. "Do you have any suspects for their murders?"

Rowley narrowed his gaze. There was no way he'd allow Hallon to take control of the interview. Right now the suspect was making excuses not to tell them about the night he'd spent with Cole and Abby. "If you could just tell us what you can recall about that night, we can be on our way."

The monotone description of Halloween night was given without any embellishment and was exactly the same as the others they'd received. He exchanged a meaningful glance with Rio and moved on to Marissa Kendrick's murder. "I'm sure you're aware that one of your friends was found murdered at the Old Mitcham Ranch on Thursday morning. Her name was Marissa Kendrick. Do you recall her?"

"You know, I don't even remember what Marissa Kendrick looks like." Hallon brushed a hand under his nose. "She is just a name from my past, is all."

"Can you account for your whereabouts on Wednesday and Thursday?" Rio took a step closer to the desk.

"Yeah, sure." Hallon turned to his computer screen and typed on his keyboard. "Wednesday I was in town from about eleven through to maybe two. I went to Guns and Ammo. After that I grabbed a bite to eat and then came home. Thursday, I took my wife, Dawn, to visit her mom. I messed around town for a time. I went to look at new saddles, visited the produce store, put in an order, and paid my bill. I went to the pizzeria for lunch."

"Did you meet up with anyone who can verify your whereabouts in town on those occasions?" Rio had adopted a bored expression.

"Only the storekeepers, I guess." Hallon removed his hat and scratched his head, smoothed down his shaggy hair, and replaced it. "No, I tell a lie. I did speak to someone that day in the pizzeria: Lily Jones, a girl I knew from college was waiting for her pizza. I shot the breeze with her for a few minutes to pass the time." He let out a long sigh. "I hope you're not going to make a big deal about that. My wife is the jealous type and if she believes I've been meeting up with some girl in the pizzeria when her back is turned, she won't be amused."

Rowley's mind went immediately to his wife, Sandy. They had a very loving and trustful relationship. He didn't have to worry if she met old school friends in town, they were as solid as a rock. "Don't worry, we have no reason to discuss this with your wife."

His phone buzzed with a message. It was from Jenna with instructions to ask if the suspects ever competed in woodcutting competitions and to ask if they still had their fraternity pins. Wondering what this had to do with the case, Rowley pushed on with the interview. "Just one other thing. Have you ever competed in woodchopping competitions?"

"I know you were raised in Black Rock Falls." Hallon smiled. "Didn't you attend the local college?"

Rowley shook his head. "Nope, I wanted a career in law enforcement so I went to UM."

"University of Montana, impressive." Hallon smiled. "Well here in Black Rock Falls lumberjack contests are an extracurricular activity. Back in those days on the football team, any way of building upper-body strength was good and competing was encouraged."

Listening with interest, Rowley toyed with the way to introduce the question about the fraternity pin. "Did you join one of the fraternities?"

"Yeah, I was in Alpha Pi." He stared into space for a few moments. "Those were the days. We thought they'd last forever."

Needing to wind up the interview and move on to the next suspect, Rowley nodded. "We sure did. Have you still got your fraternity pin? I always wear mine to reunions."

"Now that's a question." Hallon rubbed his chin. "It's not something I would toss away, so it must be around somewhere."

"What about the other members of your fraternity? Do you get to see them often?" Rio gave him a long look. "You were all like brothers, if yours was anything like mine."

"No, I don't." Hallon waved a hand as if encompassing the entire ranch. "Working here takes up all of my time, especially now as I'm doing my pa's work as well."

Satisfied he'd gotten as much from Hallon as possible, Rowley stopped recording. "Okay that's all we need for today. Thank you for your cooperation." He handed him a card. "Should you have any recollections about that night, apart from what you've told us, please give me a call." He tapped the desk with his fingers and then headed for the door.

THIRTY-SEVEN

Justin Crawley turned onto Main and headed to the produce store. As he passed the beauty parlor, he couldn't help noticing the sheriff and her deputy standing outside speaking with Lily. He slowed his truck to a crawl, watching with interest as she climbed inside the sheriff's vehicle and both the sheriff and deputy turned to speak to her in the back seat. After their recent conversation, seeing Lily with the sheriff concerned him. He contacted Wyatt Twotrees on the burner phone and explained what he'd witnessed and his earlier conversation with her. "Do you figure Lily is confessing to the sheriff?"

"*I have no idea. Did you get anywhere speaking to her?*" Twotrees sounded agitated. "*I know that the sheriff is working down a list of everyone who was on the mountain that night. They have spoken to me and Clint this morning, so I would imagine Lily is on the list as well and so are you.*"

Crawley ran a hand down his face. "I'm in town so they won't find me at home and I don't really want them speaking to my folks."

"*It's no good stressing out about it. I figure finding the bodies has opened up a whole can of worms and all we can do is stick to our story. There's no evidence at the caves, no matter what the media keeps reporting. We cleaned that place and nothing was left behind. I figure they're saying all this shit to get one of us to crack."* Twotrees let out a long sigh. *"I'll call Jess and see if they've dropped by to see him. I'll get back to you. You'll need to contact Lily again. I believe we all need to know what's going on."*

Crawley's other phone buzzed. "I have a call on the other phone. I gotta go. I'll call you later." He disconnected and slid the burner phone beneath his seat before accepting the call through his vehicle's Bluetooth connection. "Yeah, what is it, Pa?"

"The local deputies dropped by looking for you. I figure it was to give you some information about Cole and Abby. I told them you were heading for the produce store, so likely they'll catch up with you there." His pa cleared his throat. *"Terrible thing about them two kids being murdered."*

Swallowing hard, Crawley pulled his truck into the parking lot outside the produce store. He backed up to the delivery ramp and slid out of his vehicle. "Yeah, it is. I need to go. I'm just heading into the store. Thanks for the heads-up." He disconnected.

He'd just finished loading all his purchases onto the back of his truck when the sheriff's black vehicle slid in beside him and the sheriff climbed out, her deputy close behind. Crawley jumped down from the back of his truck and slammed the tailgate. He turned and almost collided with the tall deputy blocking his way to the door of his vehicle. The sheriff stood just behind him and to the right. He looked from one to the other. "Is there something I can do for you, Sheriff?"

The questions that followed were exactly what he'd expected after speaking to Twotrees. He gave them the account they required, sticking to the storyline. He, like the others, had entered lumberjack contests during his time in college but he had no idea of the location of his Alpha Pi pin. When they started asking him about Marissa's murder, his stomach clenched with anxiety. This part of the story they hadn't discussed, so he had no idea what the others had told her. Due to the flooding, he'd been driving back and forth collecting things they needed to make on-the-spot repairs. The heavy and relentless rainfall had caused roofs to leak and gutters to rip from the buildings. They had fences down all over and they had men working around the clock trying to fix everything. He'd told the truth when he'd admitted not knowing exactly where he'd been over the time Marissa went missing.

When the sheriff eventually stopped her barrage of questions, he decided not to stop at Aunt Betty's Café for a well-earned slice of pie as planned but parked opposite. He dug out his burner phone and, checking inside his notebook for the correct number, called Lily. "I saw the sheriff speaking to you. She's been visiting everyone in our group. What did you tell her? She was on my back like a rat up a drainpipe."

"I didn't tell her anything we haven't already discussed." Lily's voice echoed, as if she was speaking to him in the restroom. *"I stuck to the story we decided, to the letter."*

Irritated, Crawley stared out of the window. "You know, if you hadn't reported Marissa missing, none of us would have been in the spotlight. What you've done is given them a list of people they can investigate. Before this, as far as the sheriff was concerned, we didn't exist. Now we're all fighting for our lives."

"Marissa was my friend and she went missing. She didn't have any family to care, so what did you expect me to do? I couldn't just stand around and do nothing." Lily was close to tears.

Shaking his head, Crawley rolled his eyes. "Yeah, you could have, because now we're all under suspicion for three murders. Wyatt is calling the guys and will contact us with a plan to get out of this mess." He drummed his fingers on his steering wheel.

"From now on, keep your mouth shut." He disconnected and slid the phone back under his seat. He glanced over at Aunt Betty's Café and Twotrees' advice drifted across his mind. *Act normal*. He climbed out of the truck and ran across the blacktop to embrace the fragrance of freshly baked peach pie.

THIRTY-EIGHT

Upset by the interview with the sheriff, Lily had forgotten to bank the takings from the beauty parlor. It was always something she did on Fridays. The small room she used as an office held a sturdy safe. It was an hour or so after closing, when she finally finished counting the receipts and cash. She deposited everything into the safe and went into the beauty parlor to make sure it was neat and tidy for the morning rush. It was the same every Friday. They took appointments right up until seven and she rarely got away before ten. The townsfolk who worked nine to five appreciated the Friday evening appointments. She glanced at her watch. It was ten after eleven. Bone weary, she pulled on her coat and dragged garbage bags out the back door to the dumpster in the alleyway. She pushed open the lid, hoisted the bags inside, and then returned to lock the door.

Out of the corner of her eye, a shadow moved. Fear washed over her like a tsunami. On Fridays this end of town was deserted at this time of night. The other end of town, Antlers, the Turf and Surf, and the Cattleman's Hotel had become the popular hangouts, and Aunt Betty's usually always had customers until late, but on Friday nights the pizzeria across the road closed at ten. She carried a can of mace in her purse but stopped reaching for it when a familiar figure in a slicker and rubber boots stepped out from the shadows, smiling at her. "You scared the heck out of me. What are you doing hiding in the shadows?"

"I wasn't hiding. I've been waiting for you." He indicated to the long dark alleyway. "I can't risk being seen with you here. Let's go to the other end. No one will see us behind the dumpsters."

Unease slid over Lily. After what had happened to Marissa, she couldn't trust anyone. Her trembling fingers flitted across the catch on her purse. She managed to flip open the top but when her hand slipped inside, all she could feel was her phone and her keys. "Can't you just tell me what you want and then I'll leave and you can follow later?"

"I don't want anything. I just need to talk to you. It won't take long." He chuckled. "You're not scared of me, are you?"

When he moved closer, an ice-cold shiver ran down her spine. She didn't trust him but would get this clandestine meeting over to get rid of him. "No, why should I be? I'm no threat to anyone."

Afraid, she turned, keeping her distance, but with each step his eyes bored into her back like daggers. Lily hurried along the alleyway. Near the end, she glanced over one shoulder and glimpsed something shiny in his hand. As he walked, it swung back and forth like a pendulum on a grandfather's clock. Terror had her by the throat. He was carrying an ax. She started to run. Her high heels caught in the cobblestones and she tumbled hard to the cold damp garbage-covered ground. The air in her lungs rushed out in a whoosh and she sucked in painful breaths. As she rolled onto her back, he was on her in seconds, his large rubber boots pinning her down by her coat.

As the moon outlined his features, he raised the ax to make his intentions abundantly clear. *I'm going to die.* Terrified, as sobs shook her, she gaped at him. She didn't want to die in a filthy alleyway. Tears ran down her cheeks as she stared up at him. "Why are you doing this? Did you kill Marissa? I won't tell. I've never told anyone anything and I've kept your secret all these years." She tried to crawl away but his feet held her firmly.

Risking everything, she let out a gurgled scream and punched at his legs. Her scream came out in a breathless squeak. "Help me, somebody help me."

"Ah, Lily, no one will hear you, but I'll always remember your screams." He shook his head, the smile never leaving his face.

Pinned by her coat, she tried kicking out, but he laughed at her struggles. There was no way out. He'd trapped her. What could she possibly say to make him reconsider? Her mind became a garbled mess of fear. She couldn't think straight. Panting, she must try to reason with him. "Why me? You owe me that at least."

"You and Marissa couldn't keep your mouths shut, could you?" He swung the ax back and forth one inch above her face. "You want the truth?" He rested the ax on her nose and smiled down at her. "I killed Abby because I wanted to destroy Cole. She was mine first and he took her from me. The big man around campus had everything and could have had any girl he wanted, but he took *my* girl. I'd planned to kill her and make him watch, but Abby saw me following them. When she went into the bushes to pee, I killed him and then I killed her. She begged me not to, offered me anything I wanted, but he'd ruined her. So I killed her and you all believed me when I said it was Cole."

Horrified, shudders wracked Lily's body as she stared into eyes devoid of emotion and trembled. The cold wet ground seeped through her clothes and rats scattered back and forth, but her attention fixed on the ax swinging across her face so close it brushed her nose. Gasping, she stared at him. "I don't care. That was years ago. I still won't tell anyone. I promise."

"No, you won't." He lifted the ax high into the air. The streetlight sparkled on the sharp blade like a diamond in the night as he swung it toward her head. "Goodbye, Lily."

THIRTY-NINE

SATURDAY

It was a little after six by the time Kane finished up in the stables. He placed the grooming brushes back on the bench and gave Warrior one last rub on the nose. "I know you want to get out in the corral, but we'll give it another few days until it dries a little more. We don't want you getting hoof rot."

His phone rang, and he scanned the caller ID. Seeing it was a call on the 911 emergency line, he accepted the call. "Nine-one-one, this is Deputy Kane. What is your emergency?"

"There's a stream of blood coming out of the alleyway along-side the beauty parlor."

After sliding the barn door shut, Kane ran across the yard to the front door. He kicked off his dirty boots and headed for the kitchen. He grabbed a notepad and pen and then leaned on the kitchen counter. "Okay, can I have your name and details, please?"

"My name is Joshua Lane. I deliver supplies to the pizzeria." Lane gave him his details.

Considering all possibilities, Kane rubbed his chin. It wouldn't be out of the question for a wounded animal to seek refuge in an alleyway. Bears raided dumpsters especially alongside restaurants, where food scraps were readily available. "It might have been a wounded animal. Did you take a look?"

"I didn't see what it was, but I did see a pair of pink high heels." Lane cleared his throat. *"I have a heart condition. I didn't want to risk seeing something that might cause me to have a heart attack. There's that smell around the place as well. You know, like death?"*

Biting back a groan, Kane straightened. "Okay, Mr. Lane, I want you to go back to your vehicle, lock the doors, and wait for Deputy Rio to arrive. I'm on my way with the sheriff." He disconnected and called Rio to explain the situation.

It had been a tough week and leaving Jenna sleeping and heading into town alone seemed like a good idea, but then he dismissed it. She didn't like him being overprotective and some days it made him feel a little useless. He considered it was love that urged him to protect his wife and unborn child. He'd always been old-school in his treatment of women, as in respecting and protecting, but he found that living in this new world, where offering assistance could be deemed as offensive, troubled him. He gave himself a little shake and headed into the bedroom to wake Jenna. If this isn't an animal, it could be another murder and she'd want to be on scene from the get-go. "Jenna, you awake?"

"Yeah. I heard you talking. What's up?" She sat up slowly, pushing the hair from her eyes.

Kane explained. "Rio's on the way. He's more than capable to handle a murder scene if necessary. He'll call us when he gets on scene and give us an update. I have coffee brewing, and your decaf as well. I'll grab you a cup and then head for a shower. I stink of horses." He kissed her on the forehead and straightened.

"You go take a shower and I'll get the coffee." Jenna threw back the blankets, pushed her feet into slippers, grabbed her robe, and headed for the kitchen. "If it's a homicide, we'll need to call Nanny Raya and tell her that Tauri is going to be arriving early this morning."

Kane took a very quick shower and dressed for work. During murder cases they usually worked the weekend, other times Rio and Rowley were more than happy to take over and pocket the overtime. This weekend it would be all hands on deck. With two cases on the books, there wouldn't be any time to relax. He walked into the kitchen as Jenna disconnected from a call. From her expression, it wasn't good news. "Did you hear from Rio?"

"Yeah." Jenna folded her arms across her chest and leaned against the counter. "It's another ax murder, and Rio recognized the victim as Lily Jones. Someone murdered her in the alleyway outside the beauty parlor." She swallowed hard and met his gaze. "He said the killer decapitated her. It's a bloodbath. He's already notified Wolfe and cordoned off the area. Rowley is on scene and they've positioned their patrol vehicles to conceal the alleyway from the public."

The implications of the murder of another of the suspects in the Abby and Cole murders, deeply concerned Kane. He nodded. "They sound like they have everything under control. I'll get breakfast underway if you can rouse Tauri from sleep. They'll need us to take over while they grab a meal before starting work. I figure it's going to be another long day."

"You can say that again." Jenna headed along the passageway to Tauri's room. She turned to look at him. "I called Nanny Raya, and Blackhawk is dropping by this morning to spend some time with Tauri."

Kane grabbed eggs and bacon from the refrigerator. "That's good to know. He always enjoys his time with him." He looked down at Duke. "I haven't forgotten you." He spent a few minutes topping up the bowl of kibble and mixing a special protein drink the vet had recommended to keep him in tip-top condition. He added more cat food to the feeder as Pumpkin wrapped her sleek body around his legs. "There you go. Don't worry, Duke. We're not leaving you at home today." He washed his hands and then set about making breakfast.

It was a crisp clear morning as they rode into town. It was good to see the sun rising into a clear blue sky. Kane hadn't realized how much he'd missed it until it wasn't there. He avoided going along Main and took a few back roads to Nanny Raya's house instead. He figured keeping Tauri well away from the crime scene would be the best thing to do. His little boy's inquisitive mind would lead to questions about the sheriff's vehicles blocking the sidewalk. It wasn't something he wanted to answer and lying to his son wasn't an alternative.

After dropping by Nanny Raya's, Kane turned the Beast around and headed along Main. Both of the sheriff's vehicles were parked across the sidewalk, and Wolfe's white medical examiner's van was backed in between them with the back doors wide open.

He caught Jenna's sharp intake of breath as she stepped around Rio's truck. He followed close behind and his attention moved straight to the stream of blood running from the alleyway and down into the gutter. It had congealed into a glossy mess, with bits of leaves and dust floating on the surface. A dog had walked through it leaving a trail of pawprints that faded into nothingness. Rowley was leaning against his truck, keeping a small group of people from looking down the alleyway. The morbid fascination of some people never ceased to amaze him. They didn't seem to realize that witnessing a horrific event might stay with them for the rest of their lives. He walked over to the group of onlookers. "Go on your way. There's nothing to see here." He swung his gaze across the crowd and people reluctantly turned and walked away. He looked at Rowley. "Try to keep people away. As soon as Wolfe has finished processing the scene, we'll hose down the sidewalk. Wolfe keeps a hose in the back of his van. He often needs to wash blood from his boots."

"I'll do it." Rowley lifted his chin. "The more I work around blood, the better I'm coping with it. Before the twins were born, I'd have spewed at the sight of that mess." He sighed. "Oh and I spoke to Mr. Lane and then cut him loose. He didn't see anything, just the blood. He had deliveries to make around town, but we have his details if we need to speak to him again."

Kane nodded. "Okay, I'll let Jenna know." He turned back to the alleyway where she was waiting for him. "You good?"

"Yeah, I'll be fine." Jenna pulled on a face mask and handed one to him followed by examination gloves. She straightened her shoulders and, stepping carefully around the blood spatter, led the way along the alleyway.

FORTY

Kane followed, taking note of the footprints. They were the same as before, made from generic rubber boots. At the entrance to the alleyway, he found a rounded pattern on the ground, the same as they'd found in the barn at the Old Mitcham Ranch. The killer had followed the exact same pattern by undressing and taking his soiled clothes with him. Toward the end of the alleyway, Wolfe had erected a number of lights. The stark reality of what had happened to Lily Jones was out there for all to see. Kane had always believed that war had hardened him against even the most abhorrent crimes against mankind, but what had happened to Lily turned his breakfast into a solid ball that weighed heavy in his stomach. Again, the killer hadn't touched the victim's face, but this time had hacked off her head. He turned to look at Wolfe. "Why so much blood? Surely, she couldn't have survived very long with these injuries."

"Our minds often focus on the main subject of interest." Wolfe stood to one side. "Take another look. Can you see now why there's so much blood? Like with the previous murder, this killer had no intention of making Lily's death painless or fast."

"He cut off her hands." Jenna stared down at the corpse and then pointed at the steps leading to the back of the beauty parlor. "He left them where she could see them."

Turning back to Wolfe, Kane waited for his friend to straighten from taking the temperature of the body. "Did you notice a weapon anywhere?"

"Nope, we only arrived thirty minutes or so ago and haven't gotten to that yet." Wolfe indicated with his chin toward his assistant Colt Webber. "We've documented the scene and taken videos and photographs. If you can do a search, we'll start collecting the body parts and get her back to the morgue."

Kane nodded. "Rowley will get this blood cleaned up when you're done."

"It's fine. Webber will do it." Wolfe's eyes held a deep sadness. "Your time is better spent finding the maniac who did this."

Nodding, Kane turned as Jenna hurried along the alleyway swinging her flashlight. He followed close behind, opening dumpsters as he went and searching for the murder weapon, but found nothing. As they walked back toward Main, Jenna bent to pick up the high heels. She handed them to him and he pushed them into an evidence bag.

"I've found her purse." Jenna moved her flashlight alongside the wall belonging to the beauty parlor. After using her phone to take a photograph, she picked up the purse and turned it over in her hand. "There's no blood, so she dropped it when she was running away."

The clip on the purse was open, and a few personal items had spilled onto the sidewalk. Kane took more photographs and then collected the items. "What's inside her purse?"

"A packet of tissues, a phone, and house keys." Jenna dropped the purse inside an evidence bag and held it open for him. "What did you find?"

Kane dropped the items into the bag. "A lipstick, a hair-brush, and a stick of deodorant."

"I can see what looks like a trail of blood droplets beside the footprints over there." Jenna moved her flashlight back and forth. "I figure Wolfe needs to see them. They look different to me." She tucked her flashlight under one arm and took photographs.

Kane waited for Wolfe to walk back into the alleyway after placing the body in the back of the van. "We didn't find the murder weapon, but we found her purse and shoes." He pointed to the blood droplets in a line on the ground. "What do you make of this blood trail?"

"It's the same as the cast-off blood spatter I found on the walls and the dumpster. It tells the story of the attack better than being there." Wolfe waved a hand at the blood trail. "It could be from the murder weapon, or his hands were dripping with blood. I took samples just in case he was injured during the attack, as we are assuming he wiped his hands and changed clothes before leaving as before." He sighed. "My bet is it's from the ax." He removed his examination gloves and rolled them up into a ball. "I've documented everything and will give you a full analysis on Monday morning. If I could do this faster, I would, but the body is in such bad shape it's going to take a long time to complete the autopsy."

"I understand but I can see that this blood spatter is unusual." Jenna frowned. "The drops of blood look different. Can you explain why this occurred?"

"Not a problem." Wolfe pointed to the blood trail. "The shape of the blood droplets indicates direction. When you see both shapes, as in this case, it tells me he was swinging the ax as he walked. Each blood droplet tells a story. The pointed end faces away from the direction the killer was traveling. Swinging the ax would make blood spatter fly in both directions, so you see the blood droplets seemingly facing each other." He looked from one to the other and moved along the blood trail. "As he gets closer to the sidewalk, he stops swinging the ax. See, from the narrow end of the drips, even though they're getting smaller, they prove he was heading toward the road, not away from it." He sighed. "I'd sure like to get hold of that ax. It could be covered in DNA evidence. Many killers believe they can remove DNA from murder weapons but I can usually find traces where they wouldn't even imagine looking for them."

Absorbing the cast-off blood knowledge and locking it away for future reference, Kane nodded. "We'll do our best to find it for you."

"I know you will." Wolfe removed his face mask and smiled at them. "Once Webber has hosed down the sidewalk, I'm done here." He looked at Jenna. "I figure I could narrow down the time of death if we knew when Lily left the beauty parlor. I recall that she kept the store open late on Friday nights. I've heard the girls talking about it. I could give you an approximate time going on rigor mortis and body temperature, but I believe the window is narrower. The evidence suggests she was attacked as she left work, which would put the time of death between nine and say midnight. That's a very small window but it might catch you a killer."

"Thanks. I'll get onto it right away." Jenna removed her mask and walked back to Rio and Rowley. "Take a break and grab breakfast. I'm heading into the office to make some calls. I need to know what our suspects were doing between nine and midnight last night."

"Okay." Rio headed for his truck with Rowley close behind.

Something didn't seem right to Kane and he stood for a few moments scanning the alleyway. He turned when Jenna touched his arm. "Don't you figure it seems strange for a woman alone to leave by the back door into a dark alleyway rather than going out the front into the light?" He held up the evidence bags and opened the one with the keys. He still wore his examination gloves and headed out the alleyway and pointed the key fob at the few cars parked alongside Main. When one vehicle's lights lit up, a few yards from the front of the beauty parlor, he turned to Jenna. "It doesn't make sense why she would leave from the back door."

"Maybe she needed to dump some garbage?" Jenna rubbed her temple, thinking. "We didn't check to see if the back door of the beauty parlor is locked."

Kane nodded. "I'll look, but I figure it's locked because why would she leave with her purse if she intended to go back inside? I'll look inside the dumpster out back of the beauty parlor to see if there are any garbage bags in there filled with stuff from the store."

After hooking out the two bags on the top of the garbage, Kane tore them open and turned to Jenna. "These are from the beauty parlor." He tossed them back inside the dumpster. "I wonder if she makes a habit of dumping the garbage before she leaves on Fridays?"

"That looks like a ton of garbage." Jenna stared at the dumpster. "I figure that would be enough for a week not a day. You'd think she would get one of the apprentices or the cleaner to dump the garbage. It seems an unusual thing for an owner to do." She made a note in her notebook. "I'll be sure to ask the staff. I believe Lily was in a partnership in the business. We'll need to call the other owner and tell her what's happened." She headed toward the Beast.

Kane nodded. "I'll do that. You'll need to call the suspects and find out if they have alibis for last night. Getting a call from the sheriff will give them something to think about."

"As long as they don't come at me with an ax." Jenna gave him a wary look.

Being able to outdraw anyone he'd ever met, Kane drew his weapon fast and Jenna took a step back eyes wide. "If anyone can swing an ax faster than I can draw down on them, I'll quit my job." He slowly reholstered his weapon. "Trust me, no one is getting near you with an ax."

FORTY-ONE

They headed for the office, and once inside, Jenna pulled up the details of the male suspects. Unconcerned about the early hour, she called each of them and insisted they give her their where-abouts for the previous evening between nine and midnight. All four of them insisted they were watching *Friday Night Sports* at home. Hallon said his wife was over at his folks' house baking pies with his mother and had been since three o'clock the previous afternoon. Crawley insisted his father was with him when he watched the games, but when Jenna followed up, Crawley's mother said she went to bed early and usually her husband fell asleep in front of the TV just about the moment the game started. Wasser and Twotrees were alone all night. She ran a hand down her face in frustration. The phone calls had gotten her absolutely nowhere.

Her phone buzzed the moment she put it down. It was Norrell. "Hey, have you discovered anything interesting?" She put her phone on speaker so Kane could listen.

"Yeah, I have. The DNA under Abby's fingernails has given us a result." Norrell's footsteps clattered over tile. *"It's not a match for Cole but is good enough to use as a comparison against*

the other suspects if you can get DNA samples for them legally. Also, Wolfe has noticed a chip on the enamel of the fraternity pin. He called Kalo and asked him to find all the images of the members of the fraternity around the time of the murders and see if he can find someone wearing that pin."

Excited, Jenna punched the air. "That's fantastic. If he discovers who owned the pin, we have the killer."

"It's a very exciting discovery. I just hope it pans out." Norrell sighed. *"This wasn't the main reason I called, although it's very good news. I was considering doing another media conference. I believe it might be beneficial to your investigation if the killer believes we're hot on his trail."*

Horrified by what had happened since the last media conference, Jenna frowned. "I'm not sure that's a good idea. Are you aware that Lily Jones was found murdered this morning? She was with Abby and Cole the night they were murdered. I'm starting to believe that the killer is taking out anyone he believes is a threat."

"Oh, my goodness. No, I didn't know. I've been here since five, waiting for the DNA results to come through. You don't believe my media conference triggered him, do you?" Norrell had stopped walking and was breathing heavily.

Pushing hair from her face and tucking it behind one ear, Jenna glanced at Kane and shook her head. He responded with a shrug. "No, I don't believe it was your media conference. I figured it was because the bodies showed, and whoever was involved panicked. It's been a long time since Cole and Abby were murdered, and maybe their trust in each other is growing a little thin." She sighed. "I'm convinced that a group of people are involved, and we have a list of suspects. It will be only a matter of time before one of them breaks now that two of them have been brutally murdered. In all honesty, I don't believe any of them would consider the murders to be a warning not to say anything. When people are running scared, they look for protection and they're not going to trust the person doing this. I figure you should go ahead with your press conference. Don't give away too much information, just enough to let them know that we're onto them. Maybe it will urge one of them to come forward. In fact, I might come along and mention that anyone who was involved in the murders twelve years ago might be eligible for immunity if they come clean about what really happened that Halloween."

"Okay." Norrell blew out a long breath. *"I'll write everything down first and run it past Wolfe. He's very experienced in dealing with the media and will know what to tell them and what to withhold. When I'm done, I'll send you a copy to approve."*

Relieved, Jenna leaned back in her chair. "Thank you. I'd appreciate it. I'll speak to you later and we can arrange a time."

"Not a problem." Norrell disconnected.

"You do know the media conference could have triggered the killer." Kane stared at her across his desk. "He might well believe someone is feeding information to us. We did, after all, go and interview Josie and Marissa soon after the bodies were discovered. Then we interview Lily and she turns up dead this morning."

Jenna stood and stretched her aching back. "Did you manage to contact the owner of the beauty parlor and tell her about Lily?"

"Yeah, I did and she's a close friend of Lily's family. She wanted to be the one to speak to them about Lily's death as her mother has a serious heart condition. The beauty parlor will remain closed today. It seems to me that she has everything under control. I told her to contact Wolfe to arrange a viewing of the body and positive ID."

A knock on the door announced the arrival of Johnny Raven. The strikingly handsome, six-five, two hundred fifty pound chopper pilot and his K-9, Ben, were an asset to the team. At thirty-two, his military background meant that he slipped seamlessly into their way of doing things. A loner who'd lived off the grid until he'd discovered Wolfe's daughter Julie as the only survivor of an air crash in the mountains over the winter and saved her life. He'd not only worked with Rio and Rowley honing his hand-to-hand and weapons skills but had enrolled in a law enforcement course at the college. Before offering him the position, Wolfe and Kalo had checked out his background and he'd passed with flying colors. Jenna looked up at him and smiled. "Hey, what brings you into town?"

"My sheriff's department truck was delivered today." Raven smiled broadly. "It's been a very long time since I've driven anything like that. I came by to thank you."

"If you're going to be one of our deputies, you're going to need reliable transport." Kane stood to shake his hand. "It's good to see you again and you too, Ben." He held his knuckles out to the dog and received a friendly lick. Duke had actually got out of his basket to say hello and his thick tail was wagging at the sight of a friend.

They'd managed to secure Raven's services by offering him a retainer and then consultancy fees when they needed him for a case. Concerned about Norrell going to the Whispering Caves in the mountains to visit the crime scene, maybe Raven had arrived at the right time. Although Blackhawk would be going with her along with her team, she doubted that Wolfe would have the time to spare due to the amount of forensic work needed with the current murders. She'd considered sending Rio or Rowley with her, but right now she needed boots on the ground. She looked at Raven. He was an experienced survivalist; he knew the mountain trails and the dangers in the forest. With his dog, he would be the perfect person to send with Norrell for protection. With Blackhawk and her own team of four young men, whom Kane and Rowley had trained in self-defense and weapons, she would be in safe hands.

She stood and went to pour three cups of coffee and handed them around and placed the fixings on the desk. "I'm really glad you dropped by today because I have a job for you. If you're interested."

"Shoot." Raven spooned copious amounts of sugar into his cup and added cream.

Jenna sat down at her desk. "On Monday morning Norrell is heading to the Whispering Caves to excavate an old crime scene. It's not the safest place to be heading. Blackhawk is going along and so is her team of four forensic anthropologists, but I'd appreciate it if you would go along with Ben and keep an eye on her. I know the bears are starting to move around and she gets so engrossed in her work it's likely she wouldn't see one until it was on top of her."

"Yeah, sure. I'd love to do that." Raven sipped his coffee and sighed. "This would be about the bodies that washed down in the river. The ones that went missing over Halloween twelve years ago."

Jenna gave him an update on what had happened since finding the bodies and the current cases. "So she might need protection from a human element as well. Whoever is involved in the current cases might be a threat."

"Hmm, well, they won't get past me or Ben." Raven patted the dog on the head. "His hearing is impeccable and he can smell a stranger coming as well as a bear. Norrell will be safe with me. I can guarantee it."

Eyeing him over the rim of her coffee cup, Jenna nodded. "That's good to know."

FORTY-TWO

The media conference had been set for two and was to be held on the steps of the ME's office, so with time to spare, Jenna and her deputies canvased every residence within a wide radius of the beauty parlor in the hope that someone might have noticed something unusual the previous night. Not one person had heard or seen anything. It seemed that everyone in town watched *Friday Night Sports*. The investigation ground to a standstill, and they'd need to wait until Wolfe processed the samples taken from the crime scene and conducted an autopsy.

Exhausted and her back a constant ache, Jenna and Kane headed for Aunt Betty's Café. She lingered over lunch and noticed Kane's gaze scanning the room. "What is it?"

"Did you notice Wyatt Twotrees when we arrived? He's in the booth on the left with none other than Dustin Crawley." Kane leaned back in his chair and raised his chin toward them. "For two people who insist they never see each other, this is a little suspicious."

Acting nonchalant, Jenna dug into her peach pie. "It just got more interesting." She flicked her gaze to the door. "Here comes Wasser and Hallon."

"What do you think they're up to?" Kane stared down at his plate. "Do you figure they're meeting because we interviewed them all and then followed up with phone calls this morning?"

Lifting a forkful of pie to her lips, Jenna met his gaze. "Well, they know they're on our radar. Oh, now look who's here."

"Josie Grady." Kane reached for his coffee and took a sip. "That's the lawyer Samuel J. Cross right behind her. Why aren't they going to his office? It seems very strange to be meeting in Aunt Betty's Café, although they have taken a booth and the one beside it has a reserved sign on it. Do you figure that Susie would do that to give them some privacy if they asked her?"

Jenna shrugged. "Maybe she's heading there now to take their order. I'll wave her down on the way back and ask her. None of them are short of money, so maybe they hired that booth for an hour."

"Well, we have plenty of time before the press conference." Kane checked his watch and then smiled at her. "I might have another slice of pie. I haven't tried the cherry this week."

Leaning back in her chair and resting one hand on her belly, Jenna smiled at him. "I'll never complain about having a rest. The baby is kicking up a storm right now. It's really weird. It starts as a flutter, and then suddenly as the weeks go by, it changes. I can actually feel it stretching. It puts its little feet down and pushes into my ribs." She covered Kane's hand on the table and squeezed. "Wolfe mentioned it was a big baby. If I hadn't been checking every few weeks, I would have worried I'd made a mistake with the dates." She frowned. "Did your mom ever mention having any problems having you? Do you know what birth weight you were?"

"I don't want you to worry about this right now." Kane turned his hand over and linked their fingers. "She never mentioned having any problems, but I was her second child. My sister was the eldest."

As Kane was very good at shielding his emotions, his lowered lashes sent shivers down her spine. "You do know your birth weight, don't you? Why aren't you telling me?"

"Because it's irrelevant. My mom was approximately the same size as you, but that doesn't mean a thing. She had me thirty-six years ago, which might as well have been in the Stone Age to what doctors can do to ease the birthing process these days." He met her gaze and gave a reluctant shrug. "I weighed in at ten-and-a-half pounds and I was too long for the regular newborn crib in the hospital. My dad was very proud. I've seen photographs of him holding me moments after birth grinning with a huge cigar in one side of his mouth. In the photographs I saw of my mom around the same time, she looked very happy. That's all I can really tell you."

Understanding that new mothers had a normal fear of giving birth, she'd pushed the idea of having a large baby to the back of her mind. Kane was right, she would be in the best place possible with people she trusted. She glanced away from him as Susie walked by and gave her a wave. "I'd like another glass of milk please, and Dave would love a slice of cherry pie. I couldn't help noticing the reserved sign over there. Did Sam Cross ask you to do that so that group could have some privacy?"

"Why do you ask?" Susie looked uncomfortable by the question.

"Well, that group of people over there were the last ones to see Cole and Abby alive." Kane gave her a long searching look. "They are the names of the two bodies that washed up in the river earlier this week. The people sitting over there told us that they haven't socialized with each other since college, and we've been questioning them about the night Cole and Abby went missing. Now two of them have been murdered and they are having a meeting with a lawyer."

"Oh, I see." All the color drained from Susie's face. "Do you figure one of them might be the killer?"

Nodding slowly, Jenna raised her chin to look at her. "One or all of them. Right now, it's hard to tell."

"It was Wyatt." Susie turned her back on the group of people and started gathering the empty plates onto her tray. "He gave me fifty dollars to reserve the booth until two. We often take reservations, so it was no big deal." She took a deep breath and looked at Kane. "Are they dangerous?"

"Not to you." Kane leaned back in his chair and smiled at her with an open, friendly expression. "We figure they're killing each other to prevent them talking to us. Just go about your business as if nothing is amiss. We don't want them to believe we've been discussing them."

"Okay. I'll be right back with your pie." Susie plastered a smile on her face and headed toward the kitchen.

About fifteen minutes later, Sam Cross came over to their table and asked if he could join them. Jenna looked at him and smiled. Although Sam Cross, being a defense attorney, was never on her side, she had no reason not to be cordial toward him. "Yes, of course. What's on your mind?"

"I'm aware that you know the group of people sitting at the booth in the corner." Cross gave her a long considering stare. "They've hired me as a group to represent them in a case against the sheriff's department for harassment. It seems, as they were friends of the two deceased people you discovered in the river earlier this week, you've taken it upon yourself to go to their places of business and cause them considerable embarrassment by making it appear they're involved in the murders. Then again, this morning, you not only called them to insist they verify their whereabouts for the previous evening but followed this up with calls to their families to verify the information. This is blatant harassment as you have absolutely no evidence whatsoever that this group of people was involved in the murders of their friends."

Bristling, Jenna stared him down. "That group of people

has admitted being with Cole and Abby on the night they disappeared. It is only natural we'd question them during our investigations. One of their group, Marissa Kendrick, was found brutally murdered at the Old Mitcham Ranch. Their other friend, Lily Jones, was decapitated behind the beauty parlor last night." She took a steadying breath but didn't break eye contact. "There are no other suspects for these crimes. We have reason to believe from the evidence we've gathered over the last week that one or all of these people were involved in the murders of Cole and Abby. You're very welcome to lodge a complaint against us with the DA, but at no time did I or my deputies threaten any of them. In fact, each one we interviewed cooperated."

"It seems to me that they've something to hide if they hired you." Kane pushed his empty pie plate into the middle of the table. "It's their prerogative to lawyer up and remain silent, but that won't remove them from our suspects list." He glanced at his watch. "We need to go. We're attending a press conference."

"Stay away from my clients." Cross looked from one to the other.

Keeping her anger in check, Jenna stood and slid into her coat. She looked at him. "You'll be the first one I call when we haul them in to charge them with murder." She turned and followed Kane out of the café.

FORTY-THREE

Gripped by a sudden rush of nerves, Norrell stepped out onto the steps of the medical examiner's office to greet the press. She carried a notebook with a list of points just in case she had a sudden lapse of memory. Beside her, Wolfe gave her a nod of encouragement. Behind her, Jenna and Kane walked through the door. Having Jenna there to take questions about the progress in all the murder cases took the edge off her nerves. Although Jenna had mentioned she preferred Rio to take the media conferences, in this case, as she intended to withhold information from the press, she'd decided to do it herself. Taking a deep breath, she stepped toward the podium Wolfe had placed at the top of the steps. Being above the noisy throng of reporters helped. *Where have all these people come from?*

"Dr. Larson. James Wright, *Black Rock Falls News.*" The man rushed up the steps and stuck a microphone in her face.

"Mr. Wright, Dr. Larson is going to issue a statement." Kane stepped forward and ushered the man back down the steps. "There'll be time for you to ask your questions after that. Please remain at the bottom of the steps. Crowding around Dr.

Larson won't get your questions answered. She'll just turn around and go back inside."

Norrell placed her notes on the podium and looked out at the crowd of people staring at her. "Good afternoon. My name is Dr. Norrell Larson and I'm a forensic anthropologist working in the medical examiner's office. On Monday two bodies were discovered in the river. The mummified bodies are the remains of Cole Peters and Abby Jaye. The students of Black Rock Falls College were reported missing twelve years ago over Halloween. After careful examination, I've determined that they are victims of homicide. The bodies are extremely well preserved, and we have gathered evidence, including DNA, which we are running through data banks as we speak." She took a deep breath. "Over the last week extensive searches have been made of the area around the Whispering Caves. We have now discovered a crime scene. Evidence was found at the scene, and tomorrow morning, weather permitting, my team will begin excavating the site."

"Sheriff." A man from the middle of the crowd pushed forward. "Do you have any suspects?"

"Yes, we do." Jenna glanced over at Norrell. "Although we are waiting for DNA evidence. We're expecting to uncover more from the scene tomorrow. From what we've uncovered so far, we already have enough to make a case. What Dr. Larson finds at the scene will be the icing on the cake."

More questions were addressed to Jenna and she answered them in her usual professional way. Mr. Wright, with a nervous look at Kane, positioned at the foot of the steps, came to the front of the group again and stuck out his microphone. Turning to Wright, Norrell waited for his question.

"You mentioned DNA and yet the bodies were floating in the river for a time. Wouldn't that have contaminated the DNA? How can you be sure that the results are from the killer?"

Gripping the podium, Norrell nodded to the man. "I understand why you'd be confused. Fresh DNA has a different appearance than DNA from a long time ago. The DNA came from under Abby's fingernails. The sample of skin was dehydrated in the same manner as the bodies. There was some deterioration but not enough to damage the strand. As there are other factors involved here, which at this time we're not prepared to divulge, it is imperative that we excavate the crime scene, which is situated in the Whispering Caves." She scanned the crowd.

"You said that the bodies were mummified. Did the killer wrap them in bandages and then bury them in the caves?" A woman holding up her phone to record the conference, narrowed her gaze at Norrell.

Trying not to laugh, Norrell shook her head. "The victims were buried in dry sand and over time, rather than decomposing, the sand absorbed the moisture from the bodies, causing the dehydration."

"So how come they suddenly showed up in the river?" The same reporter held an expression of disbelief. "Do you figure someone dug them up?"

Glancing over to Jenna for support, Norrell sighed with relief when she stepped up to the podium. "Sheriff Alton will explain."

"As you are aware, over winter we had a number of avalanches in the mountains caused by seismic activity in the area." Jenna scanned the crowd. "In one section of the Whispering Caves, fissures formed in the mountainside. They filled with snow and froze. The pressure of the ice opened the cracks during the melt and a part of the mountain above the caves crumbled away. The subsequent torrential rain we've experienced over the last four weeks poured through the caves, taking the sand with it and depositing it alongside a newly formed riverbank on its way to Black Rock River. We assume that the bodies were washed along with everything else. The force of water coming down that side of the mountain is extreme. I might add, at this point, that there is no danger to the public from falling rocks at this time." She stepped away from the podium.

"Sheriff." Wright waved his microphone. "What evidence do you have and how were the victims murdered?"

"I'm unable to divulge evidence at this time." Jenna stared at him as if daring him to ask her another question.

"Do you believe this murder and the murder of Marissa Kendrick are connected? She was in that group of friends that went to the mountain that night, wasn't she?" Wright held his microphone steady.

"Undetermined at this time." Jenna lifted her chin. "When we have solid information and not hearsay, I'll issue a media statement."

Norrell stepped up again. "If there are no other questions, I have work to do. I'll release a media report when I've analyzed the data." She waited for a few moments and then turned and walked back inside the medical examiner's office.

"That was brilliant." Jenna walked beside her. "You gave them just enough to hold them off for a while."

Concerned about her trip to the mountain, Norrell looked at her. "Do you figure they will show up in a horde to watch me?"

"You might get the odd onlooker, but it's doubtful anyone would want to traipse up the mountain in this weather. Not with the number of hungry bears hunting for breakfast."

A shiver of fear skittered down Norrell's back. "I'm not really equipped to take on bears. I couldn't shoot one or anything."

"Don't worry, we don't shoot bears. Wolfe will make sure you have bear spray. You'll have Blackhawk with you, and I'm sending Johnny Raven as well. I know you haven't met him yet, but he's a big man like Dave and he'll have his dog, Ben, with him. Raven is our new K-9 unit. He lives in the forest and will be able to protect you from man and beast."

Relieved, Norrell pushed her hair from her face and smiled. "That's good to know."

FORTY-FOUR

Agitation rolls over me as the news comes to an end without one mention of Lily's murder. I find it hard to believe the sheriff could be so incompetent not to have found the body yet. Surely someone would have tripped over her or seen the blood running down the alley into the gutter. I was sure someone from the beauty parlor would have gone out the back door by now. I click off the TV, unable to watch the screen for a moment longer. Watching the smug forensic anthropologist giving her opinion on the murder scene was a joke. Although, I'm concerned there's evidence left at the Whispering Caves. Did the bodies of Cole and Abby really wash out during a storm or is someone setting me up? There are only a few of us who know exactly where we buried them. I've had my suspicions about Marissa and Lily, but now I've taken care of them they won't be running their mouths off to anyone.

Dr. Larson was way overconfident when she delivered her proclamation about the DNA evidence found under Abby's nails. No one had noticed the scratch on my neck because I'd been wearing a turtleneck, so I'm the only one who knows she scratched me. My only concern is what other evidence has been left behind. I figured we'd buried everything incriminating with them. The problem is, if Dr. Larson looks hard enough, she'll find the bloody scarf I wiped my hands on after murdering them. I recall tossing it into the grave along with my blood-spattered jacket and my gloves. It hadn't been my idea to bury everything deep and my friends' support had surprised me. I can't help smiling at the way they all fell into line. They actually believed me, but I figure poking myself in the eyes to make them water was the clincher. Everything had been fine until the bodies came floating down the river. My secret had been safe for twelve years.

We made a pact all those years ago to never give our DNA. All of us had touched the bodies and pressed our hands on Cole's and Abby's cooling flesh. It was a way to bind us all together, to make us keep the secret. Now my group is falling apart piece by piece and I can't allow it to go on any longer. I admit killing them all would solve my problem, but as the last man standing, I'd be the prime suspect and I'd never be able to prove my innocence. I need to look in other directions and make assurances that no other evidence is found against us. I'll devise another plan to save my skin. Time is my enemy.

FORTY-FIVE

MONDAY, WEEK TWO

Emily Wolfe dashed into her father's office. "Am I too late? Has she left yet?"

"Nope." Wolfe looked up from his computer screen and smiled at her. "She's out back making sure the van is packed with everything she needs. Is this really how you want to spend your day off? I figured you'd be sleeping most of the time."

Emily rolled her eyes. "I worked the weekend so I could take a day to go with her to look at the crime scene. You know I'm very interested in forensic anthropology and will be definitely adding it to my qualifications as I go along." Seeing the amusement in his eyes, she gave him a long look. "I'm tougher than you think, Dad. I put it down to the hours you kept me here working in the morgue. Sure, the shifts are long but I'm learning all the time. I actually like working with live patients. It's been a good experience for me, but I'll be grateful when it's over and I can join you here. Then I'll look into continuing my studies part-time. Having Norrell here, with her wealth of experience, I'd be crazy not to."

"I'm sure people will look on our family as being extremely

unusual, all of us working with the dead." Wolfe chuckled. "But then I'd imagine there are families of undertakers out there."

Footsteps on the tile in the passageway announced the arrival of Norrell. To Emily she was like a shaft of sunlight. Her long blonde hair and bright smile lit up the room. She'd never imagined accepting another woman to take her mom's place, but right from the start, Norrell had made it very clear she had no intention of doing that, although she did mother Anna. Often she'd found her sitting on the edge of Anna's bed reading her stories and she'd heard her talking to the little girl about their mom. It was obvious she was trying to keep her mother's memory alive to Anna, although she'd only been two when her mother passed, and her recollection would be sketchy.

"You made it, Em." Norrell gave her a hug. "That's really good. I didn't want to squash in with the guys in the van. Now we can go in the truck."

Emily had driven the mountain tracks many times and could handle the conditions. "I'll drive. I've been up the mountains many times and the conditions are pretty bad at the moment."

"That's fine by me." Norrell smiled. "I'll tell the team they can get going. We're all meeting Blackhawk at the end of the fire road. Raven will be meeting us about halfway. Somewhere along there is a cutaway that goes straight to his cabin. He cleared it himself." She looked at Emily. "Have you met him?"

Recalling the devastatingly handsome man who'd saved her life, Emily nodded. "Yeah, I've met him. He's a very nice guy. It will be good to have him along for protection."

"Yeah, Shane told me how he rescued Julie from the plane crash." Norrell nodded. "It will be nice to have another person around we can trust."

"Go and grab survival kits before you leave and take a rifle." Wolfe looked at Emily. "You carrying? I don't want you going into the forest unarmed. There's a killer in town and y'all need to stay alert."

Sighing, Emily kissed her dad on the cheek. "Yeah, I'm good. Don't forget to eat."

Leaving them to say their goodbyes, Emily headed for the closet in the passageway and grabbed supplies and liquid Kevlar vests. The light vests were worth their weight in gold. She heard Norrell walk by and head outside to speak to her team. She headed after her, grabbing the keys to one of the medical examiner's white trucks from the board as she followed her outside. She handed her the vest. "Put this on before we leave. We don't know what we're going to encounter in the forest and this offers protection. It's not bulky and you won't even know you're wearing it." She dumped the survival packs in the back of the truck, then removed her jacket and put on her own vest. "Ready to go?"

"We take the third entrance into the fire road along Stanton and then follow it to the end, where Blackhawk will be waiting for us." Norrell climbed into the truck and secured her seatbelt. "Look out for Raven. He's driving a new sheriff's department truck."

Nodding, Emily set off. She'd driven the medical examiner's trucks many times and was very familiar with them. As they turned into Main, a garbage truck backing into an alleyway to collect the dumpsters blocked the road. She glanced at Norrell. "Will your team wait for you?"

"I doubt it." Norrell gave a shake of her head. "They know we're all meeting up at the end of the fire road and I told them I would be coming along behind with you."

It seemed to take forever for the garbage truck to move along. The delay had caused a line of traffic and it was slow going until they reached Stanton. When Emily turned onto the fire road, although the gullies along each side held deep muddy water, the gravel-packed road appeared to be relatively stable, apart from deep tire tracks marring its normally smooth surface. They bounced along for a few hundred yards and the road evened out, allowing her to increase her speed, but Norrell's white van was nowhere in sight. In her rearview mirror she noticed another vehicle following along behind. "I think Raven's behind us."

"Oh, that's good." Norrell smiled. "He sounds like a very interesting man. I can't wait to meet him."

Emily stared in the rearview mirror and frowned. The vehicle behind was coming at high speed, which seemed reckless on a dirt road. The next second, the truck shunted them in the back, throwing them both forward in their seats. Terrified, Emily gripped the wheel. "That's not Raven. Hang on, he's coming again."

"Do you think he just wants to pass?" Norrell's face drained of color. "Maybe you should just pull over?"

Panic gripped Emily as another impact jarred her, twisting the truck sideways. A metallic taste poured into her mouth. She'd bitten her tongue. Increasing her speed, she drove the truck along the side of the road close to the gully, where the ground was smoother. A group of men would be waiting for them at the end of the fire road and all she had to do was outrun this lunatic. The next second, the truck was beside her and a man wearing a ski mask was peering at them through the holes. When he spun the wheel, panic gripped her. He slammed into her and the jolt went right through to her bones. The terrible sound of metal panels grinding against each other screamed in her ears. Beside her, Norrell cried out as her door buckled under the impact. The front wheels bounced and the truck came again, smashing hard and pushing them toward the rushing water.

Frantic, Emily spun the wheel and pressed down hard on the gas. The attacker was relentless and rammed them again. With a loud moan, the truck tipped over and rolled into the gully. The airbags burst out in a cloud of white, and objects from the cab flew into the air. Her Aunt Betty's Café travel mug bounced off her shoulder and a bag of candy spilled its contents over her. Pinned tight between the curtain and main airbags, Emily could see only the brown water rushing past the window. They must get out before they drowned.

Trembling with fear and shock, Emily reached out to give Norrell a shake. "Are you okay? We need to get out. Undo your seatbelt. We'll climb out the back. Your door is toast."

"Oh, my God, he's coming back." Norrell struggled to undo her seatbelt without luck. "My right arm won't move." She let out a piercing scream. "He has an ax. He's going to kill us." She frantically tried to unclip her seatbelt.

In horror, Emily gaped out of the window. The man was strolling toward them holding an ax like a baseball bat over one shoulder, as if he had all the time in the world. She reached for her weapon but couldn't get her fingers past the airbag. The next moment, the masked man swung the ax and smashed Norrell's window. Shards of glass exploded over them like diamond rain. She gaped in terror as he raised the ax again, his eyes fixed on Norrell. Emily stretched out a hand to pull her toward her but she still hung in her seatbelt. "Nooo."

The *whoop whoop* of a siren screamed in the distance. The trees lit up with red and blue flashing lights. The man cursed loudly, turned, and ran back to his truck and then took off at high speed in a squeal of tires. Heart thundering, Emily, fought against the airbags. Brown water was oozing through the seals in the door and lapping over the windshield. Beside her, Norrell was crying and blood was oozing through her shirt.

Seconds later, a sheriff's department truck with the lights flashing skidded to a halt beside them and Raven jumped out. Raising her voice above the sound of gurgling water, Emily stared at him. "Get us out of here."

"I'm on it." Raven ran to the door, placed one foot on the

side of the vehicle, and, muscles bulging, used brute strength to tear it open. The door whined as he wedged his body against it to keep it open.

Dizzy and with her back jammed to the door, Emily couldn't reach Norrell to help her. She looked at Raven. "Norrell's injured. Get her out quickly before we drown."

"I've got you." Raven pulled a knife, stabbed at the airbags, and cut through Norrell's seatbelt. His gaze moved over Emily. "If you're not injured, try and scramble toward the door." With gentle care, he lifted Norrell out and placed her on the back seat of his truck before turning back.

Gritting her teeth, Emily dragged herself toward the open door, but with the airbag, she wasn't getting far. The truck groaned and slipped deeper into the water. Panic gripped her as she fought to escape. The next moment, Raven returned, grabbed her arms, and lifted her out as if she weighed nothing. He set her down and assessed her injuries and then led her to his truck and opened the passenger door. She shook her head and leaned against the truck taking in his concerned expression. "I'm fine. I'll take care of Norrell." She smiled at his hesitancy. "It's okay. I'm doing my residency in the ER at Black Rock Falls General."

"That's good to know. Norrell will be fine—bruises, is all." Raven met her gaze with a smile. "Wolfe mentioned you being a fine medical examiner in training. So will you be working with him soon or flying the coop?"

Cheeks heating under his charm, Emily dropped her lashes. "I work with him now, but I have almost two more years of residency to go before I join the payroll. This is my home. I'm not going anywhere." She dragged her gaze away from him. "Enough about me. Call Jenna. She needs to go after that guy. He's probably the killer of those women. Where's your med kit?"

"In the back." He nodded and pulled out his phone. "I'll

call Jenna now." He made the call and then returned to her side. "They're in town and will be able to catch up to him along the highway. I doubt very much he'll risk coming back this way."

Emily helped Norrell out of her coat, and then pulled on examination gloves, noticing that Raven did the same. She grabbed tweezers from the med kit and commenced removing the glass shards from Norrell's face, chest, and arm. As she took out the glass, Raven swabbed each small laceration. When she'd finished, she stood back as he examined Norrell's arm. The skin was black in places, but she could move her fingers. She patted Norrell on the back. "There's morphine here if you need it."

"No, I'll take some Tylenol if you have any." Norrell looked at Raven. "Do you think it's broken? It hurts real bad."

"The impact hit your humerus and just a chip would be very painful, but I can't feel any fractures. You'll need X-rays to be sure." He handed her a bottle of water and two pills. He took bandages from the kit, removed the wrapping, and bandaged her arm from wrist to shoulder and then placed it in a sling. "Now let me look at you, Emily."

Emily took a step backward. "I'm fine."

"No, you're not. You have glass in your face and blood running down your neck. It's true what they say about doctors making the worst patients." Raven picked up the tweezers and poured antiseptic over them before removing the glass from Emily's face. "We need to call Blackhawk and let him know what's happened. He'll be still waiting for us at the end of the trail."

"I'm not going to the hospital, well, not yet anyway." Norrell looked at them with a determined expression. "If that was the killer, he did this to prevent me from going to the crime scene. I don't need to do anything other than instruct my team. Blackhawk said it was only a very short walk from the river to the cave."

Emily nodded. "I figure we should go too. She's right. This was done to stop Norrell excavating the crime scene."

"Have you two lost your minds? Shock could set in at any time." Raven looked from one to the other. "You're both doctors and you know the risks. You've just been in a car wreck."

"I was scared stupid but I'm not in shock." Norrell stared at him with stubborn expression. "I have Viking blood. We don't stop work because of a few small cuts and bruises."

"Okay, I guess there's no reasoning with you." Raven sighed and finished up tending to Emily's wounds. "I spent time with Julie, and I know just how stubborn Wolfe women are." He looked at Emily. "If you insist on going, you'd better call your dad."

Emily nodded. "We are stubborn and tough. I'll call a tow truck first. There's no need to worry my dad right away. He's busy today." She made the call to Millers' Garage. "They'll pick up the truck and we'll sort it out later. You won't mind filing a report for the insurance, will you?"

"Not a problem." Raven gave her a long searching look. "Just as long as you promise to tell your dad you both refused to go to the hospital. I don't want him knocking on my door late tonight. I've seen him angry and it isn't nice."

Emily chuckled. "He's great, isn't he? He and Dave are so gentle unless anyone threatens their families. It was annoying when I was younger, but now I appreciate him. I like being protected. That's a quality I respect in a man. Maybe I'm the old-fashioned kind, just like them."

"I like it too." Norrell leaned back in the seat and stroked Ben's head. "He makes me feel special."

"Okay, I guess I'll take you old-fashioned gals to the crime scene and hope we don't get into any more trouble." Raven smiled at them. "I'll grab your stuff from the truck."

As he walked away, Emily turned in her seat to look at Norrell. "I figure he's my knight in shining armor. That's twice now he's just appeared and saved my life." She lowered her voice to just above a whisper. "Coincidence or fate?"

"I'd say time will decide." Norrell rubbed her sore arm and winced. "When we're through here, I'll take the morphine. This hurts so bad, but I need to keep my head straight. I just hope we find something to nail that maniac."

Emily nodded. "So do I."

FORTY-SIX

The sun shone as Jenna walked back from the beauty parlor. They'd left the Beast beside the park and decided to stretch their legs. She'd spent the last half hour with Kane interviewing the hairstylists. She asked them if they had seen anyone hanging around the place over the last week or so or if Lily had mentioned anyone causing her a problem. All of them had given her the same reply. It had been a normal week, but Lily had been upset over Marissa's murder. She hadn't mentioned about being concerned for her own well-being. Jenna turned to Kane. "That was a complete waste of time. In fact, everything we've done in this case has been a complete waste of time. We can't interview the suspects again, unless we have a case strong enough to charge them with murder or at least interfering with a corpse. Right now we have nothing and Sam Cross isn't going to allow us to get near his clients without an arrest warrant." She sighed. "I hope Rio and Rowley have better luck with Lily's friends and family."

"What we need are DNA samples." Kane stood to one side to allow a mother pushing a stroller to go by. "Maybe we can recruit Susie or Wendy as undercover agents." He smiled at

Jenna. "If one of the suspects goes in for a meal, we could ask them to bag their cups and silverware and see if we get a hit."

Jenna snorted with laughter but the idea wasn't so farfetched. Susie and Wendy could identify all of the suspects. She could deputize them, if they agreed. "If I get desperate enough, I'll give that some serious thought but I'm hoping Wolfe will discover evidence from the autopsies on Marissa and Lily." She stared into the distance. "I know the cases are connected. We just need one tiny break."

"Hmm, and from what Blackhawk was telling us about the crime scene, Norrell will discover a ton of evidence." Kane led the way across the road to the park to allow Duke to stretch his legs. "It was good of him and his cousins to watch over the crime scene. Did he tell you they set up trail cams all around it but no one from town risked getting stuck in the mud to go there? The only way to avoid it was to go in through the res and follow the riverbank. Without a guide, they wouldn't know what Blackhawk calls the sandy trail."

Tipping her face up to grab the sun's rays, Jenna nodded. "Yeah, he explained Norrell's team would need to follow him in a convoy. The mudslides in the forest are causing a ton of problems. I called the mayor and he'll have crews out to clear the fire roads as soon as possible. It will take time. There's so much repair work to complete after the floods."

"We were lucky." Kane smiled. "No leaks anywhere."

Relaxing, Jenna sat on a park bench to watch Duke roll in the grass. Yesterday had been a lazy Sunday, and she'd spent quality time with Tauri, which was usually a luxury during homicide cases. They'd taken the horses out for a ride through the woods surrounding the ranch. Kane had checked all the fences and later tinkered with his motorcycles. Right now, she found herself at a loss what to do next. It seemed that the entire new case hinged on autopsy reports and results. The cold case hinged precariously on Norrell's discoveries at the crime scene.

Her phone buzzed. She held out the caller ID to show Kane and raised both eyebrows. "I hope nothing's wrong." She accepted the call and put the phone on speaker. "Hi, Raven, did you meet up with Norrell okay?"

"Yeah, but a silver truck ran her and Emily off the road and into a gully along one of the fire roads just as I arrived. Then some lunatic jumped onto the truck swinging an ax." Raven was breathing hard.

Horrified, Jenna gasped. "What?! Are they injured?"

"They're okay. I don't have time to explain. I need to stay with Norrell and Emily. You need to chase down this maniac. He was driving a Ford F-150." He gave the license plate. *"He kept on going along the fire road, so I figure he'll take the adjoining one to Bear Peak and get onto the highway from there. It will be slow going because I checked out that route recently and it's partially blocked by a mudslide. I figure if you left now, you'd probably catch him before he gets too far along the highway. I don't figure he's coming back this way."*

As Kane whistled Duke to his side, Jenna stood, already moving toward the Beast. "We're on our way." Once inside, she ran the plate. "It's a fleet vehicle owned by a company out at Blackwater."

"That's all we need." Kane secured Duke and slid behind the wheel. "Why can't it be simple and give us the killer's name, so we know who we're dealing with?" He used the radio to call Maggie. "Send Rio and Rowley to our position as backup, we're dealing with an unknown quantity here, over."

"I'm on it, over and out." Maggie disconnected.

Strapping on her seatbelt as Kane flicked on lights and sirens, they moved at high speed along Main. Vehicles pulled over to give them access and people stopped to stare as they flew past. Jenna's fingers closed around the grab handle and one hand went instinctively to her belly as the Beast accelerated along Stanton. The forest flashed by in a sea of green and minutes later they took the on-ramp to the highway. The truck's powerful engine roared as if in appreciation of showing its power, like a wild stallion given its head. The acceleration pushed Jenna back into her seat. Being accustomed to the old Beast and its power, the G-force from this new vehicle astounded her. She dragged her eyes away from the blacktop to glance at Kane. His face was a mask of concentration, but his stance was relaxed. He'd spent many hours putting the new Beast through its paces and knew exactly how hard he could push it.

Ahead, a line of vehicles wound up the mountain. Oncoming eighteen-wheelers rumbled past, their air brakes huffing and puffing as they tried to slow down on the steep incline. As they rounded a curve on the highway, a vehicle carrier was slowing down the traffic. Jenna sucked in a deep breath as Kane slammed his foot down on the gas and pulled out into the opposite lane. Although she trusted Kane's driving, fear slammed through her at the sight of another eighteen-wheeler cresting the top of the hill. Biting down hard on her cheek, Jenna gripped white-knuckled to the grab handle as they flashed along the line of vehicles with a *whoosh, whoosh, whoosh*.

The eighteen-wheeler sounded its air horns and was coming right at them when Kane flicked a switch and a sudden burst of acceleration pressed Jenna hard into the seat. Moments later they slid back onto their side of the road. Speechless, she gaped at Kane. "That was close."

"Nah, we had plenty of room. You don't believe I'd risk your life, do you? Not ever, Jenna." He indicated with his chin as they sped along. "Look. There's a silver pickup coming onto the highway. It's covered in mud. That's our guy."

FORTY-SEVEN

The driver of the pickup swerved onto the highway at high speed, barely missing a school bus. From his erratic driving it was obvious he'd spotted the Beast bearing down on him. To Jenna's surprise, the silver truck overtook a line of vehicles, accelerated, and then slammed on its brakes and, skidding around, headed in the other direction. Horns sounded and brakes squealed as the oncoming traffic tried to avoid him. "He's heading back to town."

"So I see. Did you get a look at him?" Kane slowed the truck. "Hang on." He pulled on the hand brake and drifted the Beast around to face the other direction.

In a split second they sped off toward town. Jenna swallowed hard. "I didn't know the Beast could do that." She hung on as Kane aimed the truck down the steep incline. "I did see the driver but he's wearing a ski mask. I have no idea who he is." She glanced at him. "If he gets into town and makes a run for it, we'll lose him."

"He won't get that far." Kane zipped past vehicles. "Call Rio. He'll be able to hole up closer to town in case we lose him."

Jenna made the call. She turned to Kane. "We'll need to

take this guy in alive. There're too many murders not to get to the bottom of what happened."

"If he comes at me with an ax, I'm gonna shoot him." Kane flicked her a glance. "He's a psychopath who has been denied his kill, so he'll be out of control. We have no idea what he'll try to do. It's kind of obvious that he attacked Norrell to stop her going to the crime scene, so we know there's a ton of evidence there against him. Right now he's got nothing to lose. He can't risk getting caught, so he'll do everything in his power to take us down. We might know about the ax, but we don't know if he's carrying a gun."

Nodding slowly, Jenna could understand his concerns. "What do you suggest we do? I know you'd prefer to remove this man from existence after what he's done. The problem is we're on this side of the law. We need to discover who else is involved. For all we know, this guy might be falling on his sword to save the others."

"I doubt it." Kane was closing in on the silver truck. "Psychopaths don't give a toss about anyone but themselves." He looked at her and blew out a long sigh. "I hate it when you put yourself in danger. Can you for once let me handle this? I'll do everything in my power not to kill him."

Shaking her head, Jenna reached out a hand and squeezed his arm. "No. I'm the sheriff and I will be standing beside you as always. We'll take him down together, but I'll let you do the shooting, if necessary. When I shoot, I aim for center mass. No doubt, if I aimed at his leg, he'd end up bleeding to death before we got him back to the office. Before you say anything, I know I'm very accurate at the shooting range, but when it comes to taking a person down and causing the least amount of damage, I figure I'll leave that up to you."

"You got it." Kane smiled at her.

The silver truck was hurtling down the mountainside, taking risks overtaking, and narrowly missing causing a wreck.

Jenna took long calming breaths as Kane weaved the Beast through traffic until they came to a long stretch of deserted highway. The Beast's engine roared as they flew along at high speed, eating up the blacktop. The distance between them closed and the silver truck swerved from side to side. Objects flew from the windows as the driver tried unsuccessfully to slow them down. "Use the PIT maneuver."

"Okay, hang on." Kane had used the precision immobilization technique many times. One tap in the right place would send a fleeing vehicle into a spin.

It was a risky move at high speed, but Jenna trusted Kane to complete it without a problem. They roared up beside the vehicle and it swerved erratically. Jenna held her breath and hung on tight as Kane executed the maneuver and the back wheels of the truck lost contact with the blacktop. It spun around, coming to rest with two wheels down the gully. The Beast pulled up behind it and Jenna's hand went to the door handle, but Kane was out of the Beast and running toward the truck. The driver jumped out swinging an ax and raving incoherently. She pulled her weapon and followed Kane.

"I'll kill you both." The driver's wild eyes stared at them.

As the ax swished back and forth, Jenna kept her distance. Behind her, vehicles had stopped to watch the action. She glanced around to see people holding up phones waiting for her to take action. "Sheriff's Department. Put down the weapon."

"Drop the weapon and place your hands on the top of your head." Kane stepped forward, his M18 pistol aimed at the man's head. "Do as we say and come quietly. It's in your best interest to cooperate. No one needs to get hurt today."

"Do you think I care about getting hurt?" The man swung the ax again. "It's the pair of you I'll be chopping into tiny little pieces." He indicated to the people in the vehicles filming him. "I'm going to be famous. When I kill the pair of you, everyone in those vehicles will cheer."

Standing her ground, Jenna exchanged a meaningful glance with Kane. "Place the weapon on the ground. Put your hands on your head. Last chance."

The man raised the ax over his head and ran toward them. A blast of gunfire echoed through the mountains and the man fell, the ax spilling from his hand and spinning across the blacktop. Kane had blasted a hole in his leg just below his knee. Cheers went up from the crowd, but Jenna ignored them. Seeing a man come at her with an ax had shaken her to her core but she'd never let him know it. She held her gun steady as Kane patted him down and cuffed him before retrieving the medical kit from the back of the Beast.

"Lie still and don't move a muscle." Kane stood over the driver. He bent and pulled off the balaclava. "Clint Wasser." He read him his rights and then stood, pulled out the M18 pistol, and glared at him. "I'll allow the sheriff to treat your injuries, but one move and the next shot will take your head off. Understand?"

"Maybe I'll aim a kick to her stomach." Wasser chuckled as if oblivious to the pain in his leg. "I figure I owe you."

Jenna turned and placed the medical kit into the truck. "Well then, I guess we'll wait for the paramedics to arrive." She pulled out her phone. "Rio get the paramedics to the highway. We've got the guy. Gunshot wound to the leg. I'll need one of you to go with him in the ambulance. I'll need both of you at the hospital. We have enough on him to charge him. I'll ask the DA to sign an arrest warrant the moment I get back to the office. Once he's through at the hospital, we'll have him taken to County. I don't want to risk leaving him in the cells overnight."

"Copy that. How bad is the injury?" The roar of Rio's engine came through the speaker.

Walking away from Kane and Wasser, she dropped her voice so no one could overhear her. "Kane shot him just below the knee, so it isn't nice. The problem is this man is extremely dangerous. We had our guns drawn and he still tried to attack us with an ax. He will try and escape custody and use everything in his power to get away. You must advise the doctor and nurses it's imperative that you stay with him every second."

"Copy that. We're five minutes away. Rowley is calling the paramedics."

Jenna nodded. "Okay, I'll attempt to clear the traffic blocking the highway. It seems they are enjoying the show." She disconnected and walked over to the line of expectant faces hanging out of windows. She took an examination glove from her pocket and retrieved the ax and turned to face the crowd. "Okay, everyone, move along now. There's nothing to see here."

"You're the best." A woman leaned out of the window. "Best sheriff ever."

To her surprise, the line of traffic dispersed in an orderly fashion and she turned back to discover that Kane had used zip ties to restrain Wasser's legs. He was wearing his stone-faced expression. She knew that expression so well. Kane was mad. "Do you figure that's necessary?"

"Yeah, when I was giving him duty of care by using a zip tie as a tourniquet, he tried to kick me in the head." Kane's expression was granite. "He's not saying too much now, is he?"

Concerned, Jenna stared at the prisoner. "Has he passed out from lack of blood?"

"Nope." Kane lifted one shoulder in a half shrug. "He banged his head on the blacktop. He'll be fine."

Examining Kane's angry expression, she narrowed her gaze. "Exactly how did that happen?"

"Maybe it's best you don't ask." Kane stared into the distance. "Here comes Rio and Rowley. I do believe I can hear the paramedic sirens as well." He shot her a glance. "While you're arranging the arrest warrant, I'll speak to Sam Cross and see if I can persuade him to allow us to interview the suspect. After he has read the charges against him, he may be willing."

Swinging the ax between two fingers, Jenna held it up to show him. "Wolfe said he would find DNA evidence on the ax if we could find it, and here it is. This may be the pivotal piece of evidence that we need to arrest Wasser for the murders of Maggie and Lily. I figure once he is charged, we'll ask the DA to arrange some type of deal with the others over the murders of Cole and Abby. To retain Sam Cross in the first place, they obviously had something to hide, but I don't believe for a second they were involved in Marissa's and Lily's murders."

"Then I suggest we get the ax to Wolfe without delay. Watch him for a moment." Kane went to the truck to collect a large evidence bag and held it out for Jenna.

Jenna pulled out her phone. "I'm going to call Emily and find out exactly what happened on the mountain. Wolfe will want to know all the details when we get there." She made the call.

"We're okay, thanks to Raven." Emily sucked in a deep breath. *"I haven't called Dad yet. He's been so busy and I didn't want to worry him. Norrell is pretty banged up. She received lacerations from the broken window and has a very badly bruised arm. Raven doesn't believe it's broken and I've had a look at it too and concur with his assessment."* She paused a beat. *"If Dad hadn't insisted on us wearing the liquid Kevlar vests, we'd be worse."*

Wiping a hand down her face, Jenna could just imagine what Wolfe would say when he found out. "What exactly happened? Tell me from the start. I have the man in custody and the ax. I have only what Raven told us to take to the DA."

Jenna listened in horror at the story Emily told her. It was as she surmised. Clint Wasser had intended to kill Norrell and Emily, and if Raven hadn't arrived on time, he would have succeeded. She leaned against the Beast and took a deep breath. For a psychopath, he wasn't as smart as he'd imagined. He should have known if Norrell had died, they'd just get another anthropologist to dig the site. She shook her head in disbelief. "Okay, I'll need you both to drop by the office as soon as you can to give us a statement."

"I have my tablet with me. I'll write one up for both of us and we'll digitally sign them. That will be enough to get things rolling and we'll drop by and sign the hard copies as soon as we leave here. Although, I figure Dad will be X-raying Norrell the moment she walks back into the office." Emily sighed. *"Give me a few minutes' head start because right now I need to call him to calm the waters before you take him the ax. Don't worry, I'll have the statements to you by the time you get back to the office."*

Jenna blew out a long sigh. "Thanks, that would be great. I'll send them to the DA along with my report and drop by as soon as we have transported the prisoner to the hospital for treatment and then dropped by to see Shane. Talk soon." She disconnected and looked at Kane. "She sounds fine. I don't figure the shock of what's happened has set in yet."

"She is tough, like you." Kane shrugged. "She's made it through many life-threatening situations without PTSD. She'd make a good soldier."

Shaking her head, Jenna stared at him. "Maybe, but if you value your friendship with Wolfe, please don't suggest that to her."

Rio and Rowley arrived, followed by the paramedics, and soon the prisoner was safely on his way to the hospital. As everyone drove away, leaving them standing on the side of the road, Jenna leaned into Kane. "I said we'd catch him, didn't I?"

"I never had any doubt." He slid one arm around her and pulled her close.

FORTY-EIGHT

Although she hadn't said a word, Jenna appeared to be tired as she climbed into the truck. Kane hadn't missed the way she rubbed her lower back. He turned to her. "It's been a long day. Do you want to take a break before we go and see Wolfe?"

"No, I'm fine. Although, I seem to be getting back pain and my ankles are swollen, but my energy level is high." She gave him a concerned stare. "I hope the adrenaline rush I got when we were flying up and down the mountain isn't detrimental to the baby."

Unable to give her a solid answer, Kane shrugged. "I guess that's something you're gonna have to discuss with Wolfe. From the books I've read about pregnancy, it says that the bump shouldn't be showing much at this stage, but it's very evident that you are pregnant. You're only a small person, maybe the extra weight is causing the backache?"

"Well then, God help me when I get to nine months." She grinned at him. "Maybe I'll need to use a wheelbarrow or something similar to take the weight." She thought for a beat. "I'll speak to Wolfe. He did mention about wanting to do another ultrasound at five months. I'm past that now."

When they arrived at the medical examiner's office, Wolfe met them in the passageway with a grim expression. Kane clicked his fingers for Duke to come to his side and then followed Wolfe into his office and placed the ax on the desk. "I'm assuming that Emily called you? Rest assured we have the man in custody. I shot him and he's currently at the hospital receiving treatment with Rio and Rowley." He pointed to the ax. "This might hold the evidence that seals this guy's fate. So far, all we have him on is attacking Norrell and Emily."

"If y'all give me a moment before I talk to you about Norrell, I'll get Webber to swab the ax and get the samples into the DNA sequencer. We have a new machine that completes rapid DNA sequencing in a few hours with higher accuracy than ever before." Wolfe picked up the ax and marched out of the door. In a few minutes he returned, went to the coffee machine, and brewed three cups of coffee. After handing them around, he went back to his chair. "Norrell called me before and explained what happened. Have you identified the man?"

"Yeah, his name is Clint Wasser. He was one of our suspects. We interviewed him but had no evidence to haul him in." Jenna added cream and sugar to her cup of decaf and sipped. "I'm sure glad I sent Raven to keep an eye on Norrell and Em."

"Yeah, I am in his debt yet again." Wolfe leaned back in his chair, coffee cup in his large hands. "From what Norrell said, Wasser was intent on killing her. He rammed the truck countless times until he pushed it into the gully. If Raven hadn't come along when he did, Wasser would have killed them with the ax just like the others."

"Emily called me. She mentioned that Norrell has a bruised arm and a few cuts from the broken glass but insisted on going to the crime scene." Jenna rolled her eyes. "They both want to get evidence against this guy."

Kane leaned forward in his chair. "Talking about evidence.

Have you found anything? We need all the help we can get to charge this guy for murder."

"I've completed the autopsy on Lily Jones. She died from blood loss. I'm not sure she would have been a very exciting kill for this murderer. When someone's hands are severed, the blood loss is extreme, and thankfully, she would have lost consciousness before he'd finished satisfying his lust for killing." He took a long sip of his coffee. "We took samples all over the crime scene and tested Lily for latent DNA, and apart from the bloody boot marks, the killer didn't leave a trace except for one laceration. It appeared different when I examined her, dirty around the edges, for want of a better explanation. It's hard to explain but I examined it microscopically and found foreign matter. I tested it and it's dried human blood. It is being tested as we speak. If it comes back as a match to Marissa Kendrick, it's the evidence you need to prove it's the same killer."

Smiling, Kane glanced at Jenna. "If the ax that Wasser was using has traces of Lily's blood as well, we'll have absolute proof that it was him."

"I'd say the chances are really high." Jenna leaned back with a sigh. "I figure he was concerned about what Norrell would find at the crime scene. So there is evidence against him there for sure."

"I'll get information to you, as soon as possible." Wolfe smiled at her. "How are you doing, Jenna? When you're done with this case, we'll need to make time for another ultrasound."

"I have a sore back and swollen ankles. Dave believes I look bigger than most second-trimester women." Jenna leaned forward in her chair. A hopeful expression crossed her face. "Are you sure we're not having twins?"

"Yeah, I'm sure." Wolfe leaned forward and rested his hands on the desk. "It would be very noticeable in the ultrasound we did earlier. I did mention last month when I examined you that the baby appears to be very large for its gestation.

As Dave mentioned, he was an extremely large baby, so this isn't at all unusual. It might mean that you deliver a little earlier, is all. If you're certain about your dates, we'll leave the delivery date at the same time." He opened his hands wide. "I can assure you it's nothing to worry about, although going forward you might need to consider just how long you intend on working. If you're having backache and swollen ankles now, it's not going to get any better and you'll need to take it a little easier toward the end. I don't mean sitting around all day doing nothing, because gentle exercise is good right up to the last minute." He gave her a long considering look. "It's not too late to call in an obstetrician. I'm only a GP when it comes to dealing with the living, as is Norrell. I could perform a cesarean in an emergency but I'm not a specialist. Would you at least consider having an obstetrician examine you and we can have them on call should the need arise?"

Holding his breath as he waited for Jenna to reply, Kane caught the flash of defiance in her eyes. Ultimately it was her decision, but he couldn't resist offering his opinion. "I know we're doing the classes and you'll have me there as well, but wouldn't it put your mind at rest knowing that there's a specialist waiting in the wings if you need one?" He searched her face, hopeful she would agree with him.

"Do you recall the night that Sandy had her twins?" Jenna looked from one to the other as she referred to Rowley's wife. "She delivered them surrounded by family. All I want is the same for our baby." She sighed. "But if you consider that it would be best to see an obstetrician just to check that everything is okay and have them on standby should the need arise, then I'll agree."

"Okay, I'll make a call." Wolfe rubbed his hands together. "I'll arrange to have them present when you have the next ultrasound. I'll make sure to tell them that you don't want to know the sex of the baby. It will probably mean looking away from the screen for a time during the examination. Sometimes these things are a little difficult to hide." He gave Jenna a broad grin and glanced at the clock on the wall. "Now, it's way past your lunchtime and you've been on your feet all day. I suggest you go and have something to eat and rest up for a while before you head back to the office."

"I guess I can email the statements and all the information to the DA over lunch." Jenna stood slowly. "I'm starving. I believed this eating for two thing was a myth until it happened to me." She patted Duke on the head. "Wanna go to Aunt Betty's, Duke?" The dog barked and wagged his tail.

Kane stood. "Thanks for the cup of coffee. It's been a long day and I figure it's gonna get longer." He followed Jenna out of the door.

FORTY-NINE

Jenna walked into her office waving the arrest warrant. "This will hold him until we have more evidence on the murders. The DA is willing to do a deal with anyone who's prepared to talk about what happened to Cole and Abby. Is Wasser back from the hospital yet?"

"Yeah, he's in interview room one with Sam Cross." Kane leaned back in his chair and smiled at her. "He's in a wheelchair but it seems I didn't inflict as much damage as I imagined. My bullet missed the bone and took out his calf muscle, so no surgery, but I'd say he's got a fair few stitches." He stood and went to the refrigerator, poured a glass of milk, and gave it to her. "I anticipated the deal offer and sent Rio and Rowley to round up the rest of the suspects. They have been bringing them in, but I can't split them all up. I placed Wyatt Twotrees and Josie Campbell in interview rooms two and three. That leaves no room for the other two."

Jenna sipped her milk. "Double them up, but leave Rio and Rowley in the rooms with them to prevent any conversation. When Cross has finished speaking to Wasser, we'll tell him there's a deal on the table and give him time to speak to his clients. Did you read them their rights?"

"I told Rio to do that before they put them in the truck." He dropped into a chair in front of her desk. "Wolfe called, and the sample he took from Lily's wound is the same blood type as Marissa. They found numerous amounts of blood on the ax. It's just as well the DA charged him with another offense because Wolfe says it's going to take around six or seven hours to get a result."

Nodding, Jenna stared at her phone when it chimed. It was Norrell.

"We've hit paydirt here, Jenna." Exuberant voices buzzed in the background. *"We've found a blood-soaked scarf, a jacket, and gloves. The name inside the jacket is Clint Wasser. They are all in good condition. The jacket we found at the bottom of a pit. It was wet but I'm sure that Shane will be able to extract DNA from the blood on the jacket. If it's from both victims, you'll have him. We're heading home now."*

Grinning at Kane, Jenna high-fived him. "That's incredible news. Everything is finally slipping into place. Now all we need is to discover exactly what happened that night on the mountain." She'd just placed her phone on the table when it chimed again. "Bobby, have you got something for me?"

"I do indeed." Kalo's excitement came through the speaker. *"I've discovered the owner of the fraternity pin. There's no doubt the owner is Clint Wasser. If you check your inbox, I found four photographs of him wearing the pin. After enlarging and enhancing the images, the damage to it is visible. I used the image of the pin taken from the hand of the victim as a reference. They're identical."*

"Great job." Kane gave Jenna a wide smile.

"That's what I'm here for. Catch you later." He disconnected.

Jenna opened her inbox and displayed the photos on her

screen. "I figure this alone sews it up for Wasser—Abby's murder and hopefully Cole's, with the evidence found in situ at the crime scene. That's enough evidence for the DA to take Wasser to trial, although it would be really nice if one of the others involved took the deal and explained what actually happened that night."

"I guess we wait and see." Kane blew out a long breath.

Twenty minutes later, Jenna made her way downstairs to the interview rooms to listen to what Sam Cross had to say. She met him in the passageway. "Is your client prepared to speak with us?"

"You can conduct your interview with him shortly. I asked to speak to my clients separately and your deputies moved them around to achieve that end." He gave Jenna an inquiring look. "I'm finding it hard to believe you didn't split up the suspects, rather than allowing them to speak to each other."

"The deputies were instructed not to allow them to speak to each other." Kane rested one hand on the handle of his weapon. "We didn't want to put them in the cells before they'd been charged as you were on your way and you gave us explicit orders not to question them."

"Only one of them is prepared to speak to you and will consider a deal." Cross frowned as he looked from one to the other. "This is not something I advised him to do, but as he has a wife and child to consider, he figured it may save him some jail time." He turned his attention to Jenna. "We can speak to Mr. Hallon now. Do you have the details of the deal?"

Trying to control her enthusiasm, Jenna shook her head. "I'll listen to what he has to say and if it's relevant to the case, I'll take it to the DA personally. He assured me that he will take everything Mr. Hallon tells me into consideration." After dropping her weapon alongside Kane's in a locked compartment in the passageway, she flashed her card over the scanner outside interview room two, and they all walked inside.

Nodding to Jess Hallon, Jenna turned on the camera and recording devices. She gave the date, time, and who was present in the room. She asked Jess Hallon to confirm that he had been read his rights and was willing to speak to them with his attorney present. "Mr. Hallon, before we discuss what happened twelve years ago over Halloween, I want to advise you that the DA is going to charge you with tampering of physical evidence, which carries up to a ten-year prison sentence in the state penitentiary, a $50,000 fine, or both. If you plead guilty and give me all the information you have about the night Cole and Abby went missing, I will personally go to the DA and ask for a deal to have your sentence reduced for cooperation. As this evidence tampering occurred at the time of their murders, there is no statute of limitations." She leaned on the desk and stared him directly in the eyes. "We know Clint murdered Abby. She had his fraternity pin clutched in her hand. We have images of Wasser wearing the damaged pin. Dr. Larson discovered skin under her fingernails, which is being DNA tested as we speak. A court order is being obtained by the DA to compel Wasser to supply a sample of his DNA." She flicked a glance at Cross, who had said absolutely nothing. "Now taking that all into consideration, tell me what happened on Halloween twelve years ago."

"I don't need to tell you the names of who was in the group that night because you know who they are." Hallon stared at his linked hands resting on the table. "Everything was fine. We were all having a good time. We built a fire near the Whispering Caves and everyone was taking turns telling stories about the axman. Cole and Abby got up and walked away hand in hand. I didn't really take much notice because they often wandered off alone together. After that, Clint said he needed to pee. I don't recall hearing anyone screaming or calling out. In the forest there's a variety of noises that could be described as screams. Owls and cats all make noises like that, and no one takes any notice." He glanced at her for a second and then back at his hands. "I don't know how long Wasser had been away. We were all talking and having a good time."

"Had you been drinking?" Kane was leaning up against the door. He stepped forward and sat down in front of the table.

"Yeah, we'd been drinking heavily." Hallon narrowed his gaze. "We were all over twenty-one. Beer and tequila shots mostly. Not just us guys, the girls were into it as well." He paused a bit and then sucked in a deep breath and stared at the table again. "Clint came back soaked in blood and carrying an ax. It was the one that Wyatt had brought to chop up wood for the fire and to scare the girls. You know like the Whispering Caves Axman?"

"What did he tell you?" Kane leaned forward in his chair.

"He said that Cole was murdering Abby with the ax when he came upon them. He said he fought with Cole and managed to get the ax away from him, but Cole pulled a knife and came at him, so he used the ax in self-defense. He was crying. We didn't know what to do but followed him back up the mountain and into a cave. Cole was lying on top of Abby and in his hand was a knife, so we all believed Clint."

Not wanting to interrupt his story, but compelled to do so, Jenna went into the folder and removed the image from Cole's autopsy clearly showing the three deep ax marks in his back. "You must have seen Cole's body. Do these wounds look like a frontal attack to you? He was struck from behind and these were the only wounds on his body."

"I recall seeing a ton of blood. I didn't get close enough to check out every wound." Hallon stared at the image and ran both hands down his face. "Now with a clear head I can see it looks like Cole was trying to run away."

"Okay, so you went with him to the bodies. What happened next?" Kane folded his arms across his chest and stared at him.

"Clint said he couldn't go to the cops because they'd figure he murdered Cole because of jealousy." Hallon's expression changed from reluctance to deep concern. "Everyone knew that he had a thing for Abby that went back a long time. So we dug a hole deep inside the cave and placed his blood-soaked clothes into it and then dragged Abby and Cole to the grave and buried them."

Taking a deep breath Jenna stared at him. "Did you check first to see if they were dead?"

"No. We could see they were dead. Clint pulled up their shirts and made us put our hands on them and swear we would never tell. They both felt cold. I will never forget it as long as I live. After that we cleaned up every inch of our camp. Clint threw the knife and ax into the river along with Abby's phone. He changed into clothes he'd brought with him. We'd planned to camp overnight and had extra clothes with us. We went down a back track to avoid the others camping on the mountain and then came back along the regular trail that everyone was using to get to the river. We made a big noise when we arrived so that everyone would notice us. We wanted everyone to believe we'd arrived late." He stared at Jenna. "We've kept Clint's secret all these years, but I can tell you he was paranoid about one of us breaking our silence." He placed a hand on his chest. "I swear to God, I did not know he'd murdered both of them. I figured as it had been in self-defense, we owed him as friends to help him. If he'd gone to trial for murder, his life would have been ruined. I admit drink probably affected our reasoning at the time, but I can tell you in all honesty, we all believed we were doing the right thing."

Nodding, Jenna looked at Sam Cross. "I'll have Maggie type up the transcript of this interview. When your client signs it, I'll send it over to the DA right away." She looked at Hallon. "Thank you for your cooperation. It's not for me to decide what happens next. As soon as the DA makes a decision, he'll come here personally to speak to you." She turned off the recording, stood, and turned to Sam Cross. "I'm ready to interview Mr. Wasser." She headed for the door.

When they'd stepped outside, she took Kane to one side. "What do you think?"

"I figure he's telling the truth. If they all decide to speak up and give the same story and not the one they've practiced over and over again, I figure the courts will go easy on them. They were a group of drunk students not thinking straight at the time who got themselves influenced by a psychopath. They've led exemplary lives since that night and aren't a threat to the public. My guess is they'll get a suspended sentence or, worst case, a year, maybe two. There are extenuating circumstances. I figure they've already done their time living with this terrible crime and not being able to tell anyone."

Part of Jenna agreed with Kane's evaluation of the interview; another part of her was dismayed that these people covered up the whereabouts of Cole and Abby, leaving their parents to wonder what had happened to them. She gathered herself and followed Sam Cross into the interview room, set up the recording device as before, and sat down to face Clint Wasser, this time with Kane at her side. "Mr. Wasser."

"Why so formal, Sheriff? Please call me Clint. It's so much nicer." Wasser smiled as if he didn't have a care in the world.

Unimpressed, Jenna placed a folder on the table. "Deputy Rio has read you the details of the arrest warrant. As we have three witnesses to the attempted murder of Dr. Larson and Emily Wolfe, I'm going to move on to the murders of Marissa Kendrick and Lily Jones."

"I didn't kill Marissa Kendrick or Lily Jones." Wasser chuckled. "They happen to be old friends of mine. Why would I kill them?"

"Friends that you haven't had contact with since you left college." Kane leaned forward in his chair and eyeballed him. "Was that because those friends discovered you covered with blood and carrying an ax after you murdered Abby and Cole, over Halloween twelve years ago?"

"No." A flicker of doubt crossed Wasser's face. "I don't know anything about their murders."

Jenna opened the folder and removed the photographs of the fraternity pin found in Abby's hand with the distinctive chip out of the enameled surface. She laid the photographs alongside the enlarged images of him wearing the exact pin. "Is this your fraternity pin?"

"You can see it's mine." Wasser shrugged. "What's that got to do with Abby and Cole?"

Although she wanted to smile, Jenna kept her expression bland. "We found it clutched in Abby's hand. She tore it from your jacket the night you murdered her, and strangely enough, we have your jacket too. It was excavated from the grave where you buried Cole and Abby. There's no doubt it's yours. The torn, bloodstained jacket has your name inside." She paused a beat to allow him to absorb the information. "Your friends have decided they don't want to go to prison to save your hide and have explained exactly what happened the night you murdered Cole and Abby. We have enough evidence to prove that you murdered Marissa and Lily as well. When Cole's and Abby's bodies showed up, you believed they were going to speak to me about that night. In fact, they all kept your secret up until today. Now they're going to save their own necks and are willing to go to court to tell the truth about that night. This is your chance to tell your story. Why did you kill them?"

"You're deluded if you believe my friends would rat on me." Wasser gave her a look that chilled her to the bone. It was the look of a serial killer. "Everything you've said is lies."

A shiver slithered down Jenna's spine and she avoided his death stare as she collected the photographs. "I'm afraid not. Ask Mr. Cross. We have DNA evidence from the ax you used to attack Dr. Larson and Emily Wolfe. Not to mention trying to attack me as well. You'll be formally charged again with four counts of homicide and sent to County to await trial. I can assure you, from the evidence we have against you and the witnesses, you'll be spending the rest of your life in the state pen." She turned off the recording device and walked out of the room.

EPILOGUE
TWO WEEKS LATER

The weather in Black Rock Falls had improved again. From her office window Jenna could see snowcapped mountaintops against a background of brilliant blue sky that went on forever. The last couple of weeks had been intense. She had spent long hours with her team correlating all the evidence against Clint Wasser. The ax had given up multiple DNA results and when Wolfe had entered them into the data bank, they'd discovered matches to a number of murders in different counties. When they hunted down where Wasser had been traveling in his work as a spare parts salesman, they matched the dates of the murders. Some of these homicides went back ten years or so, which proved that Wasser had never stopped killing since the night on the mountain twelve years previously. The information gathered from the ax would solve a multitude of cold cases throughout the state.

The excavation of the crime scene had continued but no other evidence had been discovered. Norrell had recovered completely from the incident, with only a few bruises remaining, but Wolfe had vowed to always accompany her and Emily to an excavation or crime scene in Black Rock Falls in the future. Jenna had chuckled when he'd mentioned the next time they went to an excavation, he'd be packing for bear. Since the incident she'd noticed that Raven had been around town more often than usual. The media had gotten hold of the story about how he'd rescued the women with his K-9, Ben, from a psychopathic serial killer. The orders for his protection dogs were rolling in daily.

Jenna turned away from the window as the knock came on the door and Raven walked in. "Ah, the man of the hour. Still dodging the reporters?"

"Yeah, but they're not quite as bad now, and although I've explained many times that Ben didn't get out of my truck, as I'm a K-9 unit, he's become part of the story." Raven nodded to Kane. "I do have some good news. Blackhawk is renting a cabin a short distance from mine. His work with Norrell's team means he needs to be a little closer to town. He won't be living there all the time, just when she needs him. At the excavation site, we got to talking about training dogs, so in his downtime Atohi is going to be working alongside me training K-9s and personal protection dogs. We're going to be taking puppies and raising them up for the K-9s. I have a contact in the military who would welcome the chance to get puppies with the basic training completed. I'm also getting orders from local sheriff's departments all over the state. Once I have the dogs at a high level, they want to send their deputies to me to train with the dogs. Luckily, I have a three-bedroom cabin, so they can bunk with me during this time."

Smiling, Jenna looked at his enthusiastic expression. "That's wonderful news, but does that mean we'll be losing you?"

"Not at all. Black Rock Falls Sheriff's Office will always be my primary concern." Raven nodded. "I'll be completing my qualifications in law enforcement this year. Trust me, there isn't too much to do in the mountains of a night." He smiled. "I came by to thank you. Moving back into civilization was something I never thought I'd be able to achieve. Since finding Julie in the plane wreck, and meeting so many fine people, I've discovered new goals in life. Just knowing that you, Dave, and Wolfe had faith in my ability to contribute to the team gave me the courage to take steps I would never have thought possible a year ago."

"You're very welcome." Kane stood and shook his hand. "We already consider you part of the family. We're having a cookout next weekend at the ranch. I hope you'll come by. Everyone will be there, including Wolfe, Norrell, and the girls."

I'd love to come, thank you." Raven's grin widened. "Atohi mentioned that you cook the best ribs in town." He chuckled. "And you have a motorcycle collection for me to drool over."

"I figure we're starting to build our own gang." Kane laughed. "I have a passion for building Harleys and Indians. Us guys all have a motorcycle now."

"Wow!" Raven glanced at Jenna. "Pinch me, I must be dreaming. You know I purchased a number of old cabins all over the mountain. I've discovered a wealth of old motorcycles and parts left in garages. It would be a dream come true to see one of them back on the road again."

Trying to avoid an eye roll, Jenna looked at Kane. "Seems you've found your long-lost brother."

Jenna's phone chimed. "It's Wolfe." She gave Kane a meaningful stare.

"Oh, sure." Kane headed for the door. "We'll leave you to it." He looked at Raven as they walked into the passageway. "So tell me about these old motorcycles."

Accepting the call, Jenna leaned back in her chair. "Hi, Shane, what's up?"

"I've organized an ultrasound with Dr. Elizabeth Bates. Can you make it at three this afternoon? Same place as before at the hospital."

Excited Jenna checked her watch. "Great! I'll have time to

eat, pee, and drink water beforehand as before." She sighed. "See you at three."

Excitement and trepidation gripped Jenna as she walked into the examination room. Dr. Elizabeth Bates was an extremely nice woman in her late forties who put Jenna at ease at once. She climbed onto the examination table and made herself ready. Although, one part of her wanted to see her baby, another part of her was afraid that something might be wrong. She slipped her hand into Kane's as the ultrasound gel was squeezed onto her belly. The sound of the baby's strong heartbeat settled her nerves. They both looked away from the screen, as Wolfe and Dr. Bates did a preliminary examination. She stared into Kane's eyes and they smiled at each other.

"Okay, you can look now." Dr. Bates was smiling at them. "You know most new parents are desperate to know the sex of their child. Is there any particular reason why you don't want to know, because it is evident in this case? Your baby turned around just at the right moment but I will respect your wishes."

Inside, Jenna understood the reason Kane didn't want to know the sex of the baby. After losing his pregnant first wife in a car bombing, he'd mourned her and the loss of his son. He didn't want to tempt fate by knowing and she'd respected his wishes. "We want it to be a surprise."

"That's fine." Dr. Bates looked from one to the other. "I can see it's a large baby. The organs are in excellent condition and match the overall size, but everything I see is advanced for the gestation period." She indicated to the screen. "Your baby is head up at the moment, and you can very clearly see the face and profile when it moves its head. We can take some images if you like and I will make sure I don't capture any revealing parts." She patted Jenna on the arm. "You have a very strong and healthy baby, Jenna. I can see absolutely no reason for you not to carry to term, but I would like you to have another ultrasound at seven months. By this time, I would hope the baby has turned. It will also give me a better idea of the correct delivery date. You are twenty-three weeks by your calculations, but I would estimate twenty-seven on the measurements and development." She looked at Kane. "Don't let her overwork. As the pregnancy progresses, if the baby continues to grow at this rate, Jenna will become very tired. From what Dr. Wolfe tells me, she is very stubborn about taking a rest." She looked at Jenna. "So take care of yourself, because when this child decides it wants to join us, you'll need all the strength you can muster."

"I'll do my best." Kane squeezed Jenna's hand and looked at Dr. Bates. "Can we take another look at the face? I can't believe this is happening."

The doctor moved the transducer, and the beautiful plump-cheeked little face came onto the screen. When the baby sucked its thumb everyone in the room sighed. Mesmerized, Jenna dragged her attention away from the screen to glance at Kane. Tears streamed down his face and he brushed them away and smiled at her. She cupped his chin. "I guess we'll need to decide on a name. I'd like Faith Jasmine for a girl."

"I like that. What about Jackson Daniel for a boy?" Kane's eyes had returned to the screen and he nodded slowly. "It's a strong name."

Jenna used her thumb to wipe away his tears. Happiness filled her and overflowed as she allowed her tears to fall. After waiting for so long, they were really having a brother or sister for Tauri. They'd been blessed with a healthy baby and it overwhelmed her. She nodded and hugged Kane. "I'd like that just fine."

A LETTER FROM D.K. HOOD

Dear Readers,

Thanks so much for choosing my novel and coming with me on another thrilling adventure with Kane and Alton in *Tears on Her Grave*. If you'd like to keep up to date with all my latest releases, just sign up at the website link below. Your details will never be shared and you can unsubscribe at any time. For subscribing you'll receive a free copy of one of my short stories.

www.bookouture.com/dk-hood

It's wonderful to continue writing the stories of Jenna Alton and Dave Kane and having you along. I really appreciate all the wonderful comments and messages you have all sent me during this series.

If you enjoyed my story, I would be very grateful if you could leave a review and recommend my book to your friends and family. I really enjoy hearing from readers, so feel free to ask me questions at any time. You can get in touch through social media or my website.

Thank you so much for your support.

D.K. Hood

KEEP IN TOUCH WITH D.K. HOOD

www.dkhood.com

 facebook.com/dkhoodauthor
x.com/DKHood_Author

ACKNOWLEDGMENTS

To the amazing #TeamBookouture and my very supportive editor Helen, many thanks.

I must thank my wonderful readers, who are always there to support me. It's been wonderful speaking to many of you online through the D.K. Hood Readers' Group on Facebook. I always enjoy chatting with my readers, so if you're not a member yet, drop by and join us.

PUBLISHING TEAM

Turning a manuscript into a book requires the efforts of many people. The publishing team at Bookouture would like to acknowledge everyone who contributed to this publication.

Audio
Alba Proko
Sinead O'Connor
Melissa Tran

Commercial
Lauren Morrissette
Hannah Richmond
Imogen Allport

Cover design
Blacksheep

Data and analysis
Mark Alder
Mohamed Bussuri

Editorial
Helen Jenner
Ria Clare

Copyeditor
Ian Hodder

Proofreader
Claire Rushbrook

Marketing
Alex Crow
Melanie Price
Occy Carr
Cíara Rosney
Martyna Młynarska

Operations and distribution
Marina Valles
Stephanie Straub
Joe Morris

Production
Hannah Snetsinger
Mandy Kullar
Jen Shannon
Ria Clare

Publicity
Kim Nash
Noelle Holten
Jess Readett
Sarah Hardy

Rights and contracts
Peta Nightingale
Richard King
Saidah Graham

Made in United States
Orlando, FL
19 December 2024

56037763R00169